A NOBLE INHERITANCE

ALSO BY KASEY STOCKTON

Regency Romance

The Jewels of Halstead Manor

The Lady of Larkspur Vale

The Widow of Falbrooke Court

Properly Kissed

Sensibly Wed

Pleasantly Pursued

Honorably Engaged

Love in the Bargain

All is Mary and Bright

Myths of Moraigh Trilogy

Journey to Bongary Spring

Through the Fairy Tree

The Enemy Across the Loch

Contemporary Romance

Cotswolds Holiday

I'm Not Charlotte Lucas

Love on Deck

A Noble Inheritance

Castles & Courtship
Series

KASEY STOCKTON

For Audrey, my precious girl
You are perfect exactly the way you are. I love your jokes, your
compassion, and your dance moves. But most of all, I love you
finger heart

CHAPTER ONE

VERITY

Lancashire, England
1818

The only thing more tiresome than arguing with a small child would be trying to convince my nearly grown sister to do anything she did not wish to do. At seventeen, she was old enough to reason with, but reason sometimes lost itself on the way to her understanding.

"I always take the servants' stairs," Fanny said, her voice level and stoic, her confused green eyes flitting to everything but my face. She looked at the closed door to the stairwell, then to the wall, to the floor, back to the door.

I inhaled patience. "I understand, but there was a spill, and Janet is washing the steps now. If we go down that way, we could slip and fall." The servants took great care to ensure nothing came in the way of Fanny and her routine, but sometimes necessity dictated otherwise. This was just such a time.

"But I always take the servants' stairs," she repeated.

"Fanny," I began, taking her hand. She pulled it from my

grasp. "If we walk down that way, we will ruin Janet's hard work. Do you wish to leave dirty footprints on her freshly cleaned stairs?"

A small line formed between her mousy brown eyebrows. "No."

"Then shall we take the main stairs? Just for today."

She drew in an uncomfortable, shallow breath. "We are still going to the kitchen?"

I caught Mrs. Musgrave's gaze behind Fanny's head. The housekeeper nodded. "Yes," I said with confidence. "Your breakfast is already waiting."

"Very well," my sister agreed.

I shared a victorious smile with the housekeeper before walking with Fanny down the corridor toward the grand staircase. My sister disliked this part of the house. Or any part, really, which exposed her to observation from anyone who might happen to visit. Part of me wondered if it was a routine borne of such avoidance, or if Fanny had merely been relegated to the shadows for so long that she now found comfort in them.

It took twice as long to reach the kitchens as it normally did, which put our morning to a late start. But Fanny could not be rushed.

We sat together at the end of the servants' long table and ate a breakfast of porridge and sliced apples. When that was finished, we went outside to walk the garden path to the head gardener's cottage.

"Good morning, Mr. Ramsey," I called, waving to the aged man in his doorway as we passed the front of his house. Circling to the back, I settled on the carved bench while Fanny checked the bird feeders, replenishing them as needed. I fiddled with the edge of my black shawl, pulling it tighter around my shoulders to ward off the incoming autumn chill while Mr. Ramsey pointed out a bird in the distance and spoke to Fanny about it. This was my favorite part of our mornings.

I gave Fanny another quarter-hour before approaching them. "We ought to continue on our way if we want to have enough time to draw before tea."

Fanny caught my gaze briefly before looking away. Her green eyes, so like mine in shape and hue, did not rest for long on another person's countenance. We looked so similar to one another, but we couldn't be more different.

"I would like that," she said.

"Thank you, Mr. Ramsey."

The aging gardener's smile twinkled down at me. "It is my pleasure, my lady, as always."

I dipped my head in farewell before turning back to the path skirting the gardener's house. Lamouth Park loomed ahead of us, its turrets spearing the sky with their sharp points and dark stone. It was Gothic, imposing, uninviting. But it was home.

So long as Fanny was here, so would I be.

"Mother wants you to marry the vicar's brother," Fanny said, pulling me from my frank assessment of our house. "The vicar's brother is a viscount."

I looked at her sharply. Only Mother could be heartless enough to already scheme another match for me. Regardless of how I had felt about my husband, he had only been buried a few months now, and I was in no hurry to leave my sister. "You ought not eavesdrop."

Fanny was unbothered, her voice matter-of-fact. "She told Mrs. Musgrave to prepare a menu fit for the king when he comes to dine."

Mother thought to impress a viscount into proposing marriage? Or perhaps to accentuate the fact that he would be proposing to an earl's daughter and keep him in his place— which was much more likely.

"I do not intend to leave you, Fanny." We turned on the path away from Lamouth Park, making our way through the woods.

Leaves crunched beneath our feet, and the reduced sunlight made the air crisp.

"That makes me happy," she said, pulling out the pocket watch she kept on a chain around her neck. She seemed satisfied we were not too far behind schedule and slid it back beneath the neckline of her gown.

The hamlet came into view. It was my goal to find a way to provide for myself, and if I did, I could set us up in a cottage somewhere. The only dilemma now was how I might manage it. "Would you like to live in a small house with me someday, Fanny?"

Her eyebrows drew together, her head shaking before the words escaped her lips. "Leave Lamouth? Leave Mother and Father?"

As though Mother would not welcome such a change. I shook off the unkind thought. Father would most assuredly miss us, but eventually he would not be here anymore and we would need to have a plan in place.

"It would be a very cozy cottage," I hedged. "We could plant a garden—"

"I do not wish to leave." The finality in her tone rang clear. Her hands started wringing, a sign she was growing distressed.

"We do not need to leave Lamouth," I soothed. "It was only an idea."

"I do not wish to leave," she repeated.

"And we will not." I pasted a smile on my face to cover my disappointment. "Our visit must be quick with Henrietta and the chickens, remember, or we will not have time to draw."

Fanny nodded, comforted by the return to her routine, the return to her normal. But the possibility of an unknown future hovered before me, as it had often done since my husband died. My marriage had been arranged—a convenience to keep Lamouth Park in the family. Colin had been a third cousin, and he had been the correct age to make our arrangement suitable to both parties. But pneumonia was not conscientious of rank, and even a future earl could be felled by illness.

Now that Colin was gone and the next heir was a stranger, we no longer had the comfortable assurance of living forever at Lamouth Park. One day, Father would die and a stranger would inherit the whole of it. I consoled myself that my father's health was robust, that he was a healthy, sturdy man.

Fanny bent to pet one of Henrietta's chickens, her eyes lighting up. A smile curled over my lips, satisfaction warming my chest, and I took comfort in the fact that our future was not something I needed to fret over today.

I sat in the window seat, looking out over the expanse of grass and the sheep dotting the hills in the distance. Smoke rose from the chimneys in the hamlet we'd visited that morning, creating a foggy layer over the treetops. Dust clouded on the road farther out, and I watched as a rider came down our lane faster than advisable on such terrain. The gravel did not make for sturdy footing, surely, to say nothing of the proximity to the house.

My back slowly straightened as I sat up, watching him grow nearer. His message must be of the utmost urgency to ride like that.

Fanny sat at the table in the center of the room, her focus bent over the paper in front of her, the birds taking shape beneath her charcoal pencils.

"Do you like it?" she asked when I stood, looking over her shoulder.

"They are beautiful, as always."

"Which is your favorite?"

How could I choose? The birds she'd drawn to cover the page all looked the same to me, though their positions and sizes differed. "Perhaps you might color them in, and then I will know. Would you like your watercolors?"

Fanny wrinkled her nose. "No."

I suppressed a chuckle. "Very well."

"Which is your favorite?" she repeated.

"The one at the bottom, nestled on the branch."

"I like him, too."

I was settling on my window seat again when the door opened and Janet stepped inside. She bobbed a curtsy.

"What is it?" I asked.

"Lady Huxley desires your presence in the drawing room, my lady."

"Now? I thought we were meant to meet her for tea in a half-hour."

"Now, my lady."

"Very well. Thank you, Janet."

The maid slipped out of the room.

"Come, Fanny. Mother wants to see us, so we must make haste."

She frowned. "I am not finished."

"Leave everything as it is, and we will return after tea to draw more."

"But after tea—"

"Yes, we *should* read after tea, but we are the mistresses of our own time. Would you rather read or draw?"

Fanny looked as though she was giving this great thought while I ushered her from her chair and toward the door. "I would rather draw," she said.

"Then that is what we shall do."

We had reached the door when Fanny took her hand from my grip. She never allowed me to hold it for long. At times I was better at reminding myself not to take it to heart. Fanny did not permit anyone to touch her longer than necessary. I looked down at her hands, now draped at her sides, the black charcoal smudging the outside of her palms.

"Oh, Fanny, your hands! Come, we need to clean them." I directed her to the washbasin kept in the corner of the room, wet her hands, and scrubbed until they were clean enough to meet Mother's standards.

We were taught from a young age never to keep our parents waiting. Father had left yesterday, traveling to London to participate in Parliament now that the summer recess was reaching its end, and Mother tended to be more controlling in his absences. I assumed she grew nervous when he was away and thus more exacting. I was always glad when Father returned.

I pulled Fanny down the stairs toward the drawing room, despite the knowledge she was likely growing uncomfortable, and stopped just outside the door. Our footman John stood outside, waiting for the signal to open the door while I straightened my gown, smoothed back a lock of my auburn hair, and proceeded to fix Fanny's neckline.

"Are you ready?" I asked her.

She nodded.

I inclined my head to John, and he opened the door for us to enter.

Mother sat in the center of her usual sofa, her back straighter than a plank of wood, her face ashen. When she did not critique our tardiness, I knew at once that something was not right.

We moved to the center of the carpet and bobbed curtsies before stepping back to sit on the sofa opposite her. "What is it?" I asked, looking at the note in her hands.

"There has been a terrible accident." Mother glanced up, her gaze locking on mine. "We—I—your father . . ."

Fear snaked into my chest, tightening like a coil around my lungs. "What about Father?" I asked, my voice weak.

"He was in an accident. His carriage . . ." Mother pressed her fingers to her temples in a display of anxiety I had seldom seen from her. She shook her head, whispering, "He did not survive."

Time grew still. The clock ticked louder. Mother's breathing roared in my ears, though she had not moved from her position on the sofa across from me. Fanny sat frozen beside me, and my shock shifted back into fear, clawing down my chest and into my hollow stomach.

"No," I said, the word hardly more than a whisper on my tongue. Tears filled my eyes, blurring the image of my mother as though I was looking at her through a rainy window. I wiped the tears, but they failed to slow. I wanted to pull Fanny in and seek comfort from her, but it would only make her unhappy to be touched. I curled my hands into gentle fists and drew in a long, shaky breath. Dread swirled through me, leaving me cold and sad, feeling far more alone now that my father and only ally was gone.

Oh no. If Father was no longer the earl . . .

"Who is next in line?" I asked, my voice barely passing my lips.

"His name is Daniel Palmer." Mother swallowed, her eyelids fluttering closed. She inhaled deeply, then set her gaze on me again. If she had made herself and her feelings vulnerable for a moment, it had passed. "Of Arden Castle. He has met your father in Town, though I believe you were not present."

My mind could not settle on the reality that someone else would now have claim to Lamouth Park, to this very room, to the gardener's cottage and the hamlet in the woods. Someone else would be responsible for the upkeep, for the servants, for Fanny's room.

Fanny.

Mother leaned over and picked up the bell, giving it a ring. John immediately opened the door.

"Send for Harry Johnson."

John lowered his head in acquiescence and slipped from the room.

"Father's solicitor?" I asked.

"Daniel Palmer must be notified. It would be best if he learned of this from us instead of through general gossip."

"What does this mean for us?" I asked quietly.

A look passed over Mother's face that at once frightened me. She covered it quickly, but her uncertainty was not a good sign. If Mother did not know what would become of us, anything was possible.

Anger sluiced through me in a sudden gush. "If Father and Colin had been more careful about ensuring a widow's jointure—"

"We cannot blame them," Mother snapped. "How could anyone have guessed that they would both leave us so suddenly?"

I wanted to argue further but curtailed my tongue. Had they not been so confident in the security of our line, we would not now be facing the loss of *everything*.

She drew herself up. "We will inform the new earl of his change in circumstances and assess our financial situation. Nothing more can be done now." She looked from me to Fanny. "Perhaps it is time to visit the asylum—"

"No." I spoke quickly, my hand finding Fanny's without a second thought. "We could not even afford such a thing."

"Father left a little money for Fanny."

Hope bloomed in my chest. "If he left money—"

"She cannot access it until she comes of age, but Harry Johnson will grant me funds for her care should it be needed. I have every confidence in him." Her voice was unyielding, and I could read her intentions perfectly. The money would be used to put Fanny in an asylum, or it would not be accessed at all. The solicitor would see to that.

I panicked, searching for an argument that would suffice.

"We are not yet destitute. The new Lord Huxley will likely grant us a mourning period to make our arrangements. Let us not consider any such measures until we must." Which, in my opinion, would be never.

I was not granted a reply but took her subsequent dismissal and pulled Fanny from the room at a sedate pace. Deep, black sadness spilled through my shoulders and seeped down through my body, threatening to steal my energy and will, but I fought it. There would be time to mourn Father later.

First, I needed to find a way to protect my sister.

CHAPTER TWO

DANIEL

London was a capital place to become lost. As it stood now, being invisible was my chief objective—blending into the crowds of men losing their fortunes at the tables or their wits at the pubs. For when one was lost, one could not be relied upon. If there was anything I was not, it was reliable . . . or even possessed of the desire to become such.

Lord Notley's parlor was crowded, my throat thick from the pipe smoke and overbearing perfumes. I looked again at the cards in my hand and knew I would walk out of the viscount's house a poorer man.

"Palmer?"

I looked up, catching Belford's eye. He knew in that moment I was sunk. I could see it in my friend's expression, his flat lips and suddenly averted gaze. He hated being the bank when I was losing at faro.

"Enough for tonight?" he asked, accepting my defeat and everyone's cards.

He knew me well.

I lifted my glass and swallowed the rest of my drink in one gulp. "I think I'll see what Waterley is up to. Care to join me?"

Belford glanced about the room, most likely looking for someone to take over the bank but coming up empty. "I'm here for the night."

I pushed back my chair, and the woman who had been giggling in my ear for the last quarter-hour rose with me, her hands sliding around my forearm. She'd been recently dismissed by the son of a baron, if gossip could be relied upon, and it seemed I was her target for his replacement. I wanted to shake her off but didn't wish to embarrass her. "Where to, now?" she asked.

"To find more willing friends," I said, sending a look to Belford.

He frowned. "I say, man. I've given my word to Notley that I would remain at the bank for the night, and a man's word—"

"At ease, Belford." I turned away from the table to give my seat to another when I nearly collided with a tall, familiar gentleman. I bowed, his foppish waistcoat nearly blinding me with its garishly bright colors. Were those swirls moving now? Perhaps I'd had too much to drink. I straightened, then moved to leave when he spoke.

"Young Palmer," he said.

Blast. I turned to face Lord Notley. The fop had been a friend of my father's, and he never ceased to make me feel small and insignificant, like I was still in leading strings instead of well past my majority with an estate and a life of my own. To say nothing for my well-tailored breeches. His faro parties were typically crushes, as this one was, and I had not intended to speak to the man. My luck was all in the river tonight.

"Sir," I said, pasting a smile on my face. The woman beside me clung to my arm tighter. She blinked up at him, in awe at his height, or perhaps just the height of his shirt points.

Despite his fashion obsession, Lord Notley was a force to be reckoned with in Parliament. I'd heard tales of his witty speeches and the way his words could turn the tide of a vote. To wield such power was impressive. That the man utilized this force for good only illustrated how he had maintained a close relationship with my father.

"I had the fortune of sitting with your mother last month at the theater," Lord Notley said. "Moorington is a fortunate chap, eh?"

"For ensnaring my mother? Or do you refer to his recently acquired set of grays?"

"Horses, women,"—he tilted his head side to side—"both of them are of some import. Though I've found that men who cannot decipher the difference in worth between the two hardly find either of them to be very loyal." He looked pointedly at the woman hanging on my arm, delivered a bow, and turned away.

My neck blazed. I had respect for women, and I certainly found their worth to exceed that of horseflesh. My intended slight to Lord Moorington had not at all been perceived.

Or perhaps Lord Notley had seen my intent and merely turned the insult back on me. *Well done, my lord.*

I slipped my arm from the woman's hold. I had no taste for securing a paramour at present, especially not one who required as much attention as this one seemed to. Alcohol would better serve my purposes. "Good evening," I said, giving her a bow and turning away.

"Wait, sir."

I drew in a breath, pleading for patience. "Yes?"

"Will I see you here tomorrow night?" She fluttered her lashes again, looking up at me though her chin dipped downward. If it was an attempt at appealing to me, she had missed the mark.

"That is unlikely." I nodded once more and escaped before she could waylay me further.

The butler retrieved my hat and gloves, and I jerked them on and stepped outside. Notley's words bounced about my mind while I searched for other potential meanings. Was it a slight against my habits regarding women? If so, I was glad I had not left his house with someone on my arm.

The cool air bit at me, the warmth from the day having fully receded now the sun had set. It was early autumn, the Parliament session about to begin as its summer recess had come to a close. With so many lords and ladies descending on Town, I needed to think about making an escape to the country.

I *could* return home. With Mother and Jane both married now, Arden Castle was empty but for the ghosts haunting its corridors. Those ghosts were reason enough to stay away, though they seemed to follow me as far as London on occasion. I could not even enjoy an evening of faro without summoning my father's presence to ruin my night.

His power only seemed to increase when I was in his castle.

"Sir?"

I looked up, half afraid Father's ghost had made a legitimate appearance. It was with relief that I found my servant standing before me on the paving stones instead. "Dean? What are you doing here?" *Was* he truly here? Perhaps I had drunk more than I meant to.

"I came to fetch you, sir. You've a visitor, and he won't be put off."

"Who would call now? Certainly he *will* be put off," I said indignantly. Be it misplaced irritation from my run-in with Lord Notley and the memories he conjured, but the gall of a man to insist on being seen at such a time was appalling. Unless . . . I stopped, grabbing Dean by his upper arm. "Is it about my mother? Or my sister?"

"I haven't any idea, sir."

I held on to his arm a little longer, more for stability than any need for reassurance.

"Shall I fetch a carriage?" he asked.

My arm dropped to my side. "I am perfectly capable of walking. Just help me find the right house."

"Yes, sir."

We made our way home, the streetlamps glowing orange to light our walk. Perhaps London wasn't as easy to disappear in as I'd hoped. I hadn't taken the same rooms as usual, but still I'd been located. For all I knew, Moorington, my new stepfather, was inquiring if I was still alive. It would not be the first time he had sent a buffoon to ascertain as much, and I had been equally vexed then.

Mother should have known better than to marry such a meddlesome busybody, but she'd been aware of the type of man Moorington was from the beginning. He'd proven his poor character when he required a sizable sum before agreeing to marry her. Then again, no one could measure up to my father. He was the best of men, and he never would have done something so bothersome as inserting himself in my affairs. I should know. I had been just as derelict when he was alive.

Candlelight glowed in the windows of my boarding house by the time we made it home. Dean opened the door, and I brushed past him into the parlor. A short, thin man with copper side-whiskers sat on the sofa, wringing his hands.

He stood upon my entrance. "It was thought you should be the first to hear the news, my lord, so I hastened directly to London."

"I am not . . ." I shook my head. No one had ever made the mistake of calling me *my lord* before. My father had been a force of good and well-loved by all, but never a lord. I, at less than a quarter of my father's value, was not even worthy of the mistake. "I am Daniel Palmer."

"Yes," he agreed, nodding. "Has news reached you of the carriage accident?"

Time seemed to slow as my stomach fell. "There was an accident? My mother? Jane?"

"It has naught to do with them."

"Ewan? Lachlan?" I asked, thinking of my sister's husband and son.

The stranger cleared his throat and nodded to Dean, who left the room. "Your immediate family is unharmed. Shall we sit?"

I moved to the edge of the sofa and sat as directed, more to stop the room from tilting than from any desire to be agreeable. Dean returned with a tray bearing two glasses and a decanter. He poured me a dram and handed me the brandy. I could not drink until I knew of the bad news this austere man carried.

"Who, then, was harmed?" I asked.

"Lord Huxley."

"I know the name," I said, searching through the fog muddling my brain.

"You very well *should*," muttered the man. "You are heir to his earldom."

I shook my head. "No, there was another man. Young and healthy. He was not much older than me."

"Colin Palmer?"

"Yes." I pointed at the fire-whiskered man and sipped my drink. I leaned back in my seat, self-satisfied. "The very one. He is the next earl."

"Colin Palmer died of pneumonia three months ago."

The brandy caught in my throat and I coughed, sputtering. Dean stared at me, wide-eyed, his hand reaching for the decanter. When I regained my natural breath, I sat up and stared at the stranger. "Who are you?"

"Harry Johnson, my lord, solicitor to the former Lord Huxley."

My lord. It made sense now, though I hated hearing it even more the second time. I threw back the contents of my glass and held it up for Dean to refill. He obliged me directly.

"Perhaps we ought to start at the beginning," Mr. Johnson said. "I realize your new responsibilities may seem overwhelming. I am here to assist you in whatever way I can. Lady Huxley felt it best if you did not learn of this from general gossip and dispatched me immediately. You were a difficult man to locate, my lord, and the news will surely be about London soon, if it is not already."

I shut my eyes, squeezing them closed in the hopes that this small, bewhiskered man would be gone when I opened them again.

He was still there. *Disappointing.*

I stood on shaky legs and gave him my most congenial smile.

Mr. Johnson must have mistaken that smile as my agreeing to his help. "I am putting up at the White Crown, if you are familiar with it? We can meet tomorrow, and—"

"There will be no need for that," I said.

"No? Perhaps—"

"No. We have no need to meet at all." I pressed my lips to the brandy glass, watching him search for my meaning. I tipped the glass back so the contents would burn a warm path straight to my belly. "I do not accept, sir." I put the glass on the small table with a thud, but the glass toppled off the side and rolled across the carpet.

"Do not accept?"

I turned to walk from the room. "I will be no earl."

The morning light was harsh against my closed eyelids. Pounding throbbed in my head, evidence of too much to drink the night before. Had I been sick? I pried my eyes open and looked around me, but my simple rented room was clean. I dropped my head back on the pillow in relief and immediately regretted the action when my stomach revolted, sending a bout of nausea through my body.

I was never drinking again.

Dean opened the door softly and poked his head inside, startling when he caught my eye. He'd learned long ago not to knock on mornings such as these, and I was glad to be spared a little.

"Lord Belford is here," he said in a near-whisper.

"So early?" I groaned.

Dean's mouth opened, hesitating, before he grimaced. "It is noon, sir."

Of course it was. "Tell him I will be down soon."

"Yes, my lo—"

"No," I said, sitting up and pointing at my long-time servant to the detriment of my pounding head. "We'll have none of that."

He slipped away quickly.

I was not as fast on my feet. Pulling myself out of bed and crossing the room felt like slogging through sand. I splashed water on my face and dressed enough to accept one of my oldest friends.

"Belford," I said, finding him in the parlor. He sat in the same seat the solicitor had occupied the night before, leaving me with a stale smile.

His pale eyebrows drew together in concern. "You unwell, Palmer?"

I sat on the stiff chair opposite him, refusing to claim the seat I had occupied last night, if for no other reason than wanting to distance myself from that distasteful episode. "Too much to drink."

He nodded, then looked at me warily. "I heard the news."

"There is no news. I refuse to acknowledge it."

He relaxed. Had he been worried it was on his shoulders to tell me I'd been elevated? Poor man. "You will go to the Huxley seat, then, I presume?"

"I'll do nothing of the sort."

"No, no, you are right. It is better to give the widow time to grieve. It is kind of you to allow a mourning period for her."

"You misunderstand, Belford. I do not ever intend to set foot near the Huxley seat. I have a home. Arden Castle."

He squinted, tilting his head in thought. "I suppose it is not typical, but it is done sometimes. Now that you are an earl—"

I stood and walked toward the hearth, warming my hands with the heat emanating from the fire. "You mistake me, Belford. I refuse to be the earl."

His mouth dropped open before he closed it again, his eyes narrowing. "You realize you cannot actually do that, yes?"

My father, had he been alive, would have inherited the earldom. He would have stepped into the role, perfectly at ease among the lords and possessed of the knowledge to vote appropriately. I was a usurper, a fraud. I was not worthy of the seat in Parliament, let alone the estate, tenants, land, and everything that came with the title.

"It was never meant to be mine," I whispered.

"Bloody bad luck, I say," Belford agreed. "To lose both the earl and his heir within a few months of each other. The poor family."

Yes, exceedingly pitiable. And now they had to contend with *me*. The poor family, indeed.

CHAPTER THREE

DANIEL

8 months later
May 1819

I had only been in residence at Arden Castle for a fortnight, and thus far the house had been both the refuge I sought and the penance I deserved. My father's presence was everywhere here—in his painting hanging above the mantel, his leather chair in the study, his laughter echoing in the stables where his favorite horse still resided. Memories taunted me, but the isolation provided solace in equal measure. After running from one place to the next like a veritable hurricane over the last several months, settling in my familiar home felt like an exhale.

I had thought I could find refuge in distraction, visiting my friends and never staying in one place very long. But my recent house party experience at Mr. Hale's place in Surrey had ruined me for the idea. Far too many women had grand notions of using me to become a countess. It made me sick, so I retreated to Arden for peace and *yes*, to hide.

It took the entirety of the first week to push the ghosts to the back of my mind, but now I had developed a comfortable routine —riding, hunting, avoiding the neighbors who heard I was back in Arden and wanted to see the defiant earl for themselves.

I would grow used to living here again at some point, I wagered. Perhaps it would be easier if I built a fence.

A knock on the door preceded Dean's entrance bearing a tray. "Tea, my lord?"

I glared, refusing to answer my valet as resolutely as he refused to call me by anything other than the title. "Say that again, and I'll have you horsewhipped."

"Yes, my lord." He set the tray down on the table beside my chair and walked from the room.

I needed to come up with a new threat—something he would take seriously. Something I actually meant, perhaps.

The sound of carriage wheels on the gravel outside stole my attention, and I crossed to the window to catch a peek at my visitors. When would they learn I wished to be left alone? A flash of the yellow lacquered door caught my eye. I pressed my back against the wall, out of view. Yellow? That was the spinster sisters. Hopefully I was able to hide before either of the Misses Kelby had spotted me through the window.

This was their third attempt at visiting me, and each time Dean was less helpful in moving them on their way.

Distant sounds in the empty house revealed when the sisters were permitted indoors and again when Dean came down the corridor to fetch me. I pulled out the drapes and slipped behind them, grateful they were voluminous and fell clear to the floor.

"My lord?" Dean asked, confusion lacing his tone. He stepped into the room, and his motions sounded as though they froze for a moment.

My breath was hot against the wall of thick drapes closing me in. I could feel my pulse rising, and it was ridiculous. Silly. *Not* the sort of behavior that should be exhibited by a twenty-seven-year-old man. But the last thing I wanted at present was to be forced into a genial conversation with two aged spinsters who cared for nothing more than finding me a nice, eligible female or filling their teapots with enough gossip to pour out among the other local parishioners.

Women and their bloody meddling.

I couldn't face them without a drink in me, and I'd yet to touch a drop today. Not intentionally, of course.

Dean's footsteps disappeared down the corridor. I slumped back against the wall, listening for the sound of carriage wheels making a retreat.

It did not come.

How long would I be forced to hide here? The sound of women's voices carried through the house. Their refusal to depart surprised me a little, but I imagined they were stalling until I could be located. I breathed in the musty drapes and shifted to a more comfortable position. I was going to be here for a while.

"He was last seen in here, ma'am."

"Thank you, Worthlin," one of the women said while yawning, her words stretched out and high-pitched.

Worthlin? Now the butler was attempting to locate me as well? Apparently he was no ally of mine. Why had Dean not circumvented them?

Footsteps faded again, and I waited until they disappeared entirely before lifting the drapes a little for a fresh breath. The dust was sure to make me sneeze soon, and that would give me away entirely.

A sound within the room made me grow still. Had Worthlin left one of the Kelby sisters behind? That man was facing a demotion now.

"Daniel?"

I knew that voice. Impulse made me run through a list of my

misdeeds of the day, in order to ascertain what I needed to hide. I shook off the thought. I was a grown man now.

I pushed back the drapes to find my mother standing in the center of the room, facing me as though she'd known precisely where I was, her dark brown eyes piercing me from across the room. Despite the undoubtedly long journey she must have just taken, she was every bit the countess: clean, unwrinkled traveling gown, her raven hair smoothed back into a delicate style. She embodied strength and elegance.

Oh, how I'd missed her.

"Mother." I greeted her with a bow.

"Are there children somewhere about that I am unaware of?" she asked.

"Not that I know of."

"Then why are you playing hide-and-seek?" Her innocent expression belied the teasing lilt of her words.

I could lie, but she would see through me. I could make up a farce, but she would not find it amusing. The truth, it was. "I only know one other household with a yellow carriage, and I did not see the crest on yours."

Her eyebrows lifted. "A local with a yellow—the *Kelby* sisters? Harmless, sweet old women."

"Sweet? Possibly. Harmless? Most assuredly not."

"What grievances do you have to lay at their feet?"

"Matchmaking of the most horrific and acute kind." I had overheard them when I walked through town a few days prior, so it was not a product of my imagination. Evidently there were plenty of young women in the nearby county who would make me an excellent countess, if only I were to look with greater effort.

A laugh slipped from Mother's regal lips. It was so seldom an occurrence that I found it more rewarding.

"It is my belief," I continued, "they think themselves capable of filling your role now that you are absent. Though you still manage to accomplish your share of mothering and meddling, I think, regardless of the distance between us."

Mother tilted her head. "Not as much as I would like."

If she wanted to find me a wife, she would need to spend more time with me. But since I had gone to substantial effort to make that impossible in recent months, and I did not wish to set her mind to the task now, I would not mention it.

"I've traveled a great distance, Daniel. Has that not earned me some affection?"

"Of course, Mother." I crossed the room and pulled her in for an embrace, inhaling the familiar scent of her perfume and allowing the warmth of her presence to relax me. I might've spent a good deal of effort avoiding my mother, but that did not mean it was any less comforting to see her again.

She drew in a breath and let it out on a small sigh before pulling back and looking at my face intently.

I avoided her gaze and gestured to the tea tray. "Would you care for some tea? It is still hot."

"I would, thank you." She sat in the seat I'd previously occupied and helped herself to the pot of steaming water. When her cup was prepared to her liking, she brought it to her lips and took a sip. "How long has it been since I've seen you, Daniel?"

She knew the answer to that. I pretended I couldn't see through her. "The Huttons' house party, I think."

"Almost a year ago? Good heavens. One would think you were avoiding your mama."

"Not avoiding *you* in particular," I corrected.

Silence made the discomfort loud. The distant sounds of servants unpacking what I now realized was my mother's carriage, footsteps in the marble entryway, doors opening and closing. She was here for a visit, and by the sound of things, it was not going to be a short one. How had she learned of my residence here? Whom should I dismiss for being her informant?

"My husband opted to remain at home," she said, sipping her tea again.

I could not express the joy that swooped through me for fear of hurting Mother's feelings, but I allowed a smile to flit over my lips. "Shame."

"Indeed. He might join me later, but Hammel's wife is due to have her baby next month, and Lord Moorington thought it best he remain nearby in case the child arrives early."

"Eager to know if they have an heir?"

Mother's eyes narrowed. "He is eager to meet his first grandchild. He would not dare miss it, even though I warned him that firstborns are often late. Moorington is not the villain you've painted him to be."

A man who would not marry my mother unless I agreed to provide a large financial portion for her was nothing but a villain to me, and as such he would remain. She might be blind to his faults, but I was not—nor was he to mine. "Regardless, I think we will both be more comfortable with the whole of England between us."

She looked away, hurt splashing over her eyes, and I knew a moment of regret.

"It is always good to see you, Mother," I said, giving her a congenial smile. My shoulders were tense, awaiting whatever guilt she would soon throw my way. It was no coincidence I'd yet to see her since the earldom had been unceremoniously dropped in my lap. I couldn't imagine she would let the matter lie, and in truth, I was surprised she had not found a way to descend upon me before now.

Her new family undoubtedly kept her busy.

"I am ever so glad to be here."

For a moment, I wondered if she had almost said *home*, but alas, that was somewhere in the south now.

I stood. "Shall I fetch you something of more substance?"

"No, I thank you." Mother stood, setting her mostly empty

teacup back on the tray. "I would prefer to rest until dinner. Will you ask Worthlin to ensure the table is set for four?"

My body stilled. "Whom did you bring with you?"

"I came alone. But I thought to invite the Kelby sisters to dine if they are available on such short notice."

Was she in earnest? I thought not. I flattened my lips. "You have become more amusing, Mother."

She walked ahead of me, head high and shoulders back. "I have no notion what you could mean, darling. I intend to send a note before I rest."

I laughed again. I'd avoided her for too long. Having my mother returned to Arden Castle, and *without* her meddlesome husband, felt better than I could have imagined.

But now I needed a drink.

It would appear that Mother had more of a sense of humor than I'd earlier given her credit for. I sat now at the dinner table, a Kelby sister to my left and the other beside Mother. Their graying hair was identically styled and hidden beneath white lace caps, and their gowns, though of the same style, were garishly bright pink and orange.

They were also the slowest eaters I'd ever had at my table. My fork made a screeching sound when it slid across my empty plate, and I set it down, clearing my throat.

"You must tell Jane to visit us as soon as she is able," Miss Edith said. "I desire to see that son of hers."

"She might be persuaded to join us when the weather clears," Mother replied.

"It is not advisable to travel in such rain," Miss Kelby agreed, nodding. "And with a little babe, too."

"Are you planning to host a house party this year?" Miss

Edith asked. Her wide eyes were made wider by the spectacles perched on her nose.

This was it, the moment she had been preparing herself for. I could practically see the advice begging to bubble out of Miss Edith. It was only a matter of time, when one found oneself in conversation with the Kelby sisters. They would always steer the topic to the matter of matrimony. Perhaps it was because neither of them had ever wed that they both carried an unhealthy obsession with ensuring that everyone else was given ample opportunity for it.

"That is Daniel's decision." Mother lifted her glass and took a sip. "Lord Moorington and I would always be glad of the excuse to visit Arden."

"Oh, my lord," Miss Edith beseeched me, her eyes now reminding me of an owl. "You *must* entice your mama to return later this summer."

"And dear Jane, too," Miss Kelby added.

I gave my best smile. "I will see what I can do." I would be happy for the opportunity to see my sister and her family. That was nothing I needed convincing of. But a house party? Where unwed ladies could be called to Arden to vie for my hand?

Thank you, but no.

Mother took another sip from her glass before setting it on the table. She lifted her gloves from her lap and slid them on slowly before pushing back her chair and rising. "Shall we adjourn to the drawing room? Perhaps we can play cards?"

"I am afraid we must beg leave to postpone such a treat," Miss Kelby said. "We have recently acquired a house guest, and we would be remiss if we left her home alone for too long."

Mother stilled. "In truth? You would have been more than welcome to bring her, of course. You needed only to say so."

"We could never have imposed in such a way." Miss Edith slid her gaze to me. "But she is very eager to meet Lord Huxley."

A pinch of uneasiness twisted my stomach. I did my best to

cover it, but I was not used to the name the world insisted on calling me by, and I vowed I never would grow accustomed to it.

We saw the Misses Kelby to their carriage with the promise to dine at their home in a week in order to meet their mysterious house guest. A goddaughter, evidently, and one possessed of a name I was unfamiliar with.

"That was a cruel trick," I said when Mother and I mounted the steps again to reach our house. It was unseasonably chilly for the beginning of summer, and I was eager for the weather to take a warmer turn.

"It was just desserts for the man who thought he should hide from their presence. Did I not teach you to have compassion for all people? Even the spinsters?"

"*Especially* the spinsters." I had always been taught to look after the unwed women who did not have another to rely upon. It was my responsibility as landowner to see to their needs, and Worthlin managed to ensure they were cared for. "I am not remiss in *all* of my responsibilities," I muttered.

"I did not think you were." We stepped inside and Worthlin closed the door behind us, cutting off the cool wind. Mother hesitated, waiting for the butler to leave. She worried her lip in a gesture very much unlike her, and I took that to mean she was debating whether to say what was on her mind.

Whatever it was, she had traveled a great distance to say it to me. I knew she could not have visited without cause. Since I had inherited an earldom months ago and had yet to so much as answer to the title in that time, I was fairly sure she wanted to remind me of my responsibilities. To tell me of the family I was displacing by inheriting their home. To call me to action in some way. The Lords would soon be ending its current session, and she likely thought I should have been there, too.

None of these were things I wanted to hear, however.

Clearly, I already knew them. "You must be tired from your journey."

"Daniel, wait." She held my gaze with the utmost resolution. "I know it is no small thing to become an earl. I *do* understand what it entails."

If she meant to endear me to the topic by referencing her fairly new marriage to the Earl of Moorington, she was off the mark.

She lifted one hand. "I am not asking you to do anything you are uncomfortable with—"

"Then you will not ask anything of me at all."

Her mouth tightened, her hand dropping. The careful countess was gone, and in her stead my mother stepped fully into her familiar shoes. "You cannot ignore it forever. There are people relying on you, women left behind who do not know what to make of their circumstances or what to expect now that you've inherited their home. You have the tenants of Lamouth Park to consider, and the responsibilities to England that befall an earl."

Rocks pressed upon my shoulders, weighing me with the truth of her words. "I did not ask for this. I do not want it."

"Unfortunately, that is not how earldoms operate, son." Compassion warred the frustration evident in my mother's tone. "Think of the last Lord Huxley. He left behind a wife and two daughters. Can you imagine the strain they must be under? They did not realize they would ever lose their home."

"Surely they understood that one day—"

"Lady Verity, the older of the daughters, was married to Colin Palmer. They believed themselves secure. Now she is a widow, like her mother."

I knew that. It was information presented to me earlier, but I had brushed it off then, not allowed it to settle. Her meaning now made its way to my understanding. The women had likely believed they would always remain at Lamouth, that Lady Verity's marriage to the next earl guaranteed as much.

"You ought to visit Lamouth," Mother said. "Put the women at ease. Permit them to remain as long as they need in order to find a suitable arrangement."

Except that such an action would mean accepting the mantle placed on my shoulders. I could not do so, for it was already suffocating me. How would I feel if I allowed it to take over completely? Would I even be able to breathe? "I will not go to Lamouth Park."

"Perhaps we ought to invite the women here, then?"

"Do as you wish, Mother." I dipped a bow and started walking away, needing fresh air or brandy or something to cover my faults and push them back into the shadows. "I will have no part in it."

CHAPTER FOUR

VERITY

The invitation was sent by Lady Moorington, but Mother regarded it as a direct summons from the new Lord Huxley. "He would like us to travel to him. Do they think our home unsuitable?" she mused, taking the letter back from me and setting it on the sofa cushion beside her, her gaze narrowing at the offending script.

"I very much doubt that is the issue." I smoothed my black bombazine gown over my knees as I sat in the adjacent chair, straightening my shoulders before she could instruct me to do so. "Lady Moorington mentioned her son's need to attend to business at home. Perhaps he intends to sell Arden Castle and would like to see the matter settled himself?" A man did not need two such large estates, surely. Some peers managed to hold many estates, but Father never had a need for it. Lamouth Park was enough for him.

Except for his hunting lodge in Scotland, of course. And there was the house in Mayfair for when he attended the House of Lords. He had acquired a place in Bath as well, when they attempted to cure Fanny with the waters, though last I had heard, Father was of a mind to sell it. Did he manage the sale before he died? My thoughts became shadows, gray and sad. I lifted them again. I didn't have much time before Fanny would be finished with her drawing for the day, and I had something I wanted to try with her.

Mother let out a short sigh. "I suppose we must go."

I froze. "We?"

Her gaze flicked to me. "Yes, *we*. Do you imagine I would travel to Northumberland alone? The invitation was extended to both of us, so we shall both answer it."

Both? "*All* of us, you mean?" I gently corrected her. I had read the letter. The invitation was extended to Lady Huxley and her daughters.

There was a breath of silence before Mother chose to give me a response. "We need not disrupt Fanny's schedule."

That was something we heartily agreed upon. "Then I shall remain here—"

"You will do nothing of the sort."

My heart stalled. I could not—no, I *would* not—leave Fanny in the care of the servants. Who would go about her routine with her? Persuade her to walk another path when hers was obstructed? Who would be able to reason with her when she found herself in an uncomfortable position? To take her to the village on Wednesdays or church on Sundays?

Mrs. Musgrave cared for Fanny; indeed, most of the servants did. But they were not her family. When she was in the throes of discomfort or agitation, no one else could reach her the same way I could. "If something were to happen to Fanny while I was gone . . ."

"Nothing will occur that cannot be righted upon our return."

So Mother believed our return was imminent? "I am not comfortable leaving my sister, and I am certain she would not find comfort in being left behind, either."

Mother's eyes narrowed slightly. She had never been close to either of her children. Indeed, our nurse was more sentimental toward us, and she was dismissed when I was ten, replaced by a bland governess with a penchant for Shakespeare and Greek—neither of which had appealed to Fanny. I had been my sister's champion for many years, the correspondent who found a way to please both parties—adding drawing, music, and walks outside to balance the sonnets and plays that were resolutely entering one of Fanny's ears and leaving through the other.

That I had stepped into the role of protector for my sister had been entirely natural. Six years my junior, she had needed a champion, and there was no one else willing to don the sword and shield. Now I wore the armor daily.

"If Lady Moorington invited both of your daughters, she might find it odd if only one of them arrives with you."

Mother narrowed her gaze more markedly. "Very well. Fanny will accompany us, but only if you can vow she will not be a disruption."

If you can vow she will not be a disruption. Who could promise such a thing? To say nothing of the fact that it seemed far too easy to convince her. "I will certainly do my best."

"It is settled, then, but do not give me cause for regret. Our future will be in no way secured if you remain here," she muttered.

If my mother was depending upon me to secure our future, perhaps we could come to an agreement. I would have liked nothing more than to remain at Lamouth Park with Fanny forever. Perhaps if Daniel Palmer proved an amenable man, we could contrive an arrangement to suit both our families.

Mother certainly seemed to consider it a possibility.

"Do you wish to appeal to Lord Huxley's better nature?" I asked. "Perhaps we can beg use of the dower house. Lady Moorington has no need of it. Her husband possesses a home in Surrey, I believe."

"I will not be relegated to that cottage."

It hardly warranted the name. The dower house was not

grand in relation to Lamouth Park, but I believed it was in mostly good repair and large enough to house Mother, Fanny, and me comfortably. We could remain at Lamouth until I hit upon a scheme to provide for us, at least. Mother could possibly be permitted use of the dower house for the rest of her days. If Lord Huxley was of a charitable disposition, perhaps he would be willing to grant funds to provide Mother a companion as well.

She might not wish to call the dower house her home, but I feared she had no other choice. She could not very well remain at Lamouth after the earl deigned to come.

Goodness, was *that* her plan? To dig in her heels and refuse to vacate the property?

Mother's mouth pinched, showing her limited patience for this conversation. "Lord Huxley holds a reputation as a rake, but we will not allow that to discourage us."

"Father was replaced by a rake?" He would not have appreciated that.

"Indeed. Daniel Palmer was known to ruin a young woman years ago and is a confirmed flirt. But we must make the best of it. We will write and inform them to expect us in a fortnight," Mother continued. "Perhaps we ought to have new gowns made."

With the new earl's money? We had very little of our own. "I do not have any need for new gowns."

"I wish you could put off the black before we arrive for a better first impression, but alas . . ." She trailed into a thought, exhibiting behavior I was not familiar with. "A gown in green muslin would have suited you. You always favored those hues."

"Perhaps I shall bring one for when my mourning is over—"

"In three weeks' time? That will be too late." She mumbled a bit to herself. I heard the word *impression*, but I couldn't discern anything else. "Still, I suppose you ought to bring colored gowns for when you are finished with mourning."

Too late, though? For what, exactly? It never boded well when Mother had a plan. I had been fortunate in marrying Colin in one regard: my future had been set my entire life. It was impossible to mourn that which I did not know I'd lost, and I'd never been one for flights of fancy like romance or love matches. An arrangement with my father's heir had allowed me to remain in my own home, with my sister, where almost nothing about our lives had to change—that had been most ideal. That was the arrangement I'd originally believed myself agreeing to.

Now, however, in the more than eleven months since Colin's death, I'd tasted freedom, the ability to try and make a future not just for myself, but also for Mother and Fanny. If Mother aimed to orchestrate a plan for me, I had a feeling I would not like what she had in mind.

"You needn't look so frightened," Mother said.

"What are you scheming?"

"I have yet to decide." She lifted the letter again and gave a flick of her wrist. "That is enough for today. Write to accept the invitation and give our arrival date for a fortnight from tomorrow."

"Yes, Mother." I rose and took the letter as instructed, rubbing my fingers along the creases of the paper as I walked from the room and up the stairs. At some point, Mother would need to accept our situation in life had changed. It would not be the same ever again.

I supposed I needed to take our altered situation more seriously as well. I hovered in the doorway, watching Fanny at the table in the center of the small room. A mousy brown lock of hair trailed over her cheek, nestling near her chin. Her focus was bent to the paper, so much so that she did not notice me.

Or perhaps she did sense my presence but chose not to acknowledge it.

"Fanny?"

She finished shading the belly of a sparrow, then looked up. "Yes?"

I crossed the room and gently lowered myself on the seat beside her, reaching forward to push back the loose hair. She leaned away from me. I tensed, clasping my hands together. Our journey to Bath to try the waters had not been a success. The disruption in Fanny's routine had caused her behavior to be equally erratic and unpredictable. That was the last time an asylum was mentioned.

I vowed then it would never be mentioned again.

Lunatic asylums were inhumane. That our mother could contemplate entering my sister into a house that chained women and put them on display for anyone who had a spare coin and morbid curiosity was unforgivable. I would do anything in my power to protect Fanny from such a fate.

I shoved my anger away and smiled to soften my question. "How would you like to travel to Northumberland?"

Fanny blinked, her stare blank. "I am not familiar with their birds."

My heart clenched, my hand sliding over the tabletop in her direction, though I was careful not to touch her again. "We were invited to the new Lord Huxley's home for a visit. We could make a study of the different birds we see on our journey, perhaps?"

"How long must we sit in the carriage?"

"I should think only a few days." When she didn't speak again, I tried to make it sound more palatable. "It could be an adventure. A research adventure."

The charcoal pencil twitched in her fingers, as if she wanted only to draw and I was keeping her from it. "What do you mean by a few days? Three days?" she asked.

"Four," I said. "Four is much more likely, though I need to inquire. I am not entirely certain."

"Four days to travel," she repeated, a thin line between her eyebrows. "How many days will we remain in Northumberland?"

"The invitation was extended for a fortnight." I held the letter on my lap, pinching the edge while I studied her face for any sign of emotion. Was I incorrect in assuming she would not do well alone? Her green eyes flicked from me to the paper in front of her, and I softened my voice. "Would you prefer to remain here?"

"With you?"

"No. Mother would like for me to go to Arden Castle to meet the new earl. We need to make a good impression on the man, I think, and it would seem impolite if Mother went alone to his house."

She gave a soft sigh. "Then we will go. Mother will expect it of us, will she not?"

I hadn't the heart to correct her. "It would please her, certainly."

Fanny shaded in the wing of her sparrow. "We can make a study of their birds, then we can come home."

Home. The finality in her voice squeezed my heart. Her willingness to come with us was a surprise, but perhaps that was a testament of her trust in me. "Remember, this is not our home anymore, Fanny. The new Lord Huxley has inherited the estate. It is only a matter of time until we need to find a new situation."

"If he is a kind man, he will not make me leave my birds."

Indeed. If he was a kind man, he could be induced to allow us to remain in the dower house. I would not reveal that plan to her until I knew more. "Shall we walk down to the dower house and see if it is in good repair?"

"I am drawing," Fanny reminded me, moving her pencil to focus on the shimmer in the bird's eyes.

"You are the mistress of your time, Fanny."

"Mistress of my time," she whispered, frowning. She shook her head. "I am drawing. I'm meant to draw now."

It was growing too late, anyway, I supposed. "Perhaps tomorrow after church?"

She did not look at me. "If we must."

"We will be quick about it. For now, I am going to leave you so I might write a letter accepting the invitation on Mother's behalf."

She moved on to begin the body of another bird, her focus trapped in the swooping lines and shaded feathers, while I settled myself at the writing desk. How could Mother even entertain the idea of allowing Fanny, so lacking in artifice and conceit, to be subjected to the horrors of an asylum? I had heard the tales from our chambermaid, the way they shackled women and tried all manner of experiments to heal their distorted minds.

But Fanny was not distorted or in need of drastic treatments. She was sweet. She cared for animals nearly more than she did for other people, perhaps—but could that be considered a failing of the acutest kind? I worried my lip, removing a fresh sheet of paper and dipping my quill in the ink to reply to Lady Moorington.

Whatever came of this visit, one thing was clear: I was going to find a home for us. I would keep my sister safe.

CHAPTER FIVE

VERITY

W e walked through the church doors, past rows of our neighbors in their Sunday best, until we reached our family box and filed inside. Mother sat nearest the aisle, and we quietly waited beside her for the service to begin—three women, two of us shrouded in black gowns and somber expressions, Fanny in lavender and disinterest. We were quite the sight.

Our soft-spoken vicar stood on the raised pulpit, his eyes roaming the congregation as he preached a sermon with gentle admonitions and subdued conviction. My mind wandered to the fidgeting fingers beside me. Fanny's difficulty with sitting still was not a disruption, but Mother disliked it heartily, even though no one outside of our box was likely aware.

A woman giggled softly in the pew to our left. I looked to find Miss Nelson with her head bent, stifling a giggle. Miss Toole sat beside her, struggling to temper her smile. Whatever joke had passed between them had reached the vicar's notice, and he paused to pour his attention on them briefly before resuming the sermon. They bent their heads together again in a gentle giggle, and my gut clenched briefly. I tried to subdue the jealousy. I would not exchange my life for any other, and I would not give up Fanny's company to have more varied friendships. But sometimes I still wished I could have both.

Miss Toole caught my gaze, and I turned my head away swiftly. How utterly mortifying to be caught looking at her while ruminating about my lack of friends.

"Look there," a little boy said in the pew behind us. "It's a bird."

Fanny perked up immediately, turning around. "Where?" she asked, not bothering to temper her volume.

Mother's head whipped toward her.

"We must not speak while the vicar is speaking," I whispered.

"Where is the bird?" Fanny asked the boy again, ignoring me. He must have pointed to it, for she looked up. I followed her gaze to find a blackbird up in the rafters, flitting from beam to beam, searching for a way out of the church.

Murmuring slowly heightened as the congregation's attention moved from the vicar to the struggling blackbird.

"He needs help," Fanny said, rising to better see the bird.

"Sit *down*," Mother hissed, but my sister did not heed her.

The blackbird rested briefly on the edge of a thick, wooden beam. Then he jumped to the side and flew to the opposite end of the church. He was bound to ruin his sense of direction from the flitting to and fro.

"We need to encourage him toward the door," Fanny said, her hands beginning to shake in front of her waist. She bounced on the balls of her feet and hummed nervously, her voice rising and falling with each attempt the blackbird made to locate an open window.

I stood, taking her hand in an effort to still it, but she drew away from me.

"Make her stop," Mother said quietly. Her words from earlier rang in my ears. *Vow she will not be a disruption.*

I could not fail now, or Mother would change her mind

about allowing Fanny to accompany us to Arden Castle. But how? Force would only aggravate Fanny further. The bird continued to search for freedom while the children pointed and laughed at its failed attempts. The vicar had given up attempting to maintain control over the congregation, waiting on his raised dais for order to return to the room.

I moved closer to Fanny, looking in her eyes despite how resolutely she would not look at mine. "We will not assist the bird by causing commotion."

Her gaze flicked to me briefly before searching for the bird again.

"If we are boisterous and loud, it will only frighten him," I said.

She quieted immediately, but still she bounced, her hands shaking as if she was expelling her anxious energy through them instead of her nervous humming.

The bird flew toward the open doors at the end of the room but misjudged the space and hit the edge of the frame with a *thunk*. It dropped to the ground and fell still. Fanny gasped beside me, and I reached for her forearm, stalling her from running toward it. "Wait, Fanny. Watch him."

"He's hurt!" she yelled, garnering attention from the people sitting near us.

The bird hopped up, turning its head and jumping to the side, as if testing its balance again. It hopped a few more times before flying outside and taking my frayed nerves with it. "He's safe," I said. "See, Fanny? He is unharmed."

"How can we know?" Her bent eyebrows faced the door. The only thing keeping her in our box was that Mother and I stood in front of her, barring her way.

I leaned closer and lowered my voice. "We will look outside after the service. If he is nowhere to be seen, we can safely assume his wings were not injured by his little bump. But for now we must sit quietly and be respectful while Mr. Beacham finishes his sermon."

My breath suspended, waiting for her reaction. Sometimes what I found to be perfectly reasonable logic failed to resonate with my sister. When she turned and sat again on the bench, I exhaled.

I caught Mother's thunderous expression and my blood froze, ceasing to pump through my body. She was angry, her mouth pinched, lines fanning out around her lips.

"She has not caused a stir," I said quietly. The other children in the church were louder now, some begging their mothers to allow them to follow the bird outside. The vicar cleared his throat repeatedly, attempting to gather attention again, though he was difficult to hear. It was chaos in the church. No one had their attention on Fanny anymore.

We had avoided making too much of a scene. In my opinion, it was a success.

I could see that Mother considered the situation differently. After we returned home today, we would need to make ourselves scarce until the entire episode was forgotten.

I slid the key into the lock and turned it until the tension from the door released and it relaxed against the frame. The dower house was older than I remembered, buried in shade from an aged oak tree and grimy from disuse.

"Be careful, Fanny," I warned, pushing the door open. Though the sun shone brightly on the other side of the house, we had less light in the entryway. It was dim and dirty, from what I could discern.

"Hmm?" she asked, her attention drawn to the spider web in the upper corner of the doorway.

"I only asked you to be careful. We do not know what we can

expect to find." I had imagined the house would be in good repair. It had been empty for the last decade, I knew, but Father had not knowingly left anything unkempt. I did not expect this building to be the exception.

We stepped inside and dust motes swirled around us, disturbed by the movement and the breeze that had followed us indoors. It smelled stale and musty, and I covered more than one cough while we explored the downstairs rooms.

"It is habitable," I mused while we ascended the creaking stairs. "All it needs is a good scrubbing."

I halted on the landing, and Fanny bumped into my back. "Sorry," she said.

Leaves swirled around the floor near my feet, dirt covering the planked floors. "Perhaps it is not as habitable as I believed," I muttered.

Fanny stepped around me and looked up.

A broken branch from the enormous oak tree had crashed down through the roof. The damage was extensive. The sky could be seen through cracks around the branch, and water appeared to have warped the floorboards beneath it.

It was certainly not fit to live in until that was fixed. Drat.

"Mother will not approve of this," Fanny said.

"Agreed." I toed some decaying oak leaves near my feet. "This will not do at all."

I crossed the corridor and opened the doors, looking into each room. There was plenty of space for us if we could beg enough time for the repairs, but we could not undertake such extensive repairs without approval—and finances—from the earl. I rubbed my temples.

How was I going to ensure a safe future for us? I loved my father, but drat his inability to plan for a future in which both he and Colin did not exist. Had they believed themselves invincible? I certainly had. Never once did I question my lack of dowry or the planning they had failed to do. They were responsible men and they had reasons for their choices. So why had they left us without a safety net?

Fanny's thin fingers wrapped around my wrist, gently pressing against my pulse there. "You are unhappy. Did you want to live here?"

A quiet, gentle huff slipped from my throat. She could be surprisingly astute at times. "Yes, Fanny. I wanted us to live here together."

Her brows furrowed. "I would not like to leave Lamouth or Mother."

"Indeed. Nor would I, but since the new earl now owns Lamouth, we will not be able to remain there forever. I had hoped you and Mother and I could be comfortable here after the new Lord Huxley moves into Lamouth."

She looked up, taking in the branch poking through the slanted roof. She seemed to see the room for the first time.

"We will not be living here for some time yet," I said, most likely putting words to her thoughts.

She looked around a little bit more, and I held my breath. This was the first time I'd approached the idea in a way that would make her understand that we were really going to have to leave our home.

"What of Mrs. Musgrave?" she asked.

"She will remain at Lamouth I suppose."

"Mary? Cook?"

My heart squeezed with the knowledge that Fanny was about to lose everyone in her life who made her feel comfortable. The housekeeper, our ladies' maid, the cook: women who knew and accepted Fanny with all of her many differences. But the truth remained that even if this house was in a state to be lived in, we still could not afford so many servants. Not without Lord Huxley's generosity. I hadn't the faintest idea what to expect from him. His general absence in the last eight months had not given me leave to expect much.

To say nothing for his reputation as a confirmed rake. But rakes could still be charitable, could they not? I refused to give up hope yet.

Fanny's hands started shaking, and I stepped in front of her swiftly, hoping to nip her unease in the bud. "Nothing is decided yet. We will not worry ourselves until we have just cause."

"Just cause," she said quietly, nodding. Her hands continued to shake, like she was wringing water off the ends of her fingers.

"Nothing is decided yet," I repeated. "Shall we visit Henrietta? The chickens always manage to cheer you up."

"It is Sunday."

"I am certain she'll be home."

Fanny gave a small shake of her head. "It is Sunday. We must have tea with Mother."

I suppressed the urge to sigh. Watching Fanny with Henrietta's chickens seemed far more palatable at present than suffering through a cup of tea in Mother's austere company. Especially today, when the incident in the church had likely left an unpleasant frown on my mother's face. For a woman with remarkable talent at hiding her emotions, she never bothered hiding how she felt about Fanny's episodes.

I led the way outside, Fanny following directly behind me. When I slipped the key into the lock again, I shoved it with determination. I was going to find a way to fix this house's roof and create a home for my sister, close to Mr. Ramsey's birds and Henrietta's chickens.

Somehow I would.

CHAPTER SIX

DANIEL

Mother had now remained in my company for three weeks, and it was three weeks longer than I was prepared to entertain anyone. I'd come to Arden Castle to lick my wounds, and she was not providing me enough solitude or space to do so. She took the freedom I'd offered her, hosting all manner of dinner parties with our various neighbors. While I initially thought her efforts were matrimonially minded, she soon proved me wrong with the variety of company she invited into my house.

Sunlight beamed through the far window of the drawing room, shining against the gilt clock on the mantel. It was nearly time to dress for dinner, but I was tempted to forgo the meal entirely. A nice bottle of brandy in front of the fire with my tall Newfoundland hound, Oscar, for company suited me well.

I sat across from Mother, my fingers dragging lazily through Oscar's shaggy hair while his head lolled on my knee. I knew my mother's dislike of having dogs inside, but that didn't stop me from allowing Oscar free rein of the house. I would never purposefully drive her away, but if I was able to provide additional reasons for her to leave earlier than planned, I would not change my habits too greatly.

"You'll accompany me to church this week, I hope," she said, her attention on the small screen she was embroidering.

I had managed to develop excuses the last few weeks for missing the service, but she had caught me off guard, and I struggled to think of a new reason that would not be too obvious. I bent closer to the dog, giving him more of my attention. "I am of a mind to avoid the Kelby sisters and their goddaughter at present."

The goddaughter, it turned out, was fresh from the schoolroom. *Biddable*, Miss Edith had called her.

A child would have been far more on the nose.

"Those women are harmless," Mother said.

"We have different definitions for that word, I think."

She lowered her embroidery, her fingers pinched around the needle, red thread flowing through its loop. "Not everyone's sole purpose in life is to find you a wife."

The back of my neck warmed. She spoke so plainly, giving me cause to second-guess myself. Had I exaggerated the Kelby sisters' intent? They had hosted us for dinner last week so we could meet their goddaughter, and all the talk of picnics and drives on the country lanes made their design in bringing her to my attention quite clear, I thought. Was there any other reason to call the girl biddable than to demonstrate how she would make an attractive wife?

"Perhaps not everyone," I conceded. "But the Kelby sisters' efforts regarding Miss Martin were unmistakable."

Mother pinned me in her stare. "You mean to imply that they sent for Miss Martin, all the way from Norwich, to present her to you as a potential bride? You believe they pulled her from her home, forcing her to travel alone in the rain and remain here for weeks, on the chance they might present her to you?"

"When you say it like that, you make me sound wildly vain."

She lifted both of her eyebrows as if to say that I was, indeed, as vain as I sounded. "Perhaps you ought not to believe everyone is thinking of you when they plan their summer holidays, son."

I raised my hands in defeat. "You've won, Mother."

She let the matter drop, as had been her habit recently. I had been pleasantly surprised that she did not mention the earldom again after her first day here. She must have understood that I was not yet in a frame of mind to discuss it. Or perhaps she had truly accepted that I would not be embracing the title.

I gave my dog one last scratch above the ears before pushing him gently from my knee. He settled his head over his paws on the floor, letting out a sigh of long-suffering. I crossed the room and lifted a glass from the cart. Warm, amber-colored brandy swirled in the decanter when I lifted it, and I poured it into the glass until it reached the halfway mark.

"It is still early," Mother said.

I tensed at her censure. "All this talk of responsibilities has aged the day more rapidly for me."

The sound of a carriage pulling up in front of the house stole my attention, and the glass stalled before my lips. I looked at her pointedly. "I should have known to don my jester hat. Who will be visiting us today?" I had been little more than a puppet lately anyway, and in general I was rather proud of my control. This was only my second drink today.

"I am not sure." She turned toward the window, and the confusion on her brow proved her innocence.

I took a sip of brandy, allowing the familiar warmth to soothe my irritation and lower my shoulders from my ears. I was comforted the moment it touched my lips, and each sip felt like adding a piece of armor. *Sip.* A breastplate. *Sip.* Helmet. *Sip.* Leg coverings. *Sip.* Arm coverings. *Sip.* Shield.

Mother gave a slight intake of breath and rose, crossing to the window. Her hands splayed over her stomach as she leaned toward the glass to better see. She looked back at me, guilt flashing in her eyes.

"Mother, what did you do?"

"I will remind you," she said sedately, "that you supplied permission."

"Permission for what?"

The drawing room door opened and Worthlin stepped aside, allowing three women to precede him into the room who were clearly all in different stages of mourning. The older woman had a regal bearing, her short, stout stature swathed in black bombazine. The younger women were both pretty, sharing enough of a resemblance to make them out to be sisters, most likely—though one wore black and the other lavender. Their eyes were green, almond-shaped, and striking, their features delicate and smooth, their hair different shades of brown.

I shot my mother a look. She was covering her guilt well. More women to entice me into matrimony? Interesting timing after the conversation we just had. It took a great deal of effort not to sigh loudly and vent my boredom to the whole of the room. But I was not that deep in my cups and would not do my mother the disservice of disrespecting her guests.

They were uncommonly pretty guests too, though I would not allow even that to sway me toward the altar.

"Lady Huxley," Mother said, crossing to her at once. "It has been an age. Your daughters are so grown. So beautiful."

Lady Huxley? Daughters? I looked at them sharply, recognition dawning. These were the widow and daughters of the late earl. I *had* given my permission to send for them, hadn't I? Only I had not expected my mother to act on it.

She stopped just beside me. "Please allow me the honor of introducing my son, Daniel Palmer."

She'd left off the title, for which I was immensely grateful, however odd it might seem to these women. But no one seemed to mind. Both of the women wearing black did not bother to hide their frank assessment, their eyes raking over me. I felt naked under their perusal. The young woman in lavender only spared me a passing glance before turning her attention to my hound, who had moved to lounge before the fire.

"Daniel, this is Lady Huxley." I bowed to the matron out of sheer habit, my mind whirling with what this could mean. Had my mother invited the countess and her daughters to my house to guilt me into action? It was little wonder now why she had said nothing about my failure in my responsibilities in the last few weeks.

She had been biding her time.

Lady Huxley inclined her head briefly. "My daughters." She pointed to the one in black. "Lady Verity Palmer"—she pointed to the one in lavender—"and my youngest, Lady Frances Palmer."

Lady Verity dipped in a curtsy, her long, slender arm reaching to tap her sister's elbow, as though she meant to remind her to curtsy as well. Lady Frances dipped in a belated curtsy, and I bowed to each woman in turn.

"Welcome to Arden Castle," I said, the manners instilled in me coming out now without much thought. "I hope you will find your stay comfortable."

Lady Frances slid her elbow free of her sister's hold and crossed the room, coming to kneel before Oscar in front of the fire.

"Fanny," Lady Verity said in a mildly rebuking tone. "You've not yet washed up—"

"What is her name?" Lady Frances asked, ignoring her sister.

The room was quiet.

Lady Huxley's lips flattened into a thin line, and Lady Verity wore twin spots of color in her cheeks.

I cleared my throat. "Oscar."

"Oscar," Lady Frances repeated quietly to herself. "A male?"

Had she asked *me* that question? Her attention was still on the dog.

"Is he a male?" Lady Verity asked, as if it was the most natural question in the world.

The dog's name was *Oscar*, for heaven's sake.

"He is," I said, looking between the sisters, unsure whom I should direct the answer to.

Mother stepped in. "You must be tired from your journey. Shall I show you to your rooms?"

Mrs. Hale, our housekeeper, must have been prepared for the eventuality of this visit if the rooms were ready for the women. If only someone had thought to warn me as well.

"I like Oscar," Lady Frances said.

Lady Verity crossed the room toward the fireplace. "Shall we see our rooms, Fanny? We do not wish to repulse Oscar with our traveling dirt."

If the younger sister wondered why a dog would mind dirt, she did not say so. Instead she gave Oscar another sweet scratch between the ears and pulled away, rising. She looked around the room, not quite meeting my gaze, though I had the distinct impression it was not shame which averted her eyes, but mere disinterest.

Hmm. That was unusual.

Mrs. Hale appeared in the doorway as if she could sense my mother's summons. Mother looked relieved. "Mrs. Hale, shall we show our guests to their rooms?"

"Of course, ma'am."

Lady Frances appeared reluctant to leave, bending forward to give Oscar another pat on the head. She lingered there.

Her attention to my hound was sweet. I could see her desire to remain with him. I spoke, the words leaving my lips before I could think better of them. "Oscar and I intend to remain here, Lady Frances, if you would like to return at your leisure."

She did not look at me but gave a little nod, rising and

walking to her sister's side. Lady Verity, however, flashed me a look of such gratitude it took me by surprise. Her green eyes softened, and I could tell she was refraining from saying something in response to my gesture. She tilted her head in a gentle acknowledgment before following the rest of the party from the room.

My body hummed from the interaction with the women, though I did not know why it affected me at all. My fingers were empty, longing to curl around a glass. "Odd," I said to Oscar. "Not what I'd expected."

Oscar tilted his head to the side as though he didn't understand my lack of excitement.

"You would find no fault in a guest who thoroughly scratched you behind the ears."

He slumped down again lazily.

Lady Huxley and her daughters' presence here worried me. What would they expect from me? Were they angry I had replaced their father? It was not my doing, but that didn't mean they wouldn't hold me responsible for usurping his role.

Or would they be glad to hear I had no intention of stepping into his shoes?

I returned to the cart near the wall and refilled my glass, sipping at the brandy and looking at the dog lazing on the floor. He was asleep now, due to the ministrations from the young woman. Something was strange about her, but I couldn't quite put my finger on what it was. I tipped the glass back and drained the rest of it.

If it was up to me, though, they would not be here long enough for me to find out.

CHAPTER SEVEN

VERITY

That was Daniel Palmer, eighth earl of Huxley and unprincipled rake? I could certainly see the appeal. He was too handsome to be anything else. He seemed mild-mannered for a man with a reputation for ruining young ladies, though. Were rakes not meant to be flirts?

Any hopes I had harbored that he would be as dim as he was rakish were dashed immediately. His stony expression was difficult to read, but the close way he'd watched us revealed he wasn't the bored, insouciant man he tried to make himself appear. He had been paying attention to Fanny, and it worried me a little.

What would he make of her?

If she did not prove herself, would he throw us out of Lamouth completely? Would he feel the same disgust toward her behavior that my mother did?

"You'll be just here, my lady," the housekeeper said, opening a door and gesturing toward my mother. Mrs. Hale muttered a few points of fact about the royal the bedroom was named after. "Edward the First slept in that very bed, ma'am." She left a pause to convey the magnitude of the honor they were bestowing upon my mother by giving her this room. Then she turned toward me and gestured to the next door down the corridor. "You are in here, my lady."

I followed her and peeked inside the chamber. The bed looked big enough for two. "Shall Fanny and I share?"

"We have a separate bedroom made up—"

"I think we will be more comfortable together," I said.

The housekeeper looked at Fanny, but my sister did not bother to make a reply.

"Fanny, would you like to share with me?"

"Yes," she said simply, her attention bouncing from my face to the floor. "That would be fine."

Relief fell through me like the tall, brocade drapes covering the narrow windows. I wagered she didn't care whether she slept with me or not, but I was certainly more comfortable having her nearby. What if she woke tomorrow, ready to begin her routine, and forgot where she was? What if I wasn't there to help her remember where we were and how things must be different? There was no Mr. Ramsey and his birds, no Henrietta and her chickens, and it was not our cook in the kitchen downstairs.

It was easier this way.

Mother's maid appeared in the corridor outside our chamber. "My lady has a headache."

"Cook makes a lovely, soothing posset," Lady Moorington said. She turned to Mrs. Hale. "Perhaps we can fetch her dinner on a tray this evening?"

"That would do nicely," Mother's maid, Olsen, said.

"Right away, ma'am." Mrs. Hale left us in the corridor, the keys hanging from her chatelaine bouncing with each step.

"If you need anything else, do not hesitate to ask," Lady Moorington said. "I am glad you've come, and I look forward to becoming better acquainted. We meet for dinner at seven."

She seemed to expect us to join her. I gave her a nod, and she smiled before leaving us in our room.

Fanny went to the window to look outside. I untied my bonnet and set it on the bed, then scrubbed the dirt from my face.

"I would like to see Oscar."

Where Lord Huxley would be waiting for us? I did not think it was necessarily a good idea to spend more time in his presence than we had to. I had hoped we would arrive early enough to take a walk about the grounds and acquaint ourselves with the garden, and perhaps with the animals, but it was growing too dark for that now, and we needed to change for dinner soon.

"Would you like to eat dinner with us, Fanny? Lady Moorington seems to expect it."

"Where is Mary?"

"She will probably be here soon. We need to change for dinner."

"I would like to eat with Mary."

That was customary for us, but would Lord Huxley or his mother find it rude? Would that I could forgo the dinner and eat with Fanny and Mary in the kitchen instead. But the kitchen servants here weren't used to us.

The door opened and Mary stepped inside, carrying a valise. She went to the trunk and opened it, rummaging for something. "Your mother sends a message," she said, glancing at me. "She wanted me to remind you that you must make a good impression."

"Then choose whatever gown will do that. They all look the same to me."

Mary shot me a glance. "I do not think she was only referring to your gown, ma'am."

"Good heavens," I muttered, dropping to sit on the edge of the mattress. If it were up to her, I would be propositioning the earl at dinner. *Excuse me, my lord, would you like to be my next husband? We only have to wait a week until my mourning is over and then we may have the banns read!*

Much too soon for that. It was one thing to make plans where a stranger was concerned, but now I had seen the earl. He was too handsome not to evoke some level of trepidation.

Mary pulled out a black silk dinner gown and fetched a purple one for Fanny. Colors of half-mourning were not suited to my complexion in general, so while I did not relish the entirely black wardrobe, I was glad I did not have to wear lavender.

Mary helped us dress and I waited at the door for my sister, smoothing my fingers over my long gloves to remove the wrinkles.

"Are you changing, Mary?" Fanny asked.

Mary looked at me. She was wearing the same simple gray dress she always wore. I lifted my shoulders in a slight shrug, for I could not see any reason for Mary to change.

"For what purpose, my lady?" Mary asked.

"Dinner." Fanny blinked at me. "Mary is to eat with us, is she not?"

The very idea of bringing Mary to the earl's table sent a choking cough spasming my chest. "She cannot—"

"I cannot," Mary said at the same time, her eyes perfectly round saucers. "I am happier to eat in the kitchen, my lady. I am much more comfortable there."

"But we always eat together," Fanny said.

Mary's eyes darted between me and my sister. "Would you like to eat in the kitchen with me?"

Oh, for heaven's sake. Why had I not considered all of these difficulties? Whatever would the kitchen servants think?

Fanny's nose wrinkled. "I would like to see Oscar."

"The earl's dog," I explained. "An enormous, hairy creature Fanny has taken a liking to."

"He seemed lovely. The man told me I could come see him again."

"We can visit him first," I promised. "Would you like to eat dinner with us in the dining room? Mary prefers to eat in the kitchen." The moment the words were out of my mouth, I reconsidered the wisdom in that offer. The last time Fanny ate with us in the dining room, she panicked when the duck was brought to the table. I could not recall whether Fanny or Mother was more distressed by the ensuing episode.

Fanny's hands started to tremor and she took a step back. "I prefer to eat with Mary. I always eat with Mary."

Mother would prefer that as well. It would be far simpler to present Fanny with a meal she was willing to eat down in the kitchen, where she was more likely to be comfortable, than to put her at the dining room table and watch her offend our host while she refused dish after dish.

"Perhaps we can visit with Oscar later?" I said.

"I would like to see him now. The man said I could see him now."

"The man is Lord Huxley, Fanny. He is the new earl."

"Papa was Lord Huxley."

"Yes, and now this gentleman has that title."

Her hands shook with more effort, and I lifted both of mine to stave off her additional stress. "We will go see Oscar right this moment, and then Mary will take you down to the kitchen for dinner. Will that arrangement please everyone?"

Fanny wrung her hands together and nodded. "I want to see Oscar."

"We will do that immediately." I waited for Mary to coax Fanny onto the seat at the dressing table so she could arrange her light brown hair, and my gaze slid to the darkening window. Had I made a mistake? I had thought leaving Fanny at home would be detrimental to her wellbeing, but I was beginning to wonder if bringing her here was even worse. If she made the same impression on the earl she had on my late husband, would he even be willing to help us? Or would he too believe her better suited to an asylum?

We made our way downstairs and stood at the door of the drawing room, Fanny directly behind me. I looked over my shoulder. "Are you nervous, Fanny?"

"I would prefer it if no one looked at me."

Which meant the attention must be on me. A footman opened the door for us, and I stepped inside, Fanny following behind me and Mary waiting in the corridor.

Lord Huxley sat on the sofa, one ankle resting over the other knee. He held a drink lazily in his hand and lifted his gaze slowly to us. His hair was the color of a raven's wing, his eyes a chocolate brown. It was a dangerous combination, I found, for he was the most handsome man I'd ever spent time with. I was fairly certain his eyes had been designed with the sole purpose of making young women forget themselves.

It was a good thing I was no young woman. I was a widow. My experience had given me the power to refrain from falling victim to Lord Huxley's charms.

Not that he was employing any of them at present. I dipped my head in acknowledgment and Fanny passed me, ignoring the earl and kneeling before the hound.

"You are fond of dogs, Lady Frances?"

I moved to sit across from him on the empty sofa, though he never invited me to. "Fanny. She does not answer to Frances."

If he thought it odd she would be introduced in such a way, he kept that opinion hidden behind his stony mask. I had found it odd for Mother to use Fanny's title when she never did at home, so I had no explanation ready.

"Does he know any tricks?" Fanny asked.

"He is too stubborn for that," Lord Huxley said. "Though you are welcome to teach him some. You are sure to be far more successful than I have been."

She looked back at the dog, his enormous brown head lifting to look at his master as though in offense. He flopped it back down until it rested on Fanny's lap, bringing a wide smile to her face. Her eyes brightened, and I was slightly jealous of the hound.

I had never incited such joy on my sister's face.

"Do you have any dogs of your own?" Lord Huxley asked, his voice low. It was clear from the volume alone that he was directing the question at me. Was this how he began his rakish activities? The soft, gentle words ran like velvet over my nerves.

"We do not. My mother abhors animals inside the house."

"As does mine."

My eyebrows lifted of their own volition.

"I could relegate him to the garden while she is here. But, well . . ." He lifted his cup and took a sip. "This *is* my house."

"You remind me of my late husband," I said, the words leaving my lips before I could think better of them.

"Do I?" He seemed more amused by this than anything else. "Was he handsome?"

Colin's likeness came to my mind. He was not particularly handsome, not striking like Lord Huxley at least. He was perfectly ordinary in every way—including his affections for me. In truth, Colin had been more of a friend than anything else before the incident. After it, I could not abide the sight of him. Regardless, our marriage had always been a product of convenience, and neither of us ever pretended differently.

The way he used to look forward to owning Lamouth Park never left us in any doubt of what he valued.

"He was always speaking of the rules he would change when he became master of the house," I said. "It was mostly in jest, I believe. Nothing too extravagant."

"Dogs in the drawing room?"

"His changes were more closely related to the way the

household was run. He wanted to forgo walking into dinner by rank, for example. So outdated, in his opinion."

"I suppose we *are* alike," he muttered.

"You do not sit according to rank, my lord?"

He flinched, however subtly. "You needn't call me that. I assume it is not easy for you."

That was surprisingly considerate of him. "It is no trouble, my lord, I assure—"

"Truly," he said stiffly. "I cannot abide it. You are more welcome to call me Daniel or Mr. Palmer than *my lord.*"

Perhaps Lord Huxley would not find Fanny odd after all, not when he was peculiar himself. "We are strangers," I said cautiously.

"Yes. But we are also family, are we not?" He gave me a smile, tilting his head softly to the side. "Surely it must feel strange to call another by that name."

The title Lord Huxley would forever remind me of my father, it was true, but I'd known for almost a year that it now belonged to someone else. Surely he must understand I'd prepared myself for this moment. I could separate the two in my mind. It was not an impossible feat.

"Our claim to being family is rather distant, my—" I cleared my throat, hoping he didn't notice my near blunder.

Lord Huxley glanced at me sharply, his dark brown eyes glowing. "Thank you," he said softly.

"For what?"

"Stopping yourself."

It was official. This man most certainly was more strange than my sister.

His attention on me was heavy. I lowered my gaze, unable to hold his any longer. Was he attempting to read my thoughts? I hoped he found himself unsuccessful. The last thing I needed at present was for this man to understand how desperate I was for him to accept Fanny.

"You will spoil my dog," Lord Huxley said, turning his attention to where my sister still knelt on the floor, her fingers running through Oscar's thick coat.

She ignored this remark.

"Fanny?" I said.

"Yes?" she looked up.

"Lord Huxley spoke to you."

She looked confused, her light brown eyebrows pulling together.

"Me," the earl said, drawing her attention. "It was of no consequence. I am glad you are giving Oscar such fine attention."

She looked at the dog again. "He is a gentle animal."

"I think he will love you forever now. Be careful, or he will follow you around."

Fanny said nothing to this. Her lack of response appeared rude, so I stepped in quickly. "Fanny would not mind that very much, I think."

Lord Huxley looked from my sister to me, a small line forming between his eyebrows.

The gilded clock on the mantel showed it was nearly time for dinner. I stood, smoothing down the front of my gown. "Shall we find Mary?"

Fanny scratched the dog between the ears.

"Fanny?"

"Yes." She ran her fingers once more down his side. It was never easy to tear her away from an animal. I wished that just once she would respond to me with some haste—especially with the audience we now had—but the girl did not understand the concept.

Fanny walked to the door, and I followed her. Mary stood in the corridor waiting. "Are you ready for dinner, my lady?"

"Yes."

"Shall I go with you?" I asked Mary quietly. "To explain . . ."

"Your presence is likely to make the servants uncomfortable, my lady."

"You are correct. I know that. I only wonder if it would be better for me to be there."

Mary looked from me to Fanny. "If it meets with your approval, my lady, I believe I can do a decent job of it."

"Of course you can." Mary knew Fanny as well as I did. She was familiar with the things that caused Fanny distress and what she was willing to eat. "If you need me, you will come and fetch me immediately?"

"I vow it, my lady. You need not fear. She will be well looked after."

I reached forward and squeezed Mary's arm lightly. "I know that. You have my trust."

She smiled, then called for Fanny. I watched them leave, down the corridor toward where I assumed the servants' staircase was situated. Then I drew in a heavy breath and let it out slowly. Guilt streamed through my chest, tensing my shoulders. I was not *glad* to see Fanny walk away—indeed, it worried me that she would be out of my sight in an unfamiliar place. But the knowledge that she was with someone who would watch over her, even if just for an hour or two, was a great relief.

For a short time, I could relax.

"Now, it appears it is only the two of us," Lord Huxley said from the doorway. I started at the unexpected proximity of his voice, bumping into a table set against the wall. My arm knocked into a vase of flowers and sent it flying . . . directly at the earl.

CHAPTER EIGHT

DANIEL

The vase flew at me, and I lifted my hands to catch it before it could smash into my chest and leave an oval bruise. Water and flowers splashed from the rim, soaking through my waistcoat to my skin. I gave an involuntary guffaw.

"Oh, dear," Lady Verity said, stepping forward and taking the vase of flowers from my hands. "I am sorry."

"No harm came to me or the vase." I picked my wet shirt away from the skin it now stuck to.

She stood in front of me, holding the vase, her eyes wide. "I can find a towel or something to dry your—"

"I will change. Tell my mother not to wait for me to begin dinner, please."

"Of course." She still held the vase in front of her chest, the flowers a tangled mess, a few of them littering the floor between us.

I stepped forward and took the vase from her hands, my fingers brushing her gloved ones. "You needn't hold it any longer." I placed it back on the table.

Lady Verity's cheeks blushed pink. She bent down to pick up

the flowers that had fallen. Gads, where was a footman when you needed one?

"You can leave it."

She reached for another rose. "It's no trouble."

I crouched and picked up the last few flowers near my feet. "Honestly, you needn't have troubled yourself."

"Thank you." She took the last few flowers from my hand and dropped them all in the vase. "Almost as good as new," she said, though I could detect a hint of amusement, proving she meant the opposite.

"Better, I think. You have a talent for arranging."

She leaned back and peered at the vase. It was in utter disarray, flowers poking out at strange angles, some stems broken and drooping sadly. When she lifted her face, she wore a wry smile, her lips bending up at the edges. "You are a charmer."

I scoffed lightly. Most women would simper and be glad of the attention, however sarcastically it was derived. "Or I enjoy chaos."

"I've heard as much," she muttered.

"So you've heard about me?" I tilted my head to the side, a smile threatening to curl my lips. I didn't typically flirt with ladies of quality, but the temptation at present was too great. I took a soft step toward her. "What sort of warnings did you receive?"

"There were not a great deal of them, so do not flatter yourself too much. Just that you are a rake with a propensity for drinking that makes you unpredictable." Her gaze swept over me. "I assume from this behavior that the warnings were not unfounded."

The challenge in her tone made me want to give her a reason to believe the things she'd heard. Something about the way she spoke made me think she hadn't taken those warnings seriously. Well, that was a mistake.

"That depends on how you define it." I reached for her hand, bending her fingers and bringing her gloved knuckles to my lips. Keeping my eyes on her startled face, I pressed a kiss to the back of her hand. "You are the most stunning creature to grace these corridors in an age, my lady. You will do me the honor of accompanying me into the drawing room to await dinner, I hope?"

"Were you not just about to leave so you could change your shirt?"

"I find that the present company is far too alluring to sacrifice any time for a dry shirt." I knew a moment's hesitation for what I was about to do, but squashed it. If she expected a rake, I would give her one. I lifted my other hand, faintly brushing my bent knuckles along the edge of her jaw. "You've a little something there. Here, come into the light so I might see it better."

Lady Verity followed as I pulled her gently toward the sconce, her hand still in my grip. The small orange flame lit her expression better, but I could not read the blank face she was maintaining. I stepped closer, and I could swear I heard her breath hitch. I leaned in, painting a faint smile over my lips while I inhaled. "What is that scent you wear?"

"Soap."

"Ah, so refreshing." Truly? That was the best I could come up with? I needed to try harder. I tilted her face toward the light and pretended to wipe a smudge from her jawline, but the way she watched me was disconcerting, her dark lashes fanned and eyes steady.

"Are you not accustomed to soap?"

My hand stilled, my thumb mid-swipe across her jaw, my other hand holding hers. She was a widow. She was not unused to being touched, perhaps? There was a reason she was not more undone by my attentions, I hoped. "Nothing that smells so sweet."

"Pears soap," she clarified, the most widely-used soap in

England, of course. The faint floral scent had smelled familiar. "I can obtain some for you, if you'd like."

"How generous," I murmured with one final brush over her perfectly smudge-free skin before dropping my hand. "You are not what I was expecting, my lady."

She leaned a little closer. "What were you expecting?"

I shook my head slightly. "Not this." I dropped her hand so I was no longer touching her, but I did not move my feet, instead angling slightly closer. Faint freckles dotted her nose and dusted the pale skin beneath both of her green eyes. "You are older than I expected."

Lady Verity's eyebrows shot up. "Old?"

"No. I am remarking on the fact that you are not as young as I thought you would be. It is a pleasant surprise. I prefer to spend my time with women who are not in the first blush of youth."

Her eyes widened.

Blast. I'd gone too far that time. I searched for something to say that would ease my insinuation. She surely believed I meant something risqué, as though I meant to suggest that I would be *spending time* with her. "I only mean that conversation is far more stimulating when it is not restricted to the weather or the latest *on dits*."

"I didn't take you as one with a penchant for sociable conversation."

"Then what do you call this?"

"Flirting."

A laugh tore from my chest, warming a path on its way out. Lady Verity was unexpected. Intriguing. Not in any way afraid of me. "When the woman in question is as irresistible as you are, my lady, can you blame me?"

"For pretending to wipe a blemish from my cheek? Not at all."

My body froze, but my heart was pounding hard. "I do not know what you mean."

Her smile said she knew otherwise.

I tilted my head a bit. Had I just met my match?

"Darling, what are you doing out here?" my mother asked from the base of the stairs. She looked between us, and I took a measured step back from the widow.

I smiled genially. "Waiting for you, of course. Are you ready to go in?"

Mother looked behind me but did not seem to find who she was looking for. "Should we not wait for Lady Frances?"

Lady Verity's gaze shot to the corridor where her sister had disappeared with the maid. She smiled at my mother, and I was struck by her gentle beauty. Her auburn hair was elegantly swept up, and her skin was clear against the black of her gown. "My sister will not be joining us this evening."

I hadn't realized Lady Frances wasn't returning. I assumed she'd been shown to a retiring room or some such thing. "Is she unwell?"

"She does not typically eat in the dining room with us."

"Is she out in Society?" Mother asked.

"Not quite. Mother thought to wait until she was eighteen, which will be next year." Lady Verity gave another small, strained smile. I didn't know the woman, but I assumed this was a conversation she did not wish to have by the way her eyes would not settle on either of us for very long.

Mother rallied. "Well, we are glad you brought her to Arden. This is not an ordinary social visit, anyway. Shall we eat?"

Dinner passed in much the same manner, though made slightly uncomfortable as my shirt refused to fully dry. Conversation hovered in shallow waters. Mother engaged Lady Verity with chatter about Lamouth Park and the history of her family. I had difficulty paying attention when the woman herself was not at ease. I had the strange desire to lessen her burdens, but all that did was frighten me and make me want to drink. If I drowned the strange idea, perhaps it would go away.

This was uncharted territory for me. I had *never* wanted the company of a woman of rank. The fact that I was drawn to Lady Verity was proof something was not well with me. Even the notion of spending more time in her company, pleasant as it sounded, was unconscionable. Despite my behavior before dinner, I did not trifle with women of the *ton*.

I stole a look at her. She was even more lovely now, the candles on the table warming her face.

Oh, bloody h—

I pointed to my glass so Worthlin would fill it again, then gulped the entirety in two swallows. It was uncomfortable to find myself interested in a woman of esteem—a woman who had been married to my predecessor, no less. So I did what I excelled at: I drowned the discomfort in wine until I could no longer feel it.

Worthlin filled my glass twice more before bringing me a new bottle, as directed. Mother's gaze drifted to me unpleasantly, her judgment like slick mud, tainting me. I needed to be anywhere else but this room.

Rising, I took the bottle of wine and pushed back the chair so quickly it fell with a loud, resounding crash. The sounds of gasps and forks hitting plates registered in my distant awareness, but I only had one goal: leave the room.

"Daniel," Mother admonished, speaking my name as though it was a curse.

"Good night to you both." I dipped in half, intending to bow, but my head landed on the table and it took some effort—and assistance from Worthlin, if I was not mistaken—to correct my posture again.

"Allow me to help you upstairs, my lord," Worthlin said quietly.

I ripped my arm from his hold, hot anger pouring through

me. Would they not *obey*? How many times had I requested to not be called by that wretched title? The force of my disgust pulled me from his hold too quickly, and I fell back, losing the bottle of wine in the process. It flew across the floor with a heavy thunk and a splash of red. Blast.

"My lord—"

I pushed myself up and pointed at the butler, certain steam was coming out of my head. "That is not my bloody name!"

"*Daniel!*"

I looked at my mother. Her eyes were wide with repulsion and shock. If she had not wanted the late earl's family to witness what a wretch the new earl was, she should not have invited them here. Lady Verity remained remarkably calm, given the events that had transpired so far. I tried to nod my head, unsure which direction it went, then tore out of the room.

CHAPTER NINE

VERITY

Hours had passed since the uncomfortable dinner had come to a close. Fanny was asleep on our bed, and I sat on the cold stone hearth, my knees pulled up and my chin resting on them. No fire was lit—it was too warm—but the moonlight slid through the window and illuminated this slab perfectly, bathing me in a pool of light.

Lord Huxley—or Daniel, as I had begun to think of him since that dastardly exit this evening—had ghosts nestled in his trunk, haunting him. That desperate look in his brown eyes when he fell, when he begged his servant not to call him by the title, had struck me. He had been in earnest when he requested I call him by his Christian name. I had thought he was merely flirting, that perhaps he was igniting his rakish charms for some obscene reason. But no. He was battling some darkness of his own.

I understood. I battled darkness on behalf of my sister regularly.

It was not the realization of these demons that gave me my newest idea. It was the understanding that we each had something to offer the other. Perhaps if he accepted my proposition, I could cease worrying completely.

That was it. I was decided. Enough hours had passed to sober him. I was going to Daniel's room.

I pushed up and ran my hands down my dressing gown, wiping away any soot from the hearth that might have tarnished it. My hair was in a long braid down the center of my back, and I leaned close to the mirror above the washstand, smoothing a few stray hairs away from my face.

I had never propositioned a man before. Did one bring a candle? I didn't wish to wake Fanny, so I refrained from lighting anything. My eyes had adjusted to the darkness now. Surely it would not be so difficult to find Daniel's room. By a stroke of good fortune, Lady Moorington had pointed it out when telling me where to find the family wing earlier.

Hopefully he was still in there.

I snuck into the corridor, closing the door silently, then made my way toward the family wing. Lady Moorington slept at the other end, so we would likely not be overheard if Daniel was still in his cups and failed to mind his volume. Even if we were heard, that would only help me. I was only planning to persuade him to make an agreement with me, but if we were found and he was guilted into marrying me, that would still accomplish the same task.

When I reached Daniel's door, the next step of my plan eluded me. Did I knock or merely open the door? What did his other paramours do?

My relationship with Colin had not been long-standing, and our convenient marriage was mostly in name. He'd had his room, I'd had mine, and more often than not we had retired separately. It was no wonder I'd not become pregnant in the scant two years of our marriage.

Drawing in a deep breath, I made up my mind. I would be confident, even in the face of utter uncertainty. Twisting the handle, I pushed the door open, pleased when it gave way. Light bounced from the guttering candle on the table beside Daniel's enormous, carved four-poster bed. He was reclining—mostly clothed still, thank heavens—his arm thrown over his head. I stepped inside and closed the door behind me.

Daniel lifted his arm and his head, his arched eyebrows indicating his surprise. "What the devil are you doing here?"

"Not the greeting I'd hoped for." Was the shakiness of my voice obvious? I dearly wished that was not the case.

Daniel did not so much as sit up from his reclined position. "Is there something I can help you with?"

"Your voice is much steadier now," I remarked, ignoring his question. It occurred to me that though he left the wine bottle behind when he had stormed out of the dining room, he could have fetched more from elsewhere. But he didn't sound drunk. "Are you foxed?"

"Unfortunately, not anymore."

"I can fetch something for you, if you'd like."

"I'd much prefer to learn your reason for being in my room. You did not come here by accident, I assume?"

"No." I paused. "Should I have pretended I did? I'm not used to visiting gentlemen in their bedchambers, you know."

"That is obvious," he said dryly.

"Oh." I blinked. "Am I making a mull of things?"

"It is hard to know. What *things* are you attempting?"

"Well." I drew the word out, taking a step closer to the fireplace. If I kept enough space between us, he would not misinterpret my true reason for being here. "I thought we could come to an understanding."

Daniel sat up, a note of wariness entering his eyes. "Stay where you are."

That was not a good sign. Perhaps I should have dressed differently. I dragged my braid over my shoulder. "It seems I have mistaken the situation."

"What situation is that, exactly?"

"That you are a rake." I cleared my throat.

Daniel's eyebrows shot to the top of his brow. He studied me for a moment, and I felt uncomfortably naked under his scrutiny, though I was covered from neck to toes. Did he find much lacking? Was I that repulsive to him? I'd had to put off two admirers before it was widely known I was betrothed to Colin, so I did not think I was ugly, even if I couldn't claim to be beautiful.

Perhaps my nose was too long or my eyes too wide. Maybe my chin pointed too much? I grew conscious of how I appeared now in my dressing gown, a simple long braid running over my shoulder. Did I appear like a child?

Daniel swung his legs over the side of his bed. He ran a hand through his hair. "And you thought it would be wise to visit a rake in his chamber at"—he looked at the clock on the wall—"one o'clock in the morning?"

"Is that not when you rakes are up to mischief?"

"I suppose so, though I wouldn't think mischief is confined to any hours in particular." He stood, his long, untucked shirt falling just above his knees. He still wore breeches and stockings, but nothing else. My eyes were drawn to his open collar and the dark hair visible there, but I lifted them.

Colin had been fair-haired, his chest smooth. Daniel looked his opposite in every way. It was odd to see a man who was not my late husband so relaxed in appearance, his hair falling over his forehead and a shadow of a dark beard painted over his jaw. I wanted to run my fingers over it, but that felt like a strange impulse.

Daniel stepped closer, towering over me. "What did you have in mind, my lady?"

"Well," I said, clearing my throat. My heartbeat ticked up a notch. "I am not in the first blush of youth—"

"No, you are most certainly not." He leaned forward and took my hand. "But your nervousness does you credit."

"Nervous?" I scoffed loudly. "I am *not*. I've been married, you know."

He pinched my much-too-pointed chin lightly between his fingers, looking down into my eyes. "I know."

His gaze dropped to my lips, spurring my heart into a mad dash. My blood pumped wildly, roaring in my ears, my breath coming quickly. I was not prepared for this. I had been too hasty. Was my sister's safety worth securing Daniel as a husband?

My mind flashed to the stories I'd heard, the terrible conditions in asylums—how women were treated like animals.

How could I even ask myself that? Of course it was worth it.

Daniel's lids grew heavy, his face leaning closer until he paused just before reaching my lips. The room was still, silent, his eyes hovering just above mine. "I do not trifle with well-respected ladies."

Relief and frustration swooped through me with equal measure. "You appear to be trifling with me right now."

"Perhaps a little." He leaned back a bit. "I was curious if you were in earnest."

"I am here, aren't I?" I asked, a little peeved. He did not need to know my intentions were to stop him after a kiss, to secure his hand and his promise.

He pinched my chin a little more, tilting my face up and smiling down at me. "Yes, but the question is why?"

"I would think it perfectly obvious." Evasion was the best tactic. It wasn't as if I could tell him the truth. If I revealed my need to care for and protect my sister, how could I be assured he would not be exactly like Colin and think her best suited to an asylum? I needed to be careful in how I revealed information to Daniel.

He narrowed his beautiful brown eyes at me. "It is evident that you are in search of something, and you think enticing me is the way to achieve it. But why? What does sweet Lady Verity seek? You've had a husband, so you do not need my name for any reason. You have a title, so you do not need that either. Is it the money?"

I flinched.

"Ah, so it is. But why *me*, Countess?"

"I am no countess."

"Are you not trying to become one?"

I leaned back enough for his fingers to drop from my chin, but I would not step back from him. I would not back down. "Your title is of no consequence to me."

"But my income is."

I drew in a breath. "I am not a fortune hunter."

"You must own that you've given me little reason to believe otherwise."

"Then allow me to explain."

"By all means." He swept an arm toward the trunk situated at the end of his bed. "Would you like to be seated?"

"No." I cleared my throat. "I thought—or I hoped, rather—that if I could contrive a declaration from you, then my family could remain at Lamouth. Forever."

He stared at me, and the silence in the room grew louder. "You were doing this for a house?"

That stung. I was doing this for my sister, but I didn't want to admit that, not when he looked so utterly disturbed. "There is more at stake than you can possibly understand."

"Then help me to understand," he said.

"That is rather pointless now, I believe."

"I'm not sure about that." He ran his hand over his jaw, his brown eyes dark in the dimly lit room. "Perhaps we can still come to an arrangement."

Daniel

That had *not* been what I'd meant to say. Lady Verity's eyes were rounded like a doe standing at the end of a rifle, and I believed she likely felt very much in danger. "I only meant that I am happy to create an arrangement allowing you and your family to remain at Lamouth forever."

Lady Verity ducked her chin. "Why?"

"Because I have a house. I needn't take yours."

"Lamouth is no longer my home, my—" She cleared her throat. "Sir."

"Daniel."

She let out a short breath. "It is your house now, Daniel."

"You clearly want it more than I do."

"But the tenants, the responsibilities?"

"I will employ a man to ensure they are all well cared for. I can hire *you*, if you'd like, to keep me abreast of the needs of the property." She seemed perfectly capable. The woman had pluck.

She shook her head. "That is absurd."

"What is absurd is using your beauty to secure a house I am very willing to give you for free."

Her mouth opened and she closed it again. Disbelief shone in the crease between her eyebrows. "This is all very untoward."

Rich, coming from the woman who came to my room in the middle of the night. I swallowed the impulse to point that out to her. Her preconceived assumptions could not have been further from the truth. Yes, I had a past and a reputation to match it, but I was no longer that man. I had not been that man since the night I learned of my new inheritance all those months ago. "You do not wish to believe a rake would turn you away?"

"I'm not so vain as that," she snapped. "I just . . . your plan is futile. It is unrealistic to think your sentiments might never undergo a change."

How did I convince her I meant it? "I will never accept the title, the house, or the responsibilities that come with it. I assure you, Lamouth is free for the taking."

"Until you marry and your wife chooses Lamouth as her primary residence. What are we to do then? In ten years' time we'll be uprooted?" She shook her head. "I cannot do that to my—"

I waited for her to continue, but she stopped herself again, giving her head a soft shake. "To your . . . ?" I prompted.

"It would be very uncomfortable to always wonder if we are to be turned out or if your heart has undergone a change. You may believe now you wish to remain a bachelor, but your priorities could alter."

"They won't."

"Says the rake who just refused a woman's advances. You are trying to make me believe you cannot change?"

She had me there. "That is not change, precisely. I have never trifled—"

"I know. You do not trifle with ladies." She dropped onto the trunk, resting her face in her hands and groaning softly.

"Lady Verity?"

"I think you've earned the right to call me by my name, Daniel." She spoke through her hands, her voice muffled. "We are close now after this utter fiasco."

I had the feeling I'd completely disappointed her. The way she drew inward worried me that she would think herself undesirable. She was anything but. "You are not at fault. You are a perfectly lovely creature—"

She groaned louder. "Oh stop, please. I cannot abide more flattery from you." She dropped her hands. "Drat. How am I to face you tomorrow?"

I couldn't help but smile. Her wide eyes were perfectly, innocently worried. I had the strong inclination to put her at ease. "I will not mention it. If you wish, we can pretend this never occurred, that it was merely a dream."

"A nightmare, you mean?"

"Perhaps for one of us."

Verity looked up quickly. "Nothing I can do will entice you into any sort of arrangement?"

I nearly choked. "You mean you are still interested in . . . that?"

"Marriage. A *marriage* arrangement."

Good gads, she was desperate. I'd told her she could have the house, and I'd meant it. How was that not secure enough for her?

"Oh, dear." She gasped quietly, her fingers resting over her lips. "Do you already have an understanding? Are you in love?"

"No. I have neither, and I do not intend on entering into anything of the sort."

"Whyever not?"

Because I was not good enough. Because I could never measure up. Because marriage would mean another woman telling me to stop drinking so much or expecting me to arrive on time and finding herself sorely disappointed again and again. The truth danced on my tongue. Would Verity understand? Perhaps it was the dimness of the room or the vulnerability she'd shown tonight, but I was willing to speak a little truth. "It is not in my nature to be dependable. Why would I subject a woman to that?"

A look of pity flashed in her eyes, and I directly regretted my impulsive honesty. I crossed to the door so I could open it and send her on her way.

"Wait. Daniel." Her soft voice called to me.

My hand stalled on the handle.

"We do not know one another, but I think we could enter into an agreement that would suit both parties."

"I highly doubt that."

She stepped closer, her hand rising to rest against my chest, her fingers pressing into the skin over my heart. I could feel my pulse rising, the blood pumping faster through my body. Her gentle touch was like magic; she was a witch and her fingers had cast a spell.

"A life such as the one you've led must have been lonely. If we married, I could provide you with children, and I would expect nothing from you in return except free reign of Lamouth Park."

"Nothing?" My voice was decidedly raspy. "You would be satisfied with such a marriage?"

"I seek nothing above security."

"Security," I whispered. "Any man could give you that."

She considered my words. "Perhaps many could, but only you can give me Lamouth."

The house? This came back to the house again? What the devil was so special about it? "Why?"

"It is important to me."

My heart pounded. Her pink lips were calling to me, and it was taking everything in my power to resist her allure. She was far more enticing than she realized. Evidently, I was stronger than I knew.

It was time to remove the temptation. "We can discuss this further tomorrow."

"A private conversation in the middle of the day?" she asked. "Impossible."

"You are a widow. We will not need a chaperone."

"I cannot leave my sister."

"Except for dinner?" I challenged.

"Yes. Except for dinner."

"Then I will have to be creative, I suppose."

She shook her head and dropped her hand from my chest. I immediately felt the lack, and I wanted to pull her into my arms, to see if she still smelled of fresh soap and sunshine. What had come over me? I shook the odd notion away. Despite what she'd said, this woman was a desperate fortune hunter. I would do well to remember that.

"Good night, Daniel. Please forgive my intrusion."

"This is not the end of our conversation, Verity," I reminded her.

"You promised we could pretend it was a nightmare, to act as though I did not embarrass myself so fully."

"Trust me, you have nothing to be embarrassed about."

"Oh? Do women regularly approach you so boldly and get soundly rejected?"

"Not *regularly*, no." Though after I inherited Lord Huxley's house, money, and title, they had thrown themselves at my feet. I had come to Arden Castle to escape that very thing, and it had followed me here. Only, this was the first such occurrence that hadn't wholly repulsed me. "I can honestly say that this is the first time I've been approached in my own house."

"I promise it will be the last you'll see of me." Verity dipped a curtsy and turned away, slipping through the door before I could waylay her.

The desperation in her eyes remained with me, and I found myself wishing she was wrong. I certainly hoped that wasn't the last I'd see of her. When I woke up tomorrow, she would be the first thing I sought out.

CHAPTER TEN

VERITY

I woke up to the sunlight streaming through the open window, blaring gold and orange behind my eyelids. My embarrassment from last night returned to me with a swiftness that made my muscles tense. How could I possibly face Daniel now? I groaned, pressing the heels of my hands to my eyes.

The bed was motionless beside me, so I was careful to sit up slowly and not disturb the mattress or Fanny's sleep. I crossed to the bell pull and tugged on it, yawning. When I turned around, my body went still. Fanny's side of the bed was empty.

Where was my sister? I ran to my trunk and pulled my things out, finding everything I needed to dress quickly. I was half-ready when Mary arrived.

"With haste, Mary," I said, turning my back to her so she could lace up my stays. I undid my braid and brushed through my hair while she slid my dress on.

"Are you well, my lady?" Mary asked.

"Fanny is gone," I breathed, bending to tug up my stockings while she pulled my hair back.

"She is in the drawing room," Mary said.

I stilled. "Is she upset?"

"Not that I'm aware of."

"But her routine. She said nothing about it?" At each inn on our journey here, when she awoke, her first question was if we could go in search of chickens. She could not see Harriet or Mr. Ramsey, but she wanted something along the same lines to begin her mornings. She'd done the same thing every morning for nearly fifteen years.

"Nothing to me, my lady."

I left the heap of my discarded nightclothes behind and raced from the room, walking swiftly down the staircase to the drawing room. I pushed open the door and relaxed the moment my gaze alighted on Fanny, kneeling on the rug in the center of the room petting Oscar. She wore a smile she typically reserved for animals.

A quick sweep of the room proved she was alone. I crossed the floor and sat on the edge of the sofa near Fanny. "Good morning."

She looked up fleetingly before returning her attention to the dog. "Good morning, Verity."

"You woke early."

"No, you slept late." She pulled out her pocket watch and checked the time before slipping it away again.

I supposed that was true. "Have you eaten yet?"

"Yes." The dog pawed lightly at her when she stopped scratching him between the ears, begging her to resume her ministrations. "Daniel helped me find the breakfast room."

Cold washed through me like an icy bucket of water being dumped over my head. "Daniel?"

"He's very kind. This is his castle, you know."

I knew.

"And this is his dog," she said.

Ah. It was little wonder Fanny liked him. How she came to be on such familiar terms with him, though, was a little frightening. Images flashed through my mind of Fanny in a fit of nerves because she could not see the chickens or check the bird feeders or didn't wish to eat what their cook had made for breakfast. Was Daniel now somewhere with his servants discussing what was to be done about the mad girl?

I shook the thought. "Daniel is the new Lord Huxley. He also owns Lamouth Park."

Something flickered across Fanny's brow. "He is the new earl?"

"Yes." As I had already told her, multiple times. I waited for her to say something more, but she didn't. "Has Mother been down yet?"

"No. She has a headache."

Of course she did. "Lady Moorington?"

"Who?"

"Daniel's mother."

"I have not seen her, either." Fanny sat back and looked toward the fireplace. "I can ring the bell for someone to show you where to find breakfast. Daniel told me to do that if I need anything."

"I can manage, but thank you." I had no appetite at present, anyway. It had taken far too long to fall asleep last night after leaving Daniel's room. My stupidity knew no bounds. How could I have imagined it a good idea to present myself to him in the middle of the night, like I was a prize? My naivety had won the hour, leading me to believe he would be tempted by any woman who approached him.

"I like Daniel," Fanny said.

"Do you? I would be perfectly content never to see the man again."

"Good morning, Verity." Daniel's deep voice was just behind me, throwing a wave of prickles down my neck.

I looked at my sister. "He is here, isn't he? Standing behind me?"

Fanny looked up and nodded before turning her attention

back to the dog. I shut my eyes, digging my fingernails into my palms before letting out a quick breath. I rose and pasted a smile on my face. His hair was brushed back, a dark shadow evident across his jaw where he must have recently shaved. Must he look so ruggedly handsome? "Good morning. We have dispensed with formality altogether, I see."

"Fanny insisted upon it. I could only return the favor."

Fanny never insisted upon anything. Well, that wasn't entirely true. She insisted on her routines. She was unlikely to have cared how Daniel chose to address her, though.

Lady Moorington stepped into the room shortly and delivered greetings. "Are you hungry, Lady Verity? The breakfast room has been cleared away, but I can send for something."

I swallowed. "I am not hungry."

My stomach was sick with apprehension. There was clearly amusement dancing in Daniel's deep brown eyes, but was it good or bad? What had he experienced when he spent time with my sister this morning? Would it aid me or be at my sister's expense? I had experienced far too many people mocking Fanny's odd quirks, or disregarding us as unworthy conversationalists, to not constantly be on my guard.

Mrs. Hale called for Lady Moorington, stealing her attention.

A look of confusion passed through Daniel's eyes. "Are you unwell?" he murmured. He took a step forward, but refrained from coming entirely to my side.

"I am not hungry."

"That was not my question."

I drew in a ragged breath but did my best to disguise it. "How did you find Fanny this morning?"

His gaze flicked to my sister and returned to me. "She is perfectly lovely."

What was he hiding?

"In fact," he continued, "we had devised a plan to explore the gardens, but Fanny insisted on waiting for you."

I gritted my teeth. Was I not to be allowed time to overcome my embarrassment from being rejected last night? "We wouldn't want to keep you. You must be a very busy man. I am certain we can find our way around the gardens without a guide."

"That might be best," Daniel said. He was smiling, but there was an edge present I did not understand.

"What nonsense," Lady Moorington said, leaving the house-keeper to join us. "Daniel knows this land better than anyone. There is no one more suited to be your guide." She gave her son a penetrating look that he seemed to resolutely ignore.

His teeth bared in a semblance of a smile with the shadow of a grimace. "I would be more than happy to be your guide."

"Wonderful. I wish I could join you, but Mrs. Hale needs me just now." Lady Moorington turned her attention to me. "You will be a suitable chaperone for your sister, I imagine."

I nodded.

Lady Moorington clapped her hands softly together. "Until later, then." She left the room, following the housekeeper away.

Daniel and I stood in uncomfortable silence. He did not appear to want to be our guide any more than I wanted him there.

"What do you think, Fanny?" Daniel asked, turning his attention to my sister and breaking the silence.

She looked up. "Yes?" Clearly she had not been following the conversation, but that was to be expected.

"Daniel has offered to show us the gardens. We can do so on our own, if you prefer." Fanny would undoubtedly prefer it that way. She'd never been comfortable around strangers.

Her attention remained firmly on Oscar. "I would like for him to show us the gardens."

Well, that was unexpected.

"It is decided then," Daniel said, looking everywhere but at me. "I will fetch my hat and return forthwith." He nodded sharply and strode from the room.

I watched him leave, my eyebrows pulling together. I could not tell which was chief among my emotions: anger that my extremely particular sister somehow approved of him, or embarrassment that my attempt last night had failed and he seemed to be put off by my presence. I waited until his footsteps receded before plopping down on the edge of the sofa again. "Drat, Fanny."

She did not reply.

My feet crunched on the gravel walkway as we made our way between rows of rose bushes and other shrubbery. Fanny walked ahead of us, looking for birds, while Oscar ran circles around our party. He loped to the end of the gardens and back, his tongue lolling happily.

Daniel walked by my side, watching Fanny. "Your sister is very . . ."

I tensed. Colin had begun sentences very much the same way occasionally. He never could understand her or the things she did that set her apart from typical behavior. The way her hands shook like she was flicking water from them anytime she was anxious, her humming, how inconsolable she could become . . . Where I would attempt to step in and soothe her, Colin was only ever disturbed.

Had he never put the idea of asylums in Mother's head . . . but that was in the past. Father had come to my aid and kept Fanny safe on both occasions it was brought up, but he was no longer here to defend her. Now it was up to me to keep that bit of history from repeating itself.

"Yes?" I asked, my defenses rising swiftly like a tide. "My sister is what, exactly?"

"Sweet."

I jerked my head toward him.

"Oscar likes her very much. He is particular about the company he keeps."

"More particular than his master?" I pretended to think it over. "You have shown that you can discriminate when you choose to."

Daniel coughed.

I hurried to change the subject before he could pursue it. "I think your hound must have good taste if he likes Fanny."

Daniel shot me a glance from the side. "You care for her very much."

"Of course I do. She is my sister." Was he fishing for information? I'd already revealed my desperation for Lamouth. I didn't intend to disclose more than that. "You have a sister, too, I gather?"

He nodded. "Jane. She is married to a Scotsman and they have a son, Lachlan. My mother has written to invite them to join us, but with the rain we've had lately I'm not sure if they'll be willing to travel. The roads between their home and ours can grow slick."

I looked ahead to where Fanny had paused on the path, her hand shading her eyes, her head tilted back, her gaze fixed on a tree's high branches at the edge of the copse. She'd allowed her bonnet to fall and rest against her back, the sun beating down on her light brown curls. "It is warm today."

"I hope it remains that way. If the roads dry, they'll be easier to entice to visit. And if they come, there is less of my mother's attention on me." He shot me a self-deprecating smile.

"It cannot be easy to live alone with your mother. I think I would go mad if I was forced to do that." From what I had thus far seen, Lady Moorington was of a far more loving disposition than my own mama, but I could appreciate his sentiment. "Does she visit you often?"

"No. It's been too long since I'd seen her. I only returned to Arden a few weeks before she wrote to invite your family to visit."

His words held a bitter edge, and I halted on the pathway, facing him. "You did not want us to come."

"Why do you say that?"

"Your tone. The way you phrased it. I had thought your mother was merely acting as your hostess, but it is more than that, is it not? She has orchestrated the whole of this visit?"

Daniel didn't deign to reply to me. His smile was strained. "My mother often feels she knows what is best."

I could not move. Fanny walked on ahead of us, still looking up into the tall tree, but I couldn't remove my gaze from Daniel's face. The faint lines creasing outward from his brown eyes were evidence the man smiled often, but I had not seen much of it since arriving. He had not been rude . . . merely patient. Putting up with our company for the sake of keeping his mother happy. "You did not wish for us to visit, did you?"

It made sense. He did not want the title, the house, or the responsibility. Why would he want a visit from the widow and daughters of the earl who had laid all that on his shoulders?

He was also, apparently, too much of a gentleman to answer me. Silence settled between us, heavy like an overladen raincloud.

"Then the older daughter, whom you did not want in your house in the first place, had the audacity to approach you with an arrangement in mind." I closed my eyes and clenched my hands into tight fists, nails biting into the soft flesh of my palms. "You will not credit it, but that was very unlike me."

"I credit it completely."

I opened my eyes again, surprised to find him watching me with a serious expression. His head was tilted to the side as if he were trying to make out my character. I brushed aside the severe nature of his furrowed eyebrows. "Well, that was unkind. You could at least pretend I was not wholly repulsive."

A laugh tore from his chest. "Repulsive? I did not say that."

"You did not need to. Your actions spoke loudly enough."

"Because I rejected you?" He narrowed his eyes. "I might not wish to marry for love, but that doesn't mean I will take advantage of a bereaved, penniless widow—"

"Penniless? Where did you contrive that idea?"

"From you."

Well, that was fair.

"Trust me, Verity," he said. "If I had not been taught any morals at all, we would have had an entirely different conversation last night."

Surprise whipped through me. "If I was not bereaved or you did not believe me to be in a vulnerable situation, then you might have considered my proposition?"

Daniel's mouth hung open. "Why do I have the feeling this is a trap?"

"It isn't. Not anything like last night, at least."

"That's reassuring," he said dryly. "I have to be honest. Those are not the only two things that are keeping my head correctly placed on my shoulders."

Lovely. "There is yet another reason you find me unexceptional?"

"I've never been particularly attracted to fortune hunters." He looked to the side, and his amusement fell flat. "Where is your sister?"

Fear overcame my irritation in an instant. I sucked in a quick breath, looking ahead of us on the path. It was empty. "Fanny!" I picked up my skirts and hastened forward, looking around every shrub and bush in the formal garden for my sister and her lavender gown. "Fanny!"

Daniel must have recognized the fear in my voice. He ran ahead of me, calling her name. He took the path, so I left it, running toward the copse of trees that had interested her. A flash of purple caught my eye and I turned sharply toward it. "Fanny!"

She straightened to her full height, looking at me with confusion. "Yes?"

She was unharmed, albeit a little messy, bending over to look at something on the ground. Oscar appeared from the trees and went straight to her side, and she shifted her body to protect whatever she'd been looking at. Relief flooded me. I glanced over my shoulder to wave to Daniel, but he was already heading our way.

"You should not leave my sight, Fanny. It is unfamiliar here. You could have become lost."

She looked up, glancing about as though seeing her surroundings for the first time. "Oh."

I drew in a sharp, sustaining breath. *Oh?* So insufficient a response to the subject of her safety. Sometimes I wanted nothing more than to press my hands to her cheeks and speak slowly, ensuring she understood me.

"What have you found?" Daniel asked, coming to stand at my side.

"A caterpillar." She reached down and picked up the fuzzy, striped insect. It squirmed between her fingers. "I need to keep it away from Oscar." She started toward the woods, and we followed her.

My heartbeat was still falling back to normal again. I slowed my steps, watching Fanny walk forward while the dog sniffed curiously at a tree trunk. Fanny set the caterpillar on a log, watching Oscar to be certain he did not notice it.

"If only she would pay as much attention to her own safety as she did that of a wretched insect," I muttered.

Daniel's voice came softly, replying to me, though I hadn't realized he'd even heard. "But why would she need to when she has you to do it for her?"

CHAPTER ELEVEN

DANIEL

Verity's green eyes were vibrant in the sunlight, wide and surprised.

"Forgive me," I muttered. "It was not my place to say any such thing."

Though I stood by my words. I'd yet to discern what it was about Fanny that was different. Her blatant disregard for genteel manners, which had at first made me believe she was rude, seemed far more innocent than deliberate. I'd yet to make out either Fanny or Verity's character. It was abundantly clear to me that I had not accurately taken either of their measures.

"Is it not the task of an older sister to watch out for younger sibling?"

"Some would argue that responsibility ought to fall on a governess until the child is old enough to govern themselves. Or, if not a governess, then the mother."

Verity looked away, a line forming between her eyebrows. "We have been without a governess for a number of years now. I dismissed her once I married my late husband."

"*You* dismissed her?"

"Yes." She lifted her chin. Sunlight lit her hair, making it look more red than brown. The auburn color was muted and pretty indoors, but out here it truly shone. "I had no further need of her, and neither did Fanny. Honestly, her penchant for Greek mythology was enough of a reason to dismiss her."

"You dislike Greeks? Or was it mythology that bothered you?"

Verity walked forward, following Fanny as she meandered farther into the woods. "Neither. I disliked watching her force the subject on Fanny. My sister does not have the attention for it. It was tortuous for all involved."

We made it to the other side of the copse. A low stone wall splattered with green and yellow lichen ran the length of the boundary here. I leaned my back against it and crossed my arms over my chest, watching Fanny follow a starling to the tree where it was tending to its nest.

"I can convince my mother to leave early, if you'd like," Verity said suddenly.

It took great effort to control my movements, but I did not look at her straight away. It was confusing of her to offer to leave when she had not received the thing I suspected she had come here for. She fingered the black ribbon on her bonnet, her troubled gaze resting on me.

"There is no need. I am happy to host your family at Arden for as long as you'd like to visit."

Verity lifted one eyebrow, illustrating her disbelief, and dropped the ribbon. "You need not lie to me."

"It is not a lie."

Her eyebrow remained lifted.

I wanted to say something that would force it back down. I shrugged. "I might not have felt that way when you initially arrived, but I am coming around to the idea."

"How noble of you," she said dryly.

I scoffed, the word hitting a flat note. "I assure you, I am anything but."

"Palmer!" a man called. I did not need to turn around to guess the owner of the voice, his deep baritone coming from the land abutting mine. "Or I suppose it is Huxley now?"

I turned to face my old friend, who rode on the back of a fine chestnut. His rounded cheeks were florid, reddened from the wind, his golden hair peeking out beneath a coal black hat. "Waterley," I said, unable to keep the surprise from my voice. "You've returned for the summer."

His presence here would typically be quite welcome, but I feared it would only complicate matters with our guests.

He approached the wall separating our land, towering over us from his position on the horse. "Only for a few weeks to shoot some birds."

Fanny uttered a faint scream behind me, and Verity moved to her sister's side at once.

"Belford has joined me, as have the Egerton twins." Waterley's gaze flicked between the women and me, his attention snagged by the outburst. "I would have sent 'round a note, but I did not realize you were in residence."

"It has been a long while since I've been home," I conceded. "Do not worry yourself."

"You'll join us then? We have a handful of hunts planned. Belford will be glad to see you."

Fanny's cries grew louder, and Waterley was doing a poor job of pretending he didn't notice her. He must have thought me the rudest sort for failing to introduce him to my guests, but how could I do so when one of them was crying loudly and the other was doing her best to console her? Verity tried to speak to her sister in a calming manner, but Fanny's red, splotchy face was streaked with tears, her sobs increasing in volume. What the devil had so affected her?

Waterley's attention followed mine to the ladies. A disturbed look flashed in his eyes.

I cleared my throat to reclaim his focus. "My guests seem to need my attention at present. We are respecting their mourning, so you'll understand why I cannot invite you to dine quite yet."

"You'll come visit, then?" Waterley said, his disturbed expression remaining. "Night after tomorrow? We can discuss the hunts then."

"Yes, I will be there." Surely one dinner away from Arden would not be disrespectful.

Waterley lifted his hat to me, looking once more with confusion at the women, before turning his horse and riding off. I waited until he was halfway across his field and well out of earshot before looking back at the women.

Fanny was shaking her hands, humming a disconcerting tune, her eyes wild and unable to settle on any one thing.

"Let us walk back to the house and inquire with the cook," Verity said smoothly, her voice low and rich. "Surely the gardener can lend us aid as well."

"Lend us aid," Fanny repeated.

"Shall we wipe our eyes now and return to the house?"

"Wipe our eyes," she repeated in a strained whisper.

Verity pulled a handkerchief from her pocket and held it up, showing it to her sister. "Would you like to do it yourself?" Her voice was steady and calm, as though she was speaking to a small child, but firm, as though she was the child's mother. It was oddly entrancing to watch, the way this woman took the matter in hand—whatever the situation was, though I still did not grasp what had upset the girl—and calmed her distraught sister. Her capability was commendable.

The bird chirped overhead and Verity lifted her face. "Look, Fanny. The starling returned."

Returned? I hadn't realized it had left. I supposed Fanny's hysterics had likely scared it away.

Fanny finished wiping her eyes and handed the handkerchief back to her sister, then looked up. Her hands were wringing together now, their distress lessened, and the humming had ceased. The change that had come over her was sudden in its inception and a complete mystery in its purpose. Had I not known the woman, I would have certainly believed her to be mad.

I swallowed. Maybe she *was*.

Verity looked at me, her auburn eyebrows drawn together as though she'd heard my thoughts. I swiftly adopted a bored expression, hoping I had covered whatever had been lurking on my face before.

"Shall we return to the house?" I asked, as though nothing untoward had just occurred.

"That would be good." Verity turned back to her sister. "Shall we go now? We can return to see the birds in the morning."

Fanny nodded and allowed Verity to lead her away, but pulled her hand back once we were set on the path to the house. I whistled once sharply and Oscar bounded through the trees, coming to follow behind me.

We walked toward Arden Castle and Fanny walked ahead, Oscar beside her.

"I apologize for not introducing you to my friend," I said after the walk had half-passed in silence.

"He must surely think me very rude," she said.

"Unlikely."

She looked uncertain.

"If he did find you impolite, it won't last the hour. Waterley does not consider anything for longer than is absolutely necessary. He would sooner forget I was here if he didn't have such extensive knowledge of the contents of my cellar."

Verity gave a small chuckle, and it brought a smile to my lips. "Waterley? Why does his name sound familiar?"

"He is from a prominent family. You might have become acquainted with them in London."

She shook her head. "I've not been to London."

That took me by surprise. "No marriage mart for you? Where did you meet your husband?"

"He was my father's cousin, once removed. I knew of Colin for most of my life, but we never spent much time together until after we were married. Our marriage was arranged."

That was right. She'd married the heir.

"That must have been . . ." I cleared my throat. "I am sorry."

"You've done nothing wrong."

"I should not have mentioned him in such a relaxed manner."

Verity was quiet as we walked past the rose bushes. "It has been nearly a year since Colin died. I've long since grown accustomed to his loss. It is not a trial to speak of him."

I wondered if she had too many other demands on her time and energy to focus on grief, or if she had merely grieved already. I debated asking her about the nature of Fanny's distress earlier when Waterley approached us, but I sensed she did not want to speak of it presently.

"Thank you for a most exhilarating outing." Verity dropped a quick curtsy and turned away.

"Wait," I said, grasping for her hand.

She looked back, startled.

Releasing her hand, I shoved both of mine behind my back. "Is there anything I can do for either of you?"

Her gaze flicked to her sister and back to me. "Nothing you are willing to do." Verity walked away before I could say more.

Nothing I was willing to do? She meant marrying her. She had to. The security she desired at Lamouth was far more complex than I'd realized. My earlier assumption that she was a fortune hunter was wrong, and I'd spoken the words aloud, directly to her. Shame overcame me when I stepped inside, skirting the women while they removed their outerwear and heading straight for the antechamber. I opened the cupboard set into the wall and moved aside a serving dish until I located the bottle.

Ah, there it was. I pulled it out, blowing dust from its cloudy glass.

"Daniel, I've been looking for you," Mother said, stalling in the doorway. "Lady Huxley and her daughters ought to be given a tour of the house. Do you think—"

"No, thank you, Mother." I uncorked the bottle. I didn't want her to know I had done nothing but offend the daughters—well, *one* of them—since their arrival.

"You do not know what I meant to ask."

I took a swig, and it burned the back of my throat. This was not a quality liquor by any means, but it would do the job. "You want me to lead a tour. Perhaps I can show the younger women around while you show the dowager?"

Mother's mouth opened, but she said nothing, staring at me.

"I thought so," I muttered. "This is sure to come as a disappointment, but there will be no marriage between Lady Verity and myself. Your matchmaking attempts are futile."

"Matchmaking attempts? I was doing nothing of the sort."

Frustration edged into my vision, making my arms shaky. I lifted the bottle for another sip, desperate to numb the discomfort swirling inside me. Expectations pecked at me like an insistent bird, and all I wanted was to burrow away and drink until I forgot all the pain and the memories. *Why must you be so irresponsible, Daniel? Why can you not be more like your sister? Why do you insist on making careless decisions? You know better.*

Of course I knew better. I'd been raised by paragons of virtue. But *knowing* what was right and *doing* it were two entirely different things.

Hurt and frustration splashed over Mother's face, deepening my need to succumb to oblivion. I strode past her into the corridor. "I'll be out the rest of the night. Waterley has returned."

Little did he know he was receiving an extra guest for the day.

CHAPTER TWELVE

VERITY

Lady Moorington had been all politeness at dinner, but it was clear she was distracted, though she kept up her side of the conversation well. Mother was curious about the different families in the area, and our hostess was happy to oblige her with information. I sat quietly through their conversation, wondering where Daniel was, and what his engagement this evening consisted of. Had he gone to visit another woman? That only made my embarrassment more complete. I regretted my impulse to visit his room more heartily with each passing hour.

To make matters worse, I still did not have a solution to the problem that encompassed our future. It was time to devise another plan.

"Our land borders that of the Waterley family," Lady Moorington said. "If you are familiar with Waterley House? It is a well-known estate in the area."

Mother's fork hovered just above her game hen. "I have had some business with the family. They are so close?"

Her business explained why the name was familiar to me. I must have heard it before in passing, but I could not remember the context. Though Mother was not the sort to manage any business of her own, so the nature of their relationship still eluded me.

"It is the saddest tale. The family was infected with smallpox over a decade ago, and it took both parents," Lady Moorington said. "Young Mr. Waterley and his sister were thereafter wards of their uncle, who came to live at the house and manage their affairs. The boy is a good friend of my son." Her smile grew tense, and her attention dropped to her plate.

Perhaps *that* was where Daniel was now. It would certainly be a less embarrassing destination. Unless, of course, Mr. Waterley had brought women with him for his hunting party. Did women attend such things? I hardly knew. Lady Moorington had done nothing to excuse his absence, aside from telling us that he was otherwise engaged for the evening, so that wasn't the least bit helpful.

Perhaps I could collect more information now. "We met Mr. Waterley on our walk today. Well, Lord Huxley did. I did not receive an introduction. I was too busy helping my sister when the man approached."

"That is unfortunate, but I dare say you will have another opportunity if you desire. If you were not still in mourning, I would be happy to host a dinner and introduce you to all the neighbors. As it stands now, that does not feel respectful."

Mother agreed, nodding. "We are likely to meet most of the neighbors in church, I wager."

"There are a few regular callers to Arden who will be sure to come by once they hear of our guests, anyway."

Regular callers? Women? I wanted to ask, but didn't know how to form the question without giving myself away.

"Tell me," Lady Moorington said, "was Mr. Waterley alone when you saw him?"

In truth, I hadn't paid much attention to the man. I was busy talking Fanny down from a ledge of hysteria. But the countess's question gave me pause. She seemed worried about my answer, and I wanted to know why. "He was alone, I believe."

She seemed to relax a little at this information.

A scream sounded faintly in the distance, and I lifted my head, turning my ear toward the door.

Lady Moorington gave a little laugh. "Goodness, that did not sound pleasant."

Mother tensed, her knuckles turning white as she gripped her knife and fork, frozen where they were about to cut another bite of meat.

The scream repeated, and I pushed back my chair, laying my napkin on the table and picking up my gloves.

"Verity," my mother snapped. "You would not be so rude as to leave the table."

My hand paused halfway into one of my gloves. I looked from my mother to my hostess, one subduing her anger, the other only confused. *Vow she will not be a disruption.* I chose my words carefully. "If that is my sister, I should ascertain whether or not—"

"You will sit." Her eyes were hard, and I could tell she was extremely displeased. If Mother had her way, we would pretend Fanny had never been born, but I couldn't live that way. If my sister was distressed, I would see to her. *Someone* needed to. Fanny had proven she would not find calmness on her own.

I hated embarrassing my mother in front of Lady Moorington, but there was nothing else for it. I looked between them, struggling to find the right thing to say that would please both of them and remove me from the room quickly.

Lady Moorington must have sensed my struggle. "If your sister is vexed, you by no means need to remain here. Please see to her."

"Thank you." I dipped my head in a quick curtsy, avoiding my mother's gaze. I shoved my hand into my other glove while I left the room, hastening toward the corridor where Mary and Fanny disappeared each night.

It was not difficult to find the entrance to the servants' staircase. Fanny's crying could be heard clearly. She repeatedly called out, "No! No!" It was all too familiar, the sound causing my feet to take the stairs with more haste than was likely safe, my stomach tumbling over itself in dismay and fear. A fit of nerves this loud would likely have a negative impact on the household, but I could not allow myself to worry about that yet.

Mother was likely anxious about it enough for both of us.

Fanny's cries grew louder the closer I came to the kitchen. This was the reason my mother didn't like to bring Fanny with us away from the house, the reason we never traveled at all. In this moment, I hated myself for agreeing with her, for understanding why Fanny was better off at Lamouth. Others did not understand my sister. Unfamiliar people stared at her like she was an animal, like she belonged in a madhouse, as if she suffered from lunacy.

That could not be further from the truth, but when Fanny acted out in this manner, it was difficult to convince others of that.

As she was doing now, sitting on the kitchen floor near the table, as though she'd fallen from her chair and remained where she landed. A smattering of Arden's servants were lined up against the wall, watching this occur, but no one was making an effort to help, except for Mary, who crouched near Fanny. She spoke softly, but Fanny continued to cry, repeating the word *no*, her hands fluttering, unable to still.

Drat, this was not good.

I ran past the handful of servants who stood on the other side of the room, watching with wide eyes and confusion plastered over their faces. Did they think giving her an audience was in any way helping?

In truth, it hardly mattered. I did not think Fanny even noticed her audiences—not as much as I noticed them, at least.

Mary stood abruptly and turned away, halting when she noticed me. "I was just coming to find you, my lady."

"What happened?" I asked quietly, going directly to her side.

Mary's gaze flicked to the wall of servants standing on the other side of the table and back to me.

"Just tell me, Mary."

"I think it was too much for her. The conversation was loud, with people coming to and from the dining room. Someone started singing." She shook her head, her eyes wide. "No one was talking to Fanny, but a few of them sat at the table chatting. Someone was hitting the table. They didn't do anything wrong, but it isn't like this at home. It was too much noise and bustle, I think."

I dropped to my knees in front of my sister and lowered my voice. "Were you frightened, darling?"

Her eyes looked at me and then away. She continued to chant the word *no*, and I could see discomfort making her pull into herself, her shoulders bunched to her neck, her hands fidgeting from distress. The best thing now would be to remove her from the kitchen altogether.

"Fanny, shall we go upstairs? Mary can bring your dinner, and we can eat in our room."

She fell quiet and looked up, and I held my breath while she rested her gaze on me. I reached for her hand, but she would not allow me to take it. Coaxing her up without being able to touch her was hard. I could not move her along at a faster pace than she was willing to go.

Stares burned hot on the back of my neck from the Arden servants. My own hands trembled, but I ignored them. Removing my sister from this kitchen was my priority at present.

Fanny got to her feet, and I nodded to Mary. "Would you

bring her dinner up?" The kitchen was quiet, except for Fanny's faint humming, which revealed she was still somewhat distressed.

I led her back to the stairs, and we followed Mary up them. She knew where to go better than I did. Once we reached our bedchamber, Mary set Fanny's dinner out and Fanny sat at the small dressing table to eat. Mary waited near the fireplace for me to finish making sure Fanny was comfortably situated, then I joined her.

"I wonder if it is not the best for Fanny to eat dinner in the kitchen," I said quietly, my hands still shaking from the pain of finding my sister in such a state.

Mary's brow furrowed. "It was not like this last night. Everyone went about their duties in perfect politeness, if a little quietly. I imagine they were uncomfortable having an earl's daughter in the kitchen, but tonight . . ."

"What was different? What changed? I know the servants eat early because they must serve dinner, so Fanny did not take someone's place at the table, I hope?"

"No, it was nothing of that sort." Mary looked hesitant.

"Just tell me, please."

"I think it must have occurred to them that Fanny is not like other people. They no longer guarded their tongues this evening, as if they could tell she paid them no mind."

I closed my eyes, crossing to the bed to sink on the mattress. "I should not have brought her here."

"You'd rather she have been home? If something like that would've happened and you wouldn't have been there—"

I looked up. "You would've managed to calm her eventually."

Mary shook her head. "I said all the same things you did. Lady Fanny wanted none of that when it came from my lips, but when you suggested those very same things? She stopped right away, my lady."

Frustrated tears pricked my nose. I breathed in deeply to

push them away. I would not cry about this. "Then I did the right thing? Bringing her here?"

"It is not my place to say, my lady, but I think you did not have any other choice."

It felt nice to have my own sentiments returned to me, but it did not erase the anxiety that bloomed in my chest. What would the servants say now? What sort of rumors would spread? I rubbed my temples. What would Lady Moorington think?

Or Mother? I shuddered.

"Would you like to speak to the servants?" Mary asked. "To explain?"

"What would I say?"

She looked uncomfortable. We both looked at Fanny, who quietly spooned porridge into her mouth, her head leaning back while she chewed, then tucking down to her chest every so often. I sometimes wondered what she was thinking about when she became lost in thought, especially after a fit of nerves like she'd just experienced. She likely wasn't worried about the state of the household servants' opinions. She never cared about such things.

"I suppose I could excuse her behavior, but that only gives credit to her fit, does it not?"

Mary looked as troubled as I felt. I shook my head and rested my hand on her forearm. "Go enjoy your dinner. I have Fanny well in hand now, and we won't need anything until it is time to ready for bed."

Mary tilted her head to the side a little, sorrow deep in her eyes. "I can stay, my lady."

"We do not both need to sacrifice meals, and I cannot eat now anyway."

She nodded once and turned to leave. When she was gone, I rummaged through Fanny's trunk for some paper and charcoal pencils. I took them to the dressing table and set them on the edge, keeping my hand over the top of them until she noticed me.

Fanny dropped her spoon and reached for the pencil, but I didn't relinquish it. "When you are finished with your dinner, you may draw."

She returned her attention to the porridge.

"Does that suit, Fanny?"

She nodded.

I lifted my hand from the desk and went to the bed to sit and wait. I needed to consider which explanation I ought to supply to the housekeeper, to Lady Moorington, and, most important of all, to my mother.

CHAPTER THIRTEEN

DANIEL

My head pounded like someone had led a herd of cows over it all night. I turned over in bed, anxious to fall asleep again if for no other reason than to be rid of the unrelenting throbbing in my temples.

Metal scraped against wood as my bed hangings were swept to the side, pouring orange light over my closed lids. I swore loudly.

"Good morning, my lord."

"Not for you, Dean," I mumbled, picking up another pillow to press over my head and block out the sunlight. "You just lost your position."

"Would you like tea before I bring your breakfast?" he asked, ignoring my latest threat. "I added a dram of whisky."

I moved the pillow away. "Gads, man. Why?" I understood I had drunk to excess last night, and probably the night before, and definitely far too many times in the last year, but I usually did not *begin* my day in that manner.

"Met a chap who promised it would help with the aftereffects of a late night of drinking. Claims it removes the headache faster."

Currently I wanted nothing more than that.

I sat up and let him bring me a cup of tampered tea. "I am never drinking again," I said when a wave of nausea rolled through my stomach. Well, after this tea, I meant.

"I think I've heard that before."

"Enough, Dean," I growled.

"Is it?" He said no more, which was a good thing, because my threat was close to becoming a reality had he pressed me further.

It would be no good to admit so aloud, but I couldn't help agreeing with him. I *had* said that before, far too many times. I'd meant it, too, but such a resolution was easy to forget when my hackles were up and escape appeared the best option. When others insisted on trying to control my life, I needed to find a way to take that control back. I was not proud of my methods, but they did work in the moment.

Until the next morning when regret and guilt clouded my brain worse than the headaches and nausea. Blast. There had to be a better way to cope.

The tea was . . . well, it was not tea. It hardly resembled the drink, but I gulped it down, hoping it would do what Dean claimed. Dinner at Waterley's house last night had been the raucous occasion I expected. I did enjoy being with my friends again, but had found myself wishing I was home instead. Not necessarily to have dinner with my mother and her guests but merely for the comfort of the castle.

When the men had turned to cards last night, I'd left, which was a good thing for my pocketbook but not my reputation among my friends. I hardly recalled how I got home. I certainly would have foolishly lost half my fortune had I remained. Belford tended to look out for me, but Waterley only ever had himself in mind.

Though I could not judge. When I'd drunk the rest of that

bottle of brandy and had escaped Arden, it was with entirely selfish intentions.

"Was my mother very angry last night?" I asked.

Dean smoothed out my waistcoat and laid it over a chair. "No, but I think she would've appreciated having you here."

Guilt this early in the morning was as unwelcome as an overeager rooster. "Forget I asked."

"Not that she wanted you here for your own sake," Dean said flippantly. "There was a disturbance in the kitchen. No one knew what to do."

I sat up a little straighter, lowering my cup. "What sort of disturbance? Was there a fight?"

"No, nothing of that sort. Were you aware Lady Frances takes her meals down there?"

"Dinner, yes."

Dean disappeared into the dressing room, leaving me in suspense. He returned with a fresh cravat and laid it over the waistcoat, smoothing it out.

"Well, get on with it." I could certainly discern amusement on his face, and I wanted to wipe it off.

"Lady Frances had some sort of fit during her dinner. She was screaming on the floor, and no one could say anything to stop her until they fetched the sister."

My stomach sank.

Dean lifted his eyebrows and let out a low whistle. "Some of the servants—not saying it's me, you understand—just *some* of the servants are wondering if the woman is mad."

I had asked myself that same thing, but even a brief conversation with the girl proved her mental competence. She could carry on a discussion and was fully aware of her surroundings when she chose to be. It did not make sense that someone so capable would suffer from bouts of lunacy.

I downed the rest of my tea. "I wouldn't think so." My head still throbbed when I climbed out of bed. I splashed water on my face and prepared to shave away the shadow of dark scruff on my cheeks. "Not that I am an expert on such things."

"Mr. Waterley's man would know."

"True. But it is none of our concern, nor our place to conjecture as much."

Dean's eyebrows rose. "The woman is in your house, my lord. I think that makes it your place."

It was my place to protect the people who lived in my home and the servants who worked for me—but not to reach out to the warden of a madhouse and inquire about the state of Fanny's mental stability. I had to trust my instincts, and they had told me from the outset there was nothing fundamentally dangerous about the girl. I looked at Dean through the mirror while I dragged the blade down my cheek, shaving it closely to the skin. "Was she a danger to anyone during her fit? Or a danger to herself?"

Dean shook out a fresh shirt for me. "No. She kept to herself. She wouldn't even speak to her maid. Her sister was the only person she would listen to. Before Lady Verity came downstairs, the only harm Lady Frances did was to our ears."

As I'd suspected. There was something not quite right with this family, and Verity held too much of the responsibility for her sister. I wiped the rest of the soap from my face and slid the shirt on, then tucked it into my breeches. "Where was Lady Huxley during all of this?"

"Eating dinner."

I paused, looking up. "Did she know? Was she made aware of the situation?"

"Worthlin could hear Lady Frances's fit all the way in the dining room. According to him, Lady Huxley told her daughter to leave Lady Frances be."

My teeth clenched. If only I had been there to help smooth the situation. But if the maid could not reason with the girl, what could I have done? Dean helped me finish dressing and left, taking my nightshirt with him. If there was going to be a woman disturbing the household in this way, I would need to have a talk with her sister. If nothing else, only to ascertain the girl's threat to my household—or rather, lack thereof.

I sat in the armchair near my empty fireplace and closed my eyes. First, I needed this headache to abate.

By the time my headache receded enough to warrant leaving my bedchamber, several hours had passed. I did not feel the need to seek out my mother in that time, and she blessedly let me be. My guilt was already heavy enough from leaving her on such unpleasant terms the evening before. I was perfectly aware of how deeply she disliked my spending any time at Waterley's house. She would be happy to hear Miss Waterley wasn't present last night, nor was she expected to be in the near future. At some point I needed to offer Mother that olive branch.

For now, though, a little time would give me more courage to face her.

I had always been a disappointment, and it never felt any easier to overcome. Despite the expectations laid out to me in my youth, some of us weren't meant for great things like earldoms or marriage or pleasing our mothers.

A screech sounded through my open window. I hurried to look outside, startled to see Fanny laughing on the lawn. Oscar had a stick in his mouth and Fanny was attempting to pull it free. She dislodged it, then threw it for him to chase. I immediately searched the grounds for Verity. It had not taken long to figure out that wherever Fanny went, her sister followed.

Spotted. Verity sat on the stone bench at the edge of the garden, a black bonnet over her auburn locks. I immediately closed my window and left the room. Our conversation during the night when she'd come to my bedchamber had been left dangling. It was time to finish it.

My steps were quiet when I slipped downstairs. Anything to avoid my mother for as long as I could, even sneaking outside like a child who'd broken his sister's new archery bow and didn't want to be reprimanded for it. If I recalled that situation accurately, Mother had merely waited until I returned to give me the tongue-lashing I'd earned.

The sun shone directly overhead, beating down on my face and making my temples ache softly. I pulled at my cuffs while crossing the lawn, feeling suddenly vulnerable. Fanny continued to bait Oscar into rounds of tug-of-war with a stick, then throwing it with a wide arc.

Verity hadn't seen me approach. I leaned back a little and watched her track Fanny. Her mouth was turned slightly down into a frown, and while her face seemed to follow wherever Fanny ran, her eyes seemed glazed over as if she was lost in thought.

I stepped forward. "I have always believed Oscar to be a lazy hound, but your sister is proving me very wrong."

Verity didn't so much as flinch. Her eyes shuttered, the frown replaced by a genial smile. "Perhaps all he needed was for someone to engage with him."

"I've done my best. I acquired him just a few months ago, and as you can see, he is not very young. I assumed he was set in his ways."

"He isn't good for hunting?" she asked.

"Not at all. He is an absolute wretch."

Fanny put her hand out in a circular motion, as if attempting to teach Oscar to roll over.

"Perhaps your sister can train him for me."

"To hunt?" Verity's laugh echoed through the garden. "That is more likely to set into motion a ridiculous scheme to set him free. Trust me, I should know."

"That sounds like an interesting story."

"Only if you have a good deal of time to listen to it," she muttered.

I gestured to the empty space on the bench beside her. "If you will permit me to sit with you, I would love to hear it."

She seemed uncertain, her brows pulling together just enough to be noticeable. "Why are you being friendly?"

I coughed. "Have I previously seemed taciturn and unhappy?"

"Not those words exactly." She narrowed her eyes slightly, tilting her head back to see me better. "But a man like you is typically not this friendly without purpose."

A man like me? A rake. I wanted to proclaim I had done nothing more than drink to excess and waste money at cards for the better part of the last year, so I couldn't truly claim that title anymore. But her opinion was set. I had never been very adept at praising my good behaviors. Something about inheriting the title of earl had cured me of the need to flirt to excess. Women wanted to marry me now, and they didn't care about my past if securing me meant they would become a countess. It took all the fun out of it. "Despite general opinion, my mother did raise me to be a gentleman."

Verity bit her bottom lip, looking away. Her cheeks pinked.

I wanted to move forward, away from this conversation before it could further develop. "Either way, you've piqued my curiosity. May I?"

She nodded, watching me flip back my coattails and sit beside her. The stone bench was cool to the touch and refreshing after the heat from the sun.

"My sister is very fond of animals."

"I didn't notice," I said dryly.

She ignored that comment. "Fanny was born with an overly-affectionate heart, particularly where animals are concerned. Her feelings did not pair well with a brother-in-law who was obsessed with hunting. When I married Colin and he came to live at Lamouth Park, he brought his hounds and took to shooting the fowls on our land. This was a relatively new occurrence for our estate."

"Was your father not a hunter?"

"He never cared much for it. He hosted parties on occasion when we were girls, but not frequently, and I doubt Fanny ever knew. When Colin would shoot, he was very proud of his dogs and how well-trained they were. He often boasted about his exploits, and it bothered Fanny a great deal."

I could well imagine it. Her panic after Waterley merely mentioned shooting birds had been excessive. "Do not tell me she interfered with the hounds?"

Verity looked at her sister, and I couldn't help staring at her profile. Her features were defined but delicate, and the love shining in her eyes was unmistakable. "Fanny woke up early one morning and gathered the hounds on leads that she fashioned out of rope, then took them to the local village. We walk there together every Wednesday, so she was familiar with the way. Since it was a market day, she was able to find homes for the dogs with a pair of gentlemen who were passing through."

Laughter bubbled from my chest, imagining the scene playing out. "What did she tell the men when she tried to convince them to take the dogs?"

"Her excuse to me was that they needed a new home, so I can only imagine it was something like that."

"And her goal in this transaction?"

"That is what I don't understand," Verity said, laughing. Her face relaxed, shining more beautifully. "It was unclear whether her efforts were to save the birds from being killed or the dogs from being murderers. But either way, Colin acquired new dogs to replace them, and the gentlemen she gave his dogs to likely took them home to hunt. I'm certain they were willing to accept the dogs because they were clearly of good stock."

I grinned, watching Fanny lie on the ground and roll over in an effort to show Oscar what she would like for him to do. He sat, tilting his head to the side but not budging. "Your husband must have been thrilled."

"Oh, he was livid. That was when he—" She stopped herself, clearing her throat. "Colin and Fanny were never close." She sighed. "I do hope my mother is not watching her now. She will ruin that gown."

"Will you not tell her so?"

"If I thought it would do any good, I would. I am not her mother, and I cannot command her to stop."

"Could've fooled me."

Verity jerked her head toward me. "What do you mean by that?"

I hadn't planned on mentioning it, but the conversation about Fanny had been so open, I imagined it was a good opportunity to try and discover more information about her situation. "I was told of the . . . of what occurred last night at dinner. From the sound of it, your mother was not the one who went to her aid."

The color leached from Verity's cheeks. "My mother and I do not agree on the best ways to help Fanny."

"From my servant's report, it sounded as though you were the only one who did any helping." I didn't know why I was growing defensive on her behalf, but her resolute insistence only made me want to come to her defense more. "I am beginning to suspect that your reasons for trying to strike a bargain with me have something to do with your sister as well."

Verity was silent. Her face looked etched from stone, her body unmoving. I could not discern if it was fear driving through her now, or if she was merely searching for a response.

Fanny stood again, circling her arm to give Oscar an example of what she wanted him to do. Grass clung to her back and in her messy hair. She was old enough to be reasoned with but did not seem to accept reason at times. Her fit sounded as though it was driven by lunacy, but now she was logical in her attempt to teach Oscar to roll over. Her cognitive abilities were certainly sufficient, but her emotional responses varied. I did not understand her, and I found I wanted to.

Curiosity overwhelmed me, and I turned on the bench to face Verity. "What are you hiding?"

CHAPTER FOURTEEN

VERITY

W hat was I hiding? Nothing *well*, it seemed. My hands shook, and my nails bit into my palms to keep them still. Colin's dislike of Fanny had begun in much the same manner—asking questions. It was not until she had committed the grave error of rehoming his hounds that he had declared she was better fit for Bedlam, that it would only be a kindness to find a decent madhouse to house her.

A *decent* madhouse. As though such a thing existed.

It was a good thing Father had been there to reason with Mother. But it wasn't long after that Colin had convinced them both to plan a holiday in Bath so Fanny could take the waters. That hadn't ended well, either.

Daniel watched me now, curiosity lacing his words when he asked what I was hiding. He had come out here for this reason, I was certain of it, and my answer now could greatly affect the way he viewed my sister. How many days had we been here? Two? I needed to keep her safe for twelve more days *and* somehow contrive a way for Daniel to sign a contract stating that we could remain in the house. That was the first step.

"Do we not all have secrets?" I asked, watching Fanny. She'd given up trying to teach Oscar to roll over by example and was now spinning his stick in a circle. "That's an impossible question to answer."

"It is forward of me, I'll grant you that, but I thought we did away with formalities the other night."

"You cannot know how heartily I regret that impulse."

"I do not regret it in the least. We would not have the gift of freely speaking now had you not broken down those barriers so swiftly."

"Perhaps that is precisely why I am regretting my rash actions." I looked away before settling my gaze on Daniel again. His attention was so direct—it was difficult to maintain for long. I wasn't used to being around gentlemen that were not my late husband or my father, and I certainly was not used to spending time with a known flirt.

"Have your goals changed, then?" he asked.

"Goals? Whatever do you mean?"

"Lamouth. Is that not your priority?"

"It can never be mine, so I must find something new." Somewhere safe, perhaps in the general vicinity, like the dower house if the roof was fixed. I needed to find a way to generate an income, but if he was willing to pay me to manage the house as he'd mentioned, then maybe . . .

"You are hatching a plan," he said.

Was I that obvious? "Now that you mention it, this is a good opportunity to discuss options moving forward."

"Options? Like in which churches the banns should be read or what you'll wear to our wedding?"

My cheeks bloomed with heat. "Fear not, Daniel. I will never ask you to marry me again. One rejection is more than enough."

"Pity. To be fair, you never actually proposed to me."

Was he in earnest? I wagered he wasn't. "In that case, I promise never to do so. I was wondering if we could come to another arrangement, though."

He lost the edge of amusement, his gaze flicking to me from the side. "What did you have in mind?"

Oscar barked loudly, stealing my attention, and I whipped my head around to find Fanny chasing him across the lawn toward the house. She looked a little wild, grass clinging to her gown and bits of green clinging to her messy hair, running with abandon. Oscar appeared to take issue with a pair of horses coming down the long drive carrying gentlemen on their backs.

"Wretched dog," Daniel said, breaking into a run.

"Fanny!" I called, hoping to snag her attention before she found herself in the thick of several disgruntled animals. She didn't appear to hear me. I raised the hem of my gown so it would not inhibit my movement and hurried after them, though not nearly as fast as Daniel.

Oscar reached the horses, barking wildly, and Fanny ran toward them, yelling his name.

I couldn't hear what the gentlemen were saying, but it did not sound pleasant. One of the horses was skittish. The closer I drew, the more fear I could see on the rider's face.

Once Daniel rounded the side of the building and was close to the animals, he called his dog with such authority that Oscar stopped barking and looked back to see what his master needed. "Oscar, *come*," he said in a way that made me believe no one had ever disobeyed him before. He employed the authoritative voice well, and it suited him.

Oscar barked once more, whining from his throat. "Come," Daniel repeated, and the dog obeyed. He took the dog by the scruff and walked toward the house before releasing him with a scolding, and Fanny followed.

The men on horseback—one of them I recognized as Mr. Waterley, the other a stranger—kicked into motion, crossing the drive and heading toward the stables. Wise of them to put the horses away before someone was hurt.

I took my sister by the hand. "Shall we take Oscar inside?"

"We are to see the chickens soon," she said, pulling her watch from her bodice and looking at the time. "There is not enough time to take him inside first."

"No one is expecting us, Fanny. We can take Oscar in before we see the chickens."

She seemed uncertain. "We are meant to go to the chickens in four minutes."

"Can we not change our schedule a little?"

Her mousy brown eyebrows inched together. "That would alter our schedule for the rest of the day."

"Not if we borrow the extra minutes from our chicken time. Then nothing else needs to change. Drawing and tea with Mother can proceed as planned."

Daniel's face had followed our conversation, looking from me to Fanny as our discussion proceeded. "You needn't worry about Oscar, Verity. He'll behave now." He sounded more threatening than promising.

"We cannot take Oscar to see the chickens. He will think they are his dinner," Fanny said.

Obviously. If the hound wanted to challenge a horse, he would certainly challenge squat little birds. "I wasn't suggesting—"

"We cannot take Oscar into the house or we will be late for the chickens." She was growing distressed.

"Can I have those four minutes to introduce you to my friends?" Daniel asked, stealing her attention. I looked over my shoulder to see the men walking toward us.

Fanny peeked at her pocket watch again. "Three minutes."

"Very well." An amused smile played over Daniel's lips. "Waterley, Belford, come meet my guests."

The men approached. Mr. Waterley's cheeks were rosy— likely from having received too much sun—and his golden hair waved up away from his face.

"Lady Verity Palmer," Daniel said, pointing to me, "and Lady

Frances Palmer, allow me to introduce Mr. Waterley, my nearest neighbor, and Lord Belford, one of my closest friends."

We both curtseyed to the gentlemen.

"I was sorry to hear of your father's passing," Mr. Waterley said.

My stomach clenched, as it often did when my father was mentioned. "You knew him?"

"Very little. I was a friend of your husband's in school." He tilted his head to the side, his gaze flicking from me to my sister. "He never mentioned me?"

He must have. Colin's association with the man could explain why the name Waterley had sounded familiar. "He did not speak much about those years, and what little he told me is difficult to recall at present."

"Understood." A jolly smile spread over his lips. "How long will Arden be able to boast such lovely company?"

Fanny looked at her watch again and snapped it closed. "We need to be on our way now."

I tried to bridge the gap between her bluntness and reality. "I am afraid my sister has an appointment to keep." I only hoped Daniel would not reveal the appointment was with a flock of birds. I shot him a pleading glance, and his gaze, while difficult to read, was steady. His deep brown eyes remained firmly on me for a beat longer than necessary, penetrating my nerves.

"Of course. Perhaps we can finish this conversation another time?" Mr. Waterley asked.

Daniel's attention was pulled away. "Some of my guests are observing mourning for the time being, so we have not intended to plan any social functions while they are here."

"Another chance meeting it must be, then." Mr. Waterley winked. "I should like to hear of Colin and how he fared since we parted ways at school."

Fanny was already walking away, so I took a few steps to follow her. "That would be most agreeable. Good day, gentlemen." I dipped my head to each of them, including the silent Lord Belford, and hastened to reach Fanny's side.

"We are two minutes behind schedule," Fanny said quietly.

"If we walk excessively fast, we can make up some of that time," I offered. This earned me no response, which was just as well. I intended to use this time to develop my plan moving forward. If marriage to Daniel was not an option, then something else would have to do.

Only, what would it be?

CHAPTER FIFTEEN

DANIEL

"You came," I said dryly, leading Waterley and Belford into the house.

"I didn't want to," Belford defended. "I told him we shouldn't."

That was believable. Waterley always did that which served him best, other people's opinions be hanged. My instinct had been to keep him away from Fanny, but I owned it was likely a silly concern. Even so, it hardly mattered to him that I didn't wish to subject either Verity or Fanny to his attention. If he wanted to come, he came.

Waterley scoffed. "You were foxed when you told us to stay away, Pal—er, Huxley."

My shoulders tensed. "Do not call me that."

Waterley's eyebrows raised. "You were in earnest when you said that last night? I thought you were having a lark."

We mounted the steps toward my front door, Oscar at my heels. "Whatever opinion you have of it, keep it to yourself. Huxley is not my name."

Belford looked thoughtful. "We've never called you Daniel. That will feel deuced odd."

I refrained from rolling my eyes, but only just. "Then Palmer will suffice." Without waiting for anyone to follow, I continued inside and on toward the library. "Enough about blasted names. Why have you come? I assume it is important."

Waterley cleared his throat, dropping onto the end of the sofa. "My sister is coming to visit, and she's bringing a small party with her."

My jaw clenched. It was a good thing I had yet to inform my mother that Miss Waterley was *not* in residence, for that would have been short-lived relief on her part. For my own sake, I wondered if Verity would be willing to prolong her mourning so we would not be required to welcome callers while she and her family were here.

A decanter of claret sat upon a far table, glasses stacked beside it. I crossed the room and poured the wine into two glasses, then paused, the decanter hovering over the third. *I am never drinking again.* Is that not what I thought when I woke up this morning? Is that not what I'd told Dean?

The relief a sip would provide beckoned me. Enough claret could blur the edges of my senses just enough to keep me relaxed in an otherwise anxious environment. Oscar arrested my attention, slumping in a pool of sunlight from the window. He let out a sigh as he laid his head on the floor.

The way Fanny had chased after him today brought a smile to my face, and I set the decanter back down and corked it. I carried the two glasses to my friends and deposited one with each of them. Perhaps if I could complete the visit quickly, I could find out what Fanny wanted with my chickens.

Belford looked at me strangely, then to the empty glass I'd left behind. Confusion bent his brow. I knew my friends were used to my drinking habits, but to notice when I refrained from one drink? That was lowering.

He seemed to accept the situation and tipped back his glass, swallowing half of the claret in one gulp. "There is one benefit to your sister's visit," he said, looking to Waterley. "Wherever she goes, the Malton sisters tend to follow."

This was a new development. I'd thought Belford didn't care for marriage yet. "You planning to set your cap at one of them?"

"The unmarried one, preferably," Waterley said.

Belford looked in his glass. "This is prime."

"Does he have competition?" I asked.

"Not enough money for me," Waterley said, swirling his glass. "I won't entertain the notion of less than six thousand pounds."

I coughed, grateful I had not been drinking the deep red wine, for it would now be sprayed over my rug if I had.

"Gads, man," Belford said, mildly disturbed. "Why?"

"The family business suffering, Waterley?" I asked.

He took a sip of his wine. "If I am to put up with a wife, I ought to be compensated for it."

Belford lifted his glass toward me with a goofy grin. "I pity the woman who catches your eye."

I stood to refill it for him. "Why marry at all, then?"

"Family name. Legacy. Heirs." He drank the remainder of his wine, too, and I brought the decanter over to fill it again.

Were those Verity's reasons, also? I could not discount her legacy at Lamouth Park or the appeal of producing the Huxley heirs. If she married me, she would have both of those things, much as she'd meant to have them with the previous heir. It was a lowering thought to be desired only for what I could provide. The merest whisper in the back of my mind wanted her to desire *me*.

"Where is the rest of your shooting party? The Egerton twins."

"Sleeping."

I glanced at the clock, which read past two in the afternoon.

"They could be awake now," Belford offered. "Perhaps we ought to return."

Waterley gave a slight shake of his head, his gaze resting on me. "You missed great sport last night. Stakes were high, but you can stand for it."

"It wasn't about the money." Oscar made another whining sound in his throat, which was not typical behavior for him. What did he desire? To be freed? To go to Fanny? I understood the wish. I was inordinately curious about her schedule and the need for chickens to be a permanent fixture on it. To what end did she visit them? Was it merely a social call or did they serve some greater purpose? My mouth fought a small smile at the thought.

Waterley's eyes narrowed. "What is it, then? A woman?" His brow suddenly cleared. "The widow? Or is it the school miss?"

He meant Verity and Fanny, and my defenses rose like one of Arden's thick stone walls. "Neither. I am attentive to my mother's guests, but they in no way influence my decisions."

Belford gave a small, sharp nod. "He never was one to chase women of quality, Waterley. You should know that."

"Nor have I ever been induced to set my sights on children," I added dryly. Fanny was seventeen, according to what Verity had told Mother and me. She was hardly out of the schoolroom —if at all yet. Her habit of taking dinner with the maid only reinforced her young nature.

Waterley was not convinced. He sipped at his drink and smacked his lips together, eyeing me.

The door to the library opened, admitting my mother and Lady Huxley. Both women stilled in the doorway, and I stood at once, my friends following suit.

"Forgive the intrusion. We were just coming to fetch the latest repository." Mother looked back at Lady Huxley, who was staring with wide eyes and pinched lips at my friends. A flicker of recognition passed over the widow's face.

"You are never intruding, Mother," I said gallantly.

Mother's gaze flicked to Waterley and away again. She was

too refined to make her discomfort known, but I could see it in the miniscule tightening of her jaw. "All the same, we can take our reading material to another room."

I turned my attention to the widow. "Lady Huxley, I hope you will grant me the privilege of introducing our closest neighbor, Mr. Waterley, and my friend, Lord Belford of Trillingham."

They bowed, and she gave a belated dip of her head. "I am familiar with both of your names. How fortunate you should chance to happen by. It is a pleasure."

Waterley stepped forward to bow more formally over her hand. "The pleasure is most assuredly mine. I had not realized when I brought friends home for our small shooting party I would be granted such an honor. Please accept my heartfelt condolences, Lady Huxley."

"Did you have the pleasure of knowing my husband?"

"No, but I did own the acquaintance of Colin Palmer. It was with great regret that I learned of his passing."

A look passed between the two that I could not identify, and it gave me pause. There was an understanding between them bubbling beneath the surface. My thoughts immediately jumped to Verity, but she had made mention she was not in a healthy financial position. That immediately disqualified her as a bride for Waterley.

Surely the younger sister was undoubtedly in the same financial position.

Mother went to a drawer in the chest and filed through until she found the *Ackerman's Repository* she had come for. She held it to her side. "We will not keep you any longer, gentlemen. Lady Huxley, shall we retire to the drawing room?"

They had undoubtedly chosen the library for the light, which would be sorely lacking at this time of day on the other side of the house. I shot Belford a look, and he blustered, quickly putting his glass on the sofa's end table. "We were just leaving."

Mother smiled kindly. "Do not let us force you out."

"You are doing nothing of the sort," he promised.

"Indeed," Waterley added, "my sister and her party arrive today, and I should be home to greet her." He drank the rest of his glass and set it on the small table beside Belford's.

Blast the man! Did he have to speak of his sister so carelessly? I looked at my mother quickly but could not detect any anxiety written on her face, aside from a slight tightening of her lips.

Waterley glanced at me. "You'll shoot with us this week?"

Mother looked at me sharply. Of course she didn't want me to agree to spend any time in the company of Waterley's party. With his sister present, I would've liked nothing more than to avoid them anyway. He must've known, which accounted for the way he watched me so closely.

I chose to ignore his remark.

"Mother." I tipped my head to her and then Lady Huxley. "My lady."

My friends followed me into the entryway and outside through the front door. I led them toward the stables, eager to have them gone. My mistakes were my own, and I carried the blame entirely for the faults I had. But mothers could not be depended upon for the same logic. They wanted to see the best in their offspring, and I was convinced my mother was no different. Her habit of blaming my friends for my poor choices led to uncomfortable interludes. She would never be so ill-mannered as to make her opinions known to Waterley or Belford, but I knew them, and that was enough to desire distance between the men and my home whenever Mother happened to be in residence.

"How long are they here for?" Belford asked. He must have

sensed the same disquiet I did, though I wagered he did not know why.

"Another week or so."

"Then where will they go?"

"My mother will be off to Jane's house, I hope."

"And the others?" Waterley asked.

I was tempted to not answer him, but it was a silly impulse. "To Lamouth, I suppose."

A groom noticed us approaching and brought out the horses.

"They will return to *your* new house?" Waterley asked. "You realize you are in no way obligated to them."

Perhaps not, but neither was I a monster.

Belford took his horse's reins from the groom. "Are you still set on avoiding the place?"

"Avoiding is such a nasty word." I tilted my head side to side. "I rather think they are helping me to keep the dust away. I do not want the estate, so they are welcome to it for as long as they'd like."

Waterley seemed to absorb this. "I've heard the hunting is magnificent. Colin was forever going on about how unspoiled the flocks are. Wasted opportunity, I say." He mounted his horse beside Belford and brought it around to face me.

The same unspoiled flocks that kept Fanny happy. I couldn't help but smile at the recollection of that young girl leading dogs to the market to free them.

I set my attention on my friends again. "I wager I will see you both before long."

"You are welcome to join us whenever you'd like," Waterley said. "It will not be strange, you know." He gave me a particular look that I understood immediately. His sentiments were obvious, but I disagreed with them. It hardly mattered that so many years had passed since the scandal between his sister and me—I would never be comfortable in her presence again.

No one liked to be forcibly reminded of their failures.

"Gentlemen," I said with a bob of my head. I slapped Waterley's horse on the rear and they took off.

Once they were gone from sight, I turned toward the animal pens. Crossing under the small archway, I passed through the cow enclosures to the larger yard. Pigs and goats chomped away at composted food while chickens roamed at will.

Fanny was crouched beside a white-feathered bird, her hand full of something she sprinkled on the ground in front of it. She watched the hen peck, and her sister watched her from across the yard, seated on a crate. Verity's gaze was troubled, her brow wrinkled in thought.

I approached quietly, so I would not disrupt Fanny, and leaned against the rough wooden fence beside Verity's crate. She seemed to sense my presence and turned her face up toward me, removing the shadows her bonnet had supplied.

She squinted in the sunlight, her green eyes vibrant, her elegance captivating. "I did not know you had an appointment with the chickens as well."

I suppressed the humor I felt at her words, delivered with so little feeling. "I'm afraid I'm not as organized as that."

"Then what brings you here?"

You. The thought slipped into my mind so swiftly I had not actively considered it. But upon recollection, it was the truth. Be it curiosity or an innate protective instinct these women somehow ignited in me, it was indisputable that I was drawn to them.

She waited patiently for me to gather my thoughts, her face passive, all lines of worry now carefully hidden away.

I looked at Fanny, who had now amassed a small crowd of hens around her, and my unaccountable desire to understand these women grew. I leveled my gaze at Verity and spoke the truth. "Curiosity."

CHAPTER SIXTEEN

VERITY

F anny hummed to herself as she sketched the chickens she'd fed earlier in the day. While I typically spent her drawing time seeing to household necessities or attending to my correspondence, at Arden Castle there was no such need for either of those things. I sat at the table in the morning room that had been relegated for our use and watched Fanny's chickens take shape on the page.

Which was just as well, for I had a plan to formulate. It would take some thinking to devise a scheme that would allow us to leave Arden castle soon without offending our hosts whilst also contriving an agreement that allowed us to stay in Lamouth for the time being. We were at Daniel's mercy entirely, which was part of what made his curiosity about Fanny so dratted frightening.

Whatever had he meant by that? He wanted to understand her oddities? To see for himself her purpose in seeking out chickens? Was it her unbending schedule that piqued his interest? Or her ease with animals that did not extend to her interactions with other people?

Or was it my infernal need to protect her that made him want to understand why?

Blast it all. I dropped my forehead over my bent arms on the table and groaned.

"You are distressed," Fanny said, her intonation implying she was asking a question.

The last thing I needed was for her to think she was the cause of it. I sat up and pasted a smile on my face. "It is of little consequence."

The graphite pencil twitched in her hand, her gaze flicking between me and her paper. "Is Daniel upsetting you?"

A quiet scoff left my throat. "Yes. How did you know?"

"You are exceedingly different around him."

"Different? How?"

Fanny's attention returned to shading the chicken's feathers. "You watch him more than you watch me when he is near."

My cheeks flushed at the revelation, which was two parts worrying. How long had she noticed I kept an eye on her? And how obvious was my interest in *him*?

"Tomorrow marks one year since Colin died," I said, hoping to redirect the conversation. "Which means I only need to wear mourning for two more days. What color do you think I ought to wear first?"

"Green. It is most becoming on you. Mother says so."

"I suppose I will need to see what Mary packed before I can make any decisions." I chewed on my bottom lip. "Is it very obvious that I pay Daniel extra attention?"

"Yes."

Of course it was. If Fanny of all people noticed it, who else did? I could claim that my interest in him was a product of his new role as the owner of my home, but that was only part of the reason. In truth, Daniel was intriguing. He was undoubtedly the handsomest man I'd ever seen, and he was difficult to predict. It made me want to see him more, to speak to him more in order to make out his character. I knew he once had a horrible reputation as a rake, but thus far all I had seen was a little too much drinking and a looseness in his conversation.

Those things hardly made him a *rake*, though.

"Is it time to have tea with Mother?"

Fanny pulled out her watch and checked the time. "We have seven minutes."

I stood, crossing to the window. The lawn spread out until it reached the woods, trees old and enormous stretching far into the distance. The terrain was more rugged than I had expected, and we'd yet to see as many birds as I imagined Fanny would like, but it was peaceful here. I could understand why Daniel did not wish to leave Arden. The castle itself was ancient, the walls thick and made of stone, the passages warmed from ancient hung tapestries. The bedroom walls were plastered and less medieval in appearance, but still cozy.

It was a home with character, much like the man who owned it.

When Fanny was ready, we put away her drawing things and went to the drawing room to have tea with Mother and Lady Moorington. It was with great surprise that we found Daniel seated on the sofa as well, accepting a prepared cup of tea from his mother.

"I appreciate your sense of schedule, Lady Fanny," Lady Moorington said, preparing tea for her. "It provides a good deal of structure, and I have always enjoyed structure."

"Indeed. It is a wonder you have not devised a schedule of your own already," Daniel said, earning a reproachful look.

I hazarded a glance at my mother, who was just as displeased with this conversation as I expected of her. She cleared her throat, but her lips remained somewhat pinched. "You must travel a great deal if you visit your daughter often."

"It is a product of my children living so far from me," Lady Moorington said with a slight pout. "I am forever traveling from Surrey to Scotland, but my sweet grandson is worth the effort."

"Does Mrs. Lennox come to London for the Season?"

"No, but once her little Lachlan has grown, I hope to convince her to. Her husband Ewan is very indulgent. If she wanted to come, he would bring her."

"My son-in-law was much the same way," Mother said. She sipped her tea and avoided my eye. "He was forever doting upon Verity. It would be difficult to find a man more in love, I wager."

There was a pregnant beat of silence in which Lady Moorington nodded kindly and Daniel set his gaze heavily upon me.

"Is that so?" he said. "You must feel his loss keenly."

The correct response was there, waiting on my tongue. But I could not lie when Daniel watched me so closely, and the reply soon shriveled. My gaze drifted to my lap. I was strong of character, but this was not something I wanted to falsify.

"It is the anniversary of his death tomorrow," Mother explained. "Verity is overcome."

That was true, but not for the reason she described. Colin was a good husband in the beginning. He was thoughtful, attentive, did not forever nag me. But after he had taken matters with Fanny into his own hands, setting a string of events into motion with the intent of having her placed in an asylum, my feelings for him turned black.

I loathed Colin Palmer with every fiber of my being, but for the sake of my mother's pride, I would say nothing to malign him. Neither would I lie.

The door opened and Worthlin stood in the open space, waiting for the countess's attention.

"Yes?" she asked the butler.

"You've visitors, madam. The Misses Kelby and Miss Martin."

Lady Moorington looked to Mother, seemingly for approval. Mother had a motive with this tea—her conversation had proved as much—and I would not put it past her to say she did not wish for visitors while in mourning. Fustian, of course, but she could be manipulative when she so chose.

"Do not turn your friends away on our account," I hurried to say. "We are not so formal as that. As my mother just told you, I will be out of my widow's weeds in two days."

"If you are certain?" Lady Moorington asked, looking again to Mother for approval. She received a short nod, then told her butler to see the visitors in.

Daniel brought his cup up to his mouth, a smile threatening.

I quirked my eyebrow at him, hoping he understood I was asking what he found humorous in the situation, but he merely shook his head subtly at me.

When the door opened again, two aged ladies bustled through in the brightest gowns I'd ever laid eyes on. I did not realize fabric could be so bold and sharply contrasted as the silk adorning them. Garish pink and purple stripes adorned one of the women and yellow with orange embroidery decorated the other. When they stepped into the room, a young lady followed behind in a simple pink gown that in no way resembled her chaperones.

Introductions were made, and I came to learn that the pink and purple gown belonged to Miss Edith, the yellow to Miss Kelby, and the young woman was Miss Martin, their goddaughter. Well, she was the goddaughter to one of them, but they did not specify who claimed that privilege, and it seemed they carried the responsibility equally.

Miss Martin sat primly on the edge of a chair, brought to the circle of furniture distinctly for her by Daniel, and she smiled in gratitude up at him before dipping her head coyly and remaining quiet for the duration of the tea. I did not know why her behavior irked me so greatly, except that she seemed just the sort of young lady an earl like Daniel would like to take for his countess.

Next to her, I felt like a tall, unruly monster.

"Will you attend the assemblies next week?" Miss Edith asked, looking directly at Daniel.

He coughed, covering it quickly. "I would not do my guests the dishonor of attending the function while they are visiting."

"Whyever not? Surely they would be gratified to see our fine assembly hall," Miss Kelby said, sitting tall in her seat. "There is a great assortment of families in the area and plenty of gentlemen to dance with."

Perhaps their affinity for color made them blind to the black Mother and I wore. However, by next week, I could put it off if I wanted to. Since Colin did not deserve any prolonged grief, I had only ever planned to wear mourning colors for the customary year and one day, my duty fulfilled. I would have no cause to later regret offering him any disrespect.

"Lady Verity would be glad to attend such an event, I am sure," Mother said, having come to the same realization as I had, evidently. It was not lost on me that Fanny wasn't included in her offer, but I had to agree privately that a ball in a strange town did not seem like a good place to take my sister. There was far too much there to overwhelm her, and she did not dance.

Neither did I wish to attend alone.

I jerked my head toward her. "I am more than happy to remain here and support you, Mother."

Her gaze was like fire. Whatever her plan, it involved me spending time with Daniel, I wagered, and not allowing him to have romantic moments with other young ladies. I'd been correct in my earlier assumptions. Mother wanted me to marry the earl.

It was the perfect plan, except for one small problem: the earl did not wish to marry me.

I sought his gaze and found him watching me. "You do not need to worry about our feelings," I said. "We will take no great offense at your attendance. Your friends will be glad of your company."

"Indeed," Miss Edith said. "Your addition to the event will provide us with great joy. My goddaughter was only saying this morning she hopes you will be in attendance."

Miss Martin ducked her head, her cheeks blooming a delicate pink. Her lashes lifted enough to watch Daniel for a response to this proclamation, and he did not disappoint.

"If Lady Verity will agree to accompany my mother and me, then you can count on my attendance."

Wretch. He thought to put the responsibility on me?

"Oh, please, Lady Verity," Miss Kelby said, blinking her large eyes at me. "You will not keep Lord Huxley all to yourself."

Daniel cleared his throat. "No one has that pleasure, Miss Kelby."

Fanny fidgeted beside me on the sofa. I looked to the clock on the mantel. Goodness, was that the time? It was nearly time for reading, and my sister could tell, if her behavior was any indicator. The guests did not appear to be in any way close to leaving.

"Oh, do us the honor of your acceptance, Lady Verity," Miss Martin said, her voice soft-spoken and delicate, much like the rest of her. Such pretty manners were befitting such a lovely creature, but only made me like her less.

Fanny fidgeted again and leaned in. "It is time—"

"Yes, I know," I said quietly. "Just one minute more." I turned my attention to Miss Martin, hoping the conversation would move to another topic. "I would love to go to your assemblies."

Fanny started making small humming sounds in her throat. Drat. It was beginning. I searched for an excuse, anything to give us leave to depart the tea early without offending Lady Moorington's guests. When I raised my eyes, I met Daniel's across the way. A small line formed a shadow between his eyebrows.

"Miss Martin," he said, turning to her. "Would you care to take a turn about the garden with me?"

My stomach lurched in equal parts jealousy and gratitude. The young woman looked to her godmothers in surprise, then back to the earl. "I would like that above all things, my lord."

Daniel flinched slightly, but his smile did not lessen. He stood, offering his arm. "Would anyone else like to join us? It is a lovely day outside. Lady Verity? Lady Frances?"

"Outside?" Fanny asked, her brow wrinkling. She shook her head. "I would prefer to read."

There was gentle, uncomfortable laughter around the room. I took my sister's hand and pulled her up. "I will keep you company, Fanny." She stood, Miss Martin beside her. They were very similar in appearance—both claiming light brown hair, soft features, and of a similar age and build—but they could not be more different.

Daniel led Miss Martin away, and I sent him a look of gratitude. His interference had given us reason to leave as well. I could have hugged the man, I was so glad.

Now I had to find a way to skip the assemblies without causing great offense, for there was no way I would leave my sister to go dance with strangers.

CHAPTER SEVENTEEN

DANIEL

Over the course of the last few days I'd had the Palmer women as guests in my home, it had grown apparent that the two daughters lived by the clock. Fanny checked her pocket watch more times than any dandy of my acquaintance ever had. She had her days meticulously planned, and she would not budge for anything.

Which was how I knew, when I sent a note to ask Verity to meet with me, her sister would be otherwise engaged drawing in the morning room and Verity would be free. It had not been in manipulation that I sent the note to Verity. It had been . . . strategic. If I did not speak to her alone, I doubted she would tell me the truth. Her need to protect her sister ran extremely deep.

I spun the quill in my fingers and leaned back in the over-large leather chair while waiting for Verity to reply to my polite summons. Father's desk had always felt oddly gargantuan, uncomfortable. It was not my match, but rather more like I was a child playing at being an adult and the furniture knew it. Looking around Father's study, I still did not feel as though I'd earned the right to use it for my purposes, but when there was estate business to see to, it made sense to conduct it where the ledgers and books were kept.

The door creaked open and I jerked slightly. I always felt the ghost of my father most keenly in this room. To say I was jumpy would be an understatement.

Verity hovered in the open doorway, and I gestured her inside.

"You sent for me?" she said. She wore black, but I looked forward to when she would be rid of the stark, blunt color. Yesterday at tea her mother had mentioned that today was the anniversary of Verity's late husband's death. That meant only tomorrow remained before she could put off the mourning color. I was wildly looking forward to it.

"You mentioned that Fanny enjoys going to your local village on Wednesdays. I wondered if she would have any interest in seeing ours today?"

"Oh." Her eyes widened in surprise, and she stepped further into the room. "She does not . . . That is . . ." Verity cleared her throat.

What was she not telling me? I set the quill on my desk and rose, crossing to the door she'd left open. I closed it slowly, lifting my eyebrows. "May we speak plainly?"

Verity watched me with trepidation, looking from the closed door to me again. "Certainly."

I stood near the door while she remained in the center of the room. Making her uncomfortable was the last thing I wanted. I hoped I'd proved myself in my bedroom the other night—reputation aside, I would not act dastardly toward her.

I'd learned that lesson the hard way long ago. Ladies of quality were not to be trifled with.

"It is true I walk with Fanny to our village every Wednesday, but only so we might visit with the vicar's wife. She keeps a parrot, which pleases Fanny, and has been a great friend to us."

"Ah, I see. I had thought the shops or the market might be the lure."

Verity cringed. "Fanny has not done well in overwhelming environments, historically."

"I have noticed as much."

Her green eyes flicked up to me, and something flashed in them. Was it fear? The last thing I wanted to do was stir fear in her, but I couldn't help pushing the topic a little. I wanted to understand what they were hiding.

I stepped a little closer. "You can trust me."

"Can I?" Verity did not speak with flirtation; she spoke with hesitance.

Another step closer. I felt like a predator, slowly stalking my prey. "I did not take advantage of you when given the opportunity. Neither has my character been anything but above reproach since you entered my house. I think it is fair to claim you can trust me."

"I am not worried about *that*." She shook her head slightly. "My state as a widow affords me some leniency with gentlemen. It is my sister I must protect."

"I know," I said quietly. "What I'd like to understand is why. Fanny is not a danger to herself or others, I presume? Her fit of nerves during dinner a few nights ago did not lead to any startling reports of that nature."

Verity seemed to freeze, her lips pressed together, her eyes tracking my approach. We now stood on opposite ends of the carpet. "She is no danger to anyone or anything, save her own reputation."

Ah, so it was a matter of pride. Was that why the mother did not bother to insert herself in the girl's affairs? Or much at all, save for the occasional tea? Were it not for the sisters' nearness in age, one would assume Fanny was Verity's daughter, claimed by her mother to protect her reputation or some such thing. But that was impossible and quickly dismissed.

"She has not suffered in my esteem," I said. "I understand her need for a schedule and her love of animals."

Verity's mouth broke into a soft smile. "You have been very kind to her, Daniel. I worried about how she would feel in a strange house, but aside from the odd incident, it has been mostly without crisis. It has led me to wonder if moving her to a new house would not be as difficult a trial as I'd imagined."

"Hmm." I made a noncommittal sound, hoping she'd continue. Was this why she'd wanted to marry me? To secure Lamouth for her sister's benefit? That made far more sense than my original assumptions. In the days Verity had been in my home, she had made it abundantly clear that nothing she did was with herself in mind. Coming to my room in a foolish attempt to seduce me had been foreign to her, which was clear from the outset. But discovering why she put herself in such a position has been vastly interesting.

I found myself wondering if my answer would be the same, were she to ask me again.

Father's image seemed to watch me from where it sat on the wall, reminding me of my worth. Yes, my answer would be the same now. I could never force myself on someone so good and wholesome as Verity.

"Can we speak on a matter of business?" she asked.

"Of course." I waved my hand toward the two chairs set before the hearth, inviting her to be seated, then took the chair opposite.

"There is a dower house at Lamouth," she said. "I visited it before we came here and was surprised to find it in poor repair. It wasn't like my father to let anything go in such a manner, but it appears to have been heavily neglected."

"He could have believed there would not be any use for it, perhaps, and checked on the property infrequently."

She gave me a wry smile. "That was my conclusion as well. My marriage had ensured we would have a home at Lamouth for the rest of our lives, as you well know. Mother had no need for the dower house then."

"Nor do you have a need for it now." I spoke with firm resolution. "I meant it, Verity. Lamouth is yours to do with what you will."

"And you'll hire me to oversee its needs?"

I sat up, surprised a little by the serious nature of her gaze. She meant it. She had taken me at my word and wanted to conduct a business deal. I'd expected to have to further convince her of it. "I will, if you'd like."

"Here is what I propose," she said, leaning forward. She'd given this much thought. "My sister and I would be perfectly content in the dower house, but the repairs will take some time and are bound to be expensive. I'm sorry to report a branch has fallen through the roof and there has been damage to the floors from rainfall."

Broken roof? Damaged floors? That went well beyond disrepair. "Gads, Verity. You cannot mean to live in such squalor."

She smiled. "I do not. I mean to live in it once it has been repaired."

"Yes, but . . ." I ran a hand through my hair. "You needn't live in it at all. I have told you—you can have Lamouth."

Verity sat back in her chair a little, her gaze finding the floor, concentration furrowing her brow. "I do not know how to impress upon you the importance of a permanent solution."

I'd been lounging in my seat, but her expression made me sit up a little. "Try."

She seemed to gather her thoughts. "I have already gone through the traumatic experience of losing my home, my father, and my security all at once. If I allowed myself to believe we were safe, our home secure, our future stable, and something were to happen to take that away again . . . well, I cannot allow it. I do not want to risk it. I will forever be wondering if you are in good health, if you are falling in love, if your mind has changed."

"In other words, you would think about me incessantly for the rest of your life, and that is too great a burden to bear?"

Verity shook her head, but a light of amusement had entered her shadowed eyes, and I rejoiced in it.

"I understand," I said softly. It was why she wanted to marry me. If she could produce an heir to the earldom, she would be truly secure.

As a man who sought chaos to drown the dark voices in my head, I keenly felt the need for stability and peace. As much as I desired it, though, I could not bring myself to seek it so valiantly. She impressed me.

If I had a sister such as Fanny, would I feel the same need to selflessly protect her? I *did* have a sister, but she was secure in her own right. Happily married, confident, capable. Fanny was neither married nor confident—though I imagined she was capable if the need arose.

"I need time to think." If I had time to meet with my steward or a lawyer, perhaps I could come up with a way to give her Lamouth. "We will find a solution that pleases both parties, Verity. In the meantime, I will write to the bailiff at Lamouth and direct him to begin repairs on the dower house. I think I have his direction here somewhere."

"If not, I can supply it for you."

"Thank you. You have been a great help."

"Me?" She laughed, and the sound was musical. She shook her head, as if disbelieving. "It is you who must be heartily thanked. You are the man giving us a home and an income—a place where my sister will be safe."

"Safe?" She'd caught me off guard, but I found no hint of humor in her countenance. "Gads, what sort of danger has she been in?"

Verity rose, clasping her hands in front of her waist. "Oh, nothing. Forget I mentioned it."

"You cannot say that and not explain. Are you in danger?"

"Me? No. Of course not."

"Then you must mean that Fanny is." She did not dispute that. "What sort of danger?"

"Please, Daniel," she pleaded, moving toward the door. "Forget I said anything."

"If you trust me, Verity, I can help." She certainly would not be traveling away from my home again until I ascertained what this danger consisted of.

Anxiety flashed across her face, sending a shiver through me. This was not a minor foreboding. She very much believed something threatened her sister's safety. She moved to the door again, and I grabbed her wrist, pulling her back toward me. "What is it?"

"Daniel, please—"

"I will not hurt you." I released her, the plea in her tone reminding me of the incident from years ago, that same pleading from Miss Waterley to marry her and save her reputation. I hadn't thought a boyish mistake should mean a lifetime of marriage to someone I didn't love. I had been young, irresponsible, and foolish then. I shook my head, removing the memory. This was not the moment for ghosts. "You've frightened me."

Verity shook her head. "There is no cause for alarm, I assure you. There are just . . . people . . . who believe Fanny is better suited to an asylum, and it is my aim to keep her out of one."

I was struck, my body going slack with confusion. Had I not wondered the same thing upon meeting Fanny? Had not Dean made a similar comment? Further acquaintance with the girl—however short—led me to realize that while she was different, she was far from dangerous. Why did her differences mean she deserved to be locked away? The fact was, they didn't.

"That must give you an added measure of apprehension for your future."

"Indeed," Verity said, the word rushing from her tongue on a sigh. "It is hard enough to keep to Fanny's schedule while we are away from home, but every time she embarrasses our hosts or grows anxious and has a fit of nerves, I fear she'll become inconsolable, that my mother will contact the asylum again, that—"

"Wait." I shook my head. "Again?"

Her *mother*?

Verity gave me an uneasy smile. "I am sorry, Daniel. This is not your burden. I should be returning to Fanny anyway."

She moved toward the door. I wanted to stop her again, but I'd done so too many times already. "If we cannot walk into the village, can I tempt you with another activity?"

Verity hesitated in the doorway. "It is not easy to convince Fanny to deviate from her schedule."

"She won't need to. You take a walk every morning, yes? I will commandeer you on the lawn tomorrow."

A small, genuine smile curved over her lips, though she still seemed uncertain. "You may try, but Fanny is not easily persuaded to stray from her original plan."

"I'd like to try."

Verity nodded slightly. "Tomorrow, then."

I went back to my desk and sat at the chair behind it, pulling out a sheet of paper to begin my letter to Lamouth's bailiff. For some reason, the desk did not feel quite as large as it had earlier.

CHAPTER EIGHTEEN

VERITY

Mary stood at the dressing table behind Fanny, pulling her hair into the loose knot she was most comfortable in. I stood behind them, pacing back and forth. I'd gone over the conversation with Daniel in my mind since it took place yesterday and come to the same conclusion each time: he had a kind heart and only wanted to help. Making Fanny vulnerable and revealing my fears about her being dragged to an asylum had *not* been a mistake.

I would repeat the words to myself over and over again until I believed them. I ought to believe them, for Daniel had given me no cause to think otherwise. But I'd once thought the same of Colin, and he'd proved me wrong.

Fanny stood, finished readying for the day. I led her outside, having already breakfasted in our room, toward the location we'd last seen the starling. We checked every morning for it in the tall tree on the edge of Arden's property but had yet to find it again.

Daniel waited for us in the garden, hiding a large silk contraption behind him. "Good morning, ladies." He dipped in a bow, which Fanny and I returned.

"We are off to look for the starling," I explained as we reached him on the path.

Daniel lifted the contraption, and I realized immediately what it was. "Would you care to help me fly my kite first?"

Fanny looked up at the earl for the first time. "It is a bird."

"Indeed." Daniel held it up, turning it this way and that so the light from the sun would reveal the shine of the silk. "My father gave it to me when I was a child, and it has taken many flights over the years."

It really was a beautiful kite. "It must look marvelous once you have it in the air," I observed.

"Like a real bird, I think." He turned his attention to Fanny. "But I will let you be the judge of that."

"Would you like to join Daniel?" I asked her. "We can look for the starling afterwards."

Fanny consulted her watch and nodded. "Yes. I should like to see the kite fly."

"You will tell us what to do?" I asked.

Daniel's dark eyebrows lifted. "Have you never flown a kite before?"

"Never."

His smile widened. "You are in for a treat."

Daniel directed us to the long lawn so we would have plenty of room. Wind whipped around us, pulling at my bonnet. Once we were in the right location, Daniel gave Fanny the string, and I stood beside her. "Now I will run and hold the kite up. When I release it, you will be responsible for helping it fly. Keep a firm hold on the string, and you will know what to do."

She looked at me uneasily.

"I will be beside you the entire time," I said. "But you won't need my help. You can do this."

Fanny's attention shifted to the string in her hands that was wound on a spool.

Daniel shrugged out of his coat and laid it over a stone

bench at the edge of the garden. He walked toward us again, rolling up his shirtsleeves to just below his elbow, revealing strong forearms, the muscle bunching as he worked. How arduous did he imagine this kite-flying was going to be? All he had to do was run and launch it into the air, I believed.

He took it in his hands, gave us a little grin, and took off. The string pulled taut and ripped out of Fanny's hands, launching the spool onto the grass between them.

Daniel's steps slowed when he looked behind him to find what had gone wrong.

Fanny shook her hands out. "It did not turn."

"That is my fault," Daniel said, jogging back toward us. "I should have explained better. You must hold it loosely enough for the string to unravel as I run further away." His chest heaved a little from running to and fro, and I averted my gaze.

"Hold it loosely," Fanny repeated to herself.

"Yes. Shall we try again?"

She picked up the spool and held it loosely in her hands, waiting for him to try again.

He must have sensed that no verbal confirmation was coming and put himself into position. "Ready?"

"Yes."

Daniel took off. The spool spun in Fanny's loose grip until Daniel was a good length away from us, then it flew from her hands once more, dragging on the grass behind Daniel as he ran. He must have sensed it, for he looked back and turned to jog toward us again.

"I held it loosely," Fanny said.

"Yes, too loose. You must still keep something of a grip on it."

She looked at her hands, troubled.

"Shall we try again?"

"You may," Fanny said, gesturing to Daniel and then me.

"I think you ought to try one more time," I said.

"Agreed," Daniel said, picking up the spool of string and rewinding it again before reaching it toward Fanny.

She accepted it, albeit reluctantly, and turned it about in her hands.

Daniel took off again.

I tucked a loose lock of hair behind my ear, watching him run and Fanny focus on the spool of string in her hands. She turned it as he went, holding it but allowing it to unravel still. When Daniel was a good distance away he launched the kite into the air. Fanny pulled back on the string and the kite soared above our heads, diving on the wind and righting itself.

"You are doing it!" I shouted.

A smile curved over Fanny's mouth, but her concentration did not break from the silk bird floating overhead.

My grin was so wide I felt it would split my face in two. I looked at Daniel and found him watching Fanny, his joy radiating as purely as mine. He turned his smile on me and raised one fist in the air in triumph.

I clapped my hands together. "You've done it!"

"I have," Fanny agreed. Her concentration remained in the sky and her smile very much in place. "We have," she corrected. "Together."

Daniel approached us, and we shared a smile. My stomach warmed, my heart increasing in speed the longer he looked at me. Hope planted itself deep in my chest, burying in my heart and threatening to sprout and grow. Could Daniel be different? His patience with Fanny, his genuine happiness, his lack of judgment—he was kindness itself.

I found I liked him very much.

Daniel

Once the kite lost its lift and plummeted to the ground, we rewound the string and made it fly again. Fanny seemed perfectly willing to continue the exercise for the remainder of the day, and after witnessing the pure joy on both sisters' faces, I could very much do the same. My heart beat a rapid tattoo, and I didn't think it was just from all the running back and forth I was doing to launch the kite into the air.

"Oh, the time," Fanny said, dropping the kite to check her pocket watch. The silk bird dove and spun until it landed hard on the grass away from us.

Verity clasped her hands in front of her lightly and spoke in a soothing tone. "We can change the schedule for the day if you'd like to fly the kite longer." She looked to me for approval.

"I have nothing on my schedule, so I am available as long as you'd like."

Fanny shook her head. "We must look for the starling."

I picked up the spool of string and started winding it, stepping forward slowly until I reached the kite. "What starling is this?"

Fanny pointed toward the copse of trees. "She has built a nest in a tree near the stone wall, but we have not seen her return to it since the first day."

"The day Mr. Waterley came upon us," Verity explained.

I recalled them watching a bird then.

"We need to go now," Fanny said, starting toward the trees.

Verity shot me an apologetic look. "You are welcome to join us."

An opportunity to further spend time with these women was a treat I didn't want to deny myself. I couldn't explain why I felt drawn to them—to Verity's beauty and strength, to Fanny's sweet innocence. My feelings toward them were as contrasting as the sun and the moon, but they were no less strong for their differences. "I would love to come."

I jogged to the stone bench at the edge of the garden and set down the kite, laying my coat over the top to keep it anchored there.

I caught up to the women quickly. Fanny set a fast pace, and Verity kept up. We picked our way through the trees and came out the other side. The long field that butted my property was not empty, and I stifled a curse. The very last thing I wanted to do right now was introduce Miss Waterley to my guests. Could I direct their attention further into the trees until my neighbors had passed?

Waterley lifted his arm in recognition. Well, blast. They'd noticed us. It appeared I had no choice but to subject Verity to the acquaintance of my initial downfall.

"Palmer!" Belford called when they were still a fair distance away. "Well met, my friend."

I remained beside the women. Fanny paid no mind to the group moving toward us, instead continuing to search the trees for the starling or its nest. I did not know which.

Miss Waterley walked toward us, her arm linked through Miss Malton's. She was just as lovely as I recalled, her blonde hair so fair it was nearly white, rolled into curls that bounced near her sparkling blue eyes. She looked away demurely, but the way her gaze kept seeking mine left no mystery as to her intent —she would not give me the cut direct. Miss Malton looked very much the same as before as well: pretty, brunette, and sporting a pout while she picked her way through the field in what I could only imagine were inadequate shoes.

"Shall I introduce Waterley's party?" I asked quietly. Aside from Waterley and Belford, whom she had already met, it was only Miss Waterley, Miss Malton, and one of the Egerton twins —they were identical, and I never could tell whom I was speaking to.

Verity nodded. "If you'd like to."

If that was the criteria, I absolutely would not. But social constraints rested upon me, and I had no other choice but to make the victim in my largest, fullest mistake known to Verity.

We approached the long, drystone wall and waited for the rest of Waterley's group to meet us there.

Waterley's smug smile screamed of an ulterior motive, but I didn't want to assign such a trait to my friend. Whatever could he possibly find victorious about bringing his sister to see me?

"It is a windy morning for a walk," I said when they finally reached us.

Miss Waterley's gaze was direct. "We were coming to see you, my lord."

I bowed, if for no other reason than to avert my eyes from her gentle countenance. She had long ago been seared in my mind, her image flashing at the most inopportune moments. Seeing her again in the flesh after so much time had passed was as painful as I'd imagined it would be. I could not look at her without being reminded resolutely of my failure.

When we were caught in a compromising situation, she'd asked me to honor her with my name. I'd refused, under the false impression we would be able to hide our misdeeds from the world. I had not thought it was worth marrying the girl over a handful of stolen kisses.

We were fortunate to have been found when we were, or there could have been far more at stake.

After that, my liaisons with women never crossed the boundaries into ladies of quality. In the last year, however, I had not so much as kissed any woman.

My gaze sought the ground while I fought a flood of memories I didn't want to face.

Verity's hand found mine and brushed it softly, the back of her fingers over my knuckles. The stone wall hid her compassionate gesture, and it pulled me from my carriage ride down memory lane.

I straightened, turning my attention to Verity. I sought

strength in her green gaze, and she gave it willingly. To think that this woman had come to me only a few days ago and offered herself as my wife. I could have agreed to the scheme then, taken her to the church, and claimed her as my partner, and I wouldn't have realized the gemstone I would be acquiring in marriage. She was selfless in the truest sense of the word.

But I was glad I had refused her. I'd learned my lesson when I foolishly played with Miss Waterley's heart, and I would never do that again. Verity deserved better than me, anyway. Even if she only had a mind for Fanny now, that would surely not always be the case. Someday she would fall in love, and she would be glad she hadn't shackled herself to such an undeserving fool.

I pushed away the melancholy and focused my attention on my guests. "Lady Verity, Lady Frances, allow me to present Miss Waterley, Miss Malton, and Mr. Egerton."

The women all curtsied and exchanged pleasantries, and Egerton bowed.

I had to find a way to divert the group before they could finagle an invitation to the house. Mother would have a difficult time seeing Miss Waterley, and I wanted to prevent that.

"Shall we walk together?" I asked. "I've yet to show my guests the walled garden."

Miss Waterley glanced at Miss Malton before turning her attention on me again. "It has been an age since I've seen the garden. It would be a joy to show it to your friends."

Thunder and turf. I'd forgotten the moments we shared in those walls. We had been meeting in secret long before we were found together, and that garden had been one of our destinations. She was bound to think I'd meant something by the offering to walk there. Miss Waterley's sense of ownership was unmistakable. I ignored it, turning my attention back on Verity. Her concerned eyes were watching her sister, though. Blast. I hadn't considered Fanny's schedule.

"The bird is not here," Fanny said.

"We will look again tomorrow," Verity promised. "Shall we look at the walled garden with the rest of the party? We can—"

"Do you think she moved her nest?" Fanny asked.

It seemed to take a moment for Verity to decide what to say.

"How far is the stile?" Miss Malton asked.

"It is only just around the bend," Miss Waterley said with authority. "Here, I will show you."

"We shall be around shortly," Belford said.

Egerton hurried forward and offered Miss Waterley his arm. She took it, pulling him along, but not before turning back over her shoulder to look at me briefly. I tore my gaze away first. I would give her no reason to interact with me more than she needed to.

"I haven't any idea, Fanny," Verity was saying now, her voice soft and placating. "We can look again later. I have never seen a bird move a nest, but you would know more about it than I would."

"She could build a new nest elsewhere," Fanny explained, growing agitated. "Unless one of Daniel's friends killed her."

I was startled into responding. "Gads, Fanny. Whatever do you mean?"

She looked back to the tree where the starling last was seen. "Your friends are here to hunt." She spoke so matter-of-factly it took me by surprise. She'd been paying attention to my friends?

I could lie to her, but she was far too smart for that.

I cleared my throat. "Well, yes, but they will not hunt starlings. Your bird is safe."

"She would not be considered decent target practice?"

"No." Even Waterley would not do something so dreadful . . . I believed. "Your starling is safe from their guns."

Fanny flinched. I thought of the story Verity had shared, when Fanny had given the hunting dogs away. Her care for all animals ran deeply.

"Daniel's friends are expecting us to walk in the garden with them now," Verity said. "We would not want to embarrass Daniel by being rude or ignoring his friends, would we?"

"No." Her brow furrowed. "I like Daniel."

My chest swelled with inordinate warmth. I never thought gaining the approval of a seventeen-year-old girl would give me cause to feel such triumph.

"I do too," Verity said, avoiding my gaze. "Daniel has been a kind friend to us both. We will walk in the garden before we see the chickens, because we are the mistresses of our time. Our schedule will be different today so we are not rude to his friends."

Fanny seemed to struggle with this pronouncement.

"I am very grateful, Fanny," I said, hoping to help ease her discomfort. Truthfully, I did not care if they begged leave to see Fanny's hens, but Verity was more adept at managing her sister and I gave her space to do so as she saw fit. "We can send for Oscar to walk with us, too, if you'd like."

She shook her head. "He is a danger to the hens. We will walk in the garden without him, so he is not tempted to follow us to the chickens."

I suppressed a chuckle. Oscar roamed the house and grounds at will and had never before threatened the hens, but I understood her hesitation. "Yes, my lady."

Fanny looked at me with her brow wrinkled in confusion. "You do not call me that. Mary calls me that."

"And the servants here, I hope."

Fanny shook her head. "Only Mary calls me that."

I wanted to ask why she had not received the deference she deserved from my servants, but a quelling look from Verity silenced me.

"Shall we?" I asked, offering Verity my arm.

She looked at it with hesitation, and I recalled my rolled-up sleeves and missing coat. Label me careless, but I didn't worry overmuch for my exposed arm. It was the least of our concerns at present. I just wanted to escort the lady somewhere. "My arm functions the same whether or not a sleeve adorns it."

"You shouldn't say such things. You do not know who is lurking nearby or what assumptions they might make."

"Doesn't your status as a widow keep us safe from the assumptions of lurking ears?"

"Widows can still fall prey to gossip, Daniel."

"I know. I shouldn't be so careless." I pulled my arm away. "Forgive my thoughtlessness."

Verity slid her hand over my forearm and tugged me forward. "Oh, never mind all that. Let us find your friends before they are forced to come find us."

I pulled my arm close to my side so Verity would follow suit, and was not disappointed. She drew up next to me, allowing me to escort her to the clearing where the rest of the group would soon be waiting. Fanny followed us, humming to herself, but I couldn't be bothered to pay attention to the tune. My mind was riveted by the feeling of this woman's hand on my arm, her fingers pressing into my skin, and how I had never felt anything quite as captivating before.

CHAPTER NINETEEN

VERITY

Miss Waterley had one motivation for seeking Daniel out this morning: to finagle some sort of invitation from him. I had never met the woman before in my life, but the fact was indisputable. During our time here thus far, I had yet to hear any mention of the lavish parties held at Arden Castle in the past, but evidently, they were all Miss Waterley could think of presently. Each new corner we turned or moss-covered statue we found had another memory attached to it that Miss Waterley felt compelled to share with us, and somehow they all ended with mentions of a dinner, ball, or card party she'd attended at Arden Castle in the years before.

It was equally clear upon watching Daniel that while Miss Waterley's stories became more animated, he only withdrew further. If I had not mistaken things between them, I would assume there was an old, heavy history woven through their families—or perhaps just between these two.

A disagreeable thought, that. I wasn't naïve enough to believe Daniel didn't have a past. We'd been comfortably tucked away in his house since arriving at Arden and nothing had been introduced to us yet in this regard.

"Is the fountain in good order, my lord?" Miss Waterley asked.

Daniel faced away from the group, his hands clasped lightly behind his back. By the way his attention drifted along the plants and lazily took in the garden, it was evident he hadn't heard her—or wanted it to appear that way.

Maybe he was making a point that he would not respond when he was called by the title he loathed. He'd asked her once already to refrain, but she didn't heed him.

"Lord Huxley?" she asked.

He turned slowly to face her, his expression blank.

She smiled, her face transforming from one of gentle confusion to a rare beauty. She was classical in all possible ways, her blonde hair angelic, her features small and evenly balanced. As jealous as I felt, I could not find myself surprised that a liaison had once existed between them. "Is the fountain in good order?" she repeated.

He did not say anything for a moment. "I wouldn't know. I never come out here."

"Ever?" She gave a little laugh. "I remember visiting this magical place quite frequently."

"That was a long time ago, and much has changed since then, has it not? It would be safe to say the garden and I are veritable strangers now. As distanced as I am from this place, it is inevitable."

She seemed to take this personally, her smile slipping. "Strangers? Hardly." She turned toward her brother. "Will you allow that to go unchallenged? To call us strangers when our families have been so close all these years."

Mr. Waterley looked uncertain, which only fueled my belief that there was some lurid history between the families. "I believe Palmer was speaking of the garden."

Fanny left the shrubbery she was analyzing—I was certain she found a spider web of interest or some such thing—and came to stand directly beside me. "Can we leave the garden now?"

"That is not polite, Fanny," I whispered, quietly enough to not be overheard. "We will leave when Daniel's guests leave."

"When will Daniel's guests leave?" she asked, not bothering to modulate her volume.

Everyone grew silent. Miss Malton shared a shocked look with Miss Waterley, one that made me want to fill an ewer with water from the mossy fountain and splash it in their faces. I drew in a deep breath through my nose and pushed that ill-conceived notion away. "Patience, Fanny."

She pulled out her watch and looked at it again before snapping it closed. "But I would like to see the hens now. We always visit the hens now."

"We've changed our schedule today, remember? So as not to be rude to our host. We are the mistresses of our time."

Fanny's voice escalated, and I feared her behavior would soon follow suit. I walked a fine balance between pushing Fanny to do things that were uncomfortable for the sake of helping her grow, and doing what I could to avoid a fit so her reputation would remain intact. Most of the time my priorities lay in avoiding dramatics, for one awful fit was all our mother needed as motivation to contact the asylum again.

I looked briefly to the sky in search of the perfect thing to say to abate her agitation. Her hands began to flap before her slightly, a humming emanating from her throat. I whipped my head toward her, vastly aware every set of eyes was fastened on Fanny.

"I want to leave," she said, her hands flapping more.

"We never meant to interrupt your afternoon," Mr. Waterley said, watching Fanny with disturbed interest. "Please do not remain on our account."

Fanny looked back at me, her humming ceasing but her hands continuing to flutter. Her chest heaved as though she'd run a great distance. "He has given us permission. Is it no longer rude to leave?"

My cheeks warmed, and I hoped they imitated faint rouge, hiding my embarrassment. I hated anyone thinking my sister was rude when she was only factual, and everyone was staring at her as though she was . . . mad. My entire body clenched in discomfort.

Miss Waterley turned away, dismissing us. Her nose wrinkled and mouth turned down, eyes widening toward her friend as if she sought confirmation that Fanny was feral. She stopped before a statue of a woman, the stone head bent in anguish, then leaned toward Miss Malton and spoke, not bothering to lower her voice. "She reminds me of that creature Uncle had to fetch for the asylum last year. Brother, do you feel the same?" Miss Waterley shuddered. "She wore that dreadful cloak."

My body froze, much like the statue Miss Waterley stood beside. Asylum? It was the most dreadful word, evoking the highest feelings of loathing within me. Fanny tugged impatiently at my sleeve, but I could not move, my feet stuck in the marshy grass.

Mr. Waterley tilted his head to the side. "I suppose so. The statue is much quieter, though."

His sister laughed, and my stomach clenched uncomfortably. "You know I am not referring to the statue, brother," she whispered in a voice far too loud to truly be called such.

"Did I tell you, Palmer?" Mr. Waterley said. "My uncle is thinking of expanding the building. I thought to ask your advice."

Daniel looked uncomfortable. Fanny was nearly to the stone arched entrance of the garden, but I felt rooted in place.

"I can't see what value my opinion would hold on the matter."

Egerton laughed. "Palmer has no experience with madness, does he?"

"No," Daniel said firmly. Was he avoiding my eye, or was I searching for guilt where none lay?

The women looked past me to my sister, driving my disquiet deeper.

"Not advice in that way," Mr. Waterley said. "I cannot conceive if the cost of the additions will be worth the effort. It is not as though the increase of patients constitutes such a large expenditure, but my uncle is persistent in his wants."

Was Mr. Waterley's uncle the owner of an asylum, or was Mr. Waterley the owner? It sounded as though this was the man who needed to give permission for the expenses, and they must have been close if both Waterley siblings were witness to the uncle collecting a patient. I hadn't realized we were near such a location. Fanny was already out of sight, so my feet itched to follow her, but I could not move yet. Fragments of past conversations filtered into my mind. "What was the name of your uncle?"

The entire party looked at me with some surprise. I had not added much to the conversation yet, and I'd already been dismissed, my sister out of sight completely.

"Dr. Walter Waterley."

The name was familiar. It tripped the memories of those conversational fragments again, and I shook the fear that crept over my bones.

"What do you say, Palmer?" Mr. Waterley asked, heedless of my distress.

Daniel's gaze flicked to me and back to his friend. "It sounds to me as though you already have your answer." His dark eyes were further shadowed, lending his countenance discomfort and secrecy. I wanted to believe Daniel hadn't kept this information from me intentionally, but his ill ease put that into question.

He had allowed Fanny and me to spend the morning with a

man whose uncle ran an asylum, whose name sounded frighteningly familiar, and Daniel didn't think to warn me?

I dipped a general curtsy to the group before turning on my heel and following my sister out of the walled garden. My steps were quick and sure, my mind made up. I was going to deposit Fanny somewhere that would occupy her and seek my mother out. I wanted to know why the name Waterley sounded familiar. I had a sneaking suspicion but hoped she would disabuse me of the notion immediately.

If it was for the reason I feared, then Fanny and I were leaving Arden Castle at once.

There was a general bustle of noise and commotion in the walled garden behind me, but I blocked the sound. I didn't care to hear the jokes made by their party or how Miss Waterley was next choosing to assert her history with the family. If she managed to install herself as the next countess at Lamouth, I would not be able to contain my irritation.

I caught up to Fanny as she rounded the great castle walls. "I need to speak to Mother," I said. "Can we put off the chickens for another time? You can draw—"

"I want to see the hens. You need not come if you do not care to visit them today."

"It does not feel safe to separate."

She lifted her gaze to me briefly. "We have gone there every day."

It was true. She knew the way—even now she was leading me to the chickens, not the other way around. The men who worked with the animals didn't bother Fanny. One of them, Mr. Smith, had taken a liking to her and pointed out different interesting facts when he had the time. If anything, Fanny was safer in the pens than she was in the house with a mother who was potentially conspiring to place her in a madhouse.

Especially if mother had dragged us here for the reason I was beginning to suspect.

Another shiver shot through my body. It would probably be better if I spoke to Mother while Fanny was outside, so she would not accidentally overhear.

"Will you come inside when you're finished visiting the hens? We can meet in the sitting room to draw."

Fanny didn't bother to speak, but dipped her head before continuing on her path toward the animals. I watched her walk for a few moments before I shook off my anxiousness as best I could and turned toward the house. The group was leaving the walled garden, and I noticed Daniel saying goodbye to them as they walked toward their property. He hadn't noticed me that I could tell, so I quickened my steps to reach the house before he could.

I closed the door and peeked in the drawing room, but it was empty. I mounted the stairs toward my mother's chamber, but no answer came when I knocked. Where was she?

Perhaps the sitting room. I opened the door, finding Mother with her embroidery on the sofa in the center of the room.

She looked up when I closed the door.

"Where is Lady Moorington?" I asked.

"Discussing something with the housekeeper."

"Is she to return soon?"

"Not that I am aware of."

My nerves would not settle enough for me to take a seat, but I moved further into the room. "Good. There is something I need to speak to you about, a matter of some delicacy."

Mother put her needle down at that and raised her gaze to me. "Is it about the earl?"

"No. It's Fanny."

She made an irritated sound in her throat. "You are forever going on about your sister. Do you think of nothing else?"

"*Someone* needs to think of her," I said, allowing my frustration to color my words.

Mother stiffened. She did not acknowledge my remarks by

responding to them. "Your focus should be on securing the earl as a husband."

Her thoughtlessness made me regret my initial actions toward Daniel. He was worth more than the title he carried. I never should have reduced him to it. "That hardly matters. He won't have me."

She peered at me. "You mean you've tried?"

"Whatever your plan is, I fear you must devise an alternative." It was not a direct answer, but I didn't feel she ought to know about my attempt to secure Daniel. If she knew what I was willing to do, she would undoubtedly exploit my desperation.

Mother set her embroidery in a basket and moved it aside, then stood. "That is unacceptable. We have nothing if you do not make a good match."

It was a sentiment I too carried. I understood her fear. But Daniel was not our only option. "There are other men. We can arrange something—"

"Why? You have a completely suitable man in this very house. Marriage to him would allow us to keep our home. You are everything desirable in a wife, and our name is spotless." She narrowed her eyes. "Is it Fanny? Does the earl take issue with her?"

"Of course not."

"Then why do you believe he is so uninterested?" She leaned back a little. "Does he fear you will not produce an heir? We must make him see reason. You were only married for two years, which is certainly not enough time to induce worrying."

My hands curled into fists and my nails bit into my palms. I didn't want to admit my failure in securing Daniel. Aside from making myself vulnerable to Mother's schemes, it was embarrassing. I should never have tried it. "Will you tell me why the name Waterley sounds familiar?"

She ceased moving, her mouth pinching together. Her

silence only added to my dread. "He was a friend of Colin's," she said smoothly. "Did you not know?"

"I was in the drawing room when he mentioned it, but I do not recall Colin ever speaking of him to me."

"You must not have been listening well."

"Mother, you will not fob me off so easily. Why does his name sound familiar to me?"

Her lips pinched together, anger shooting from her eyes. "Waterley Hospital Lunatic Asylum."

I tried to hide my dismay, swallowing hard. "Is it close to us here?"

"Yes. I admit, I did not realize how close it was until we arrived. I only knew it was in the county."

"And Mr. Waterley called," I said, finishing her thought.

Her eyes darted down to her lap before lifting stubbornly to meet mine. "Do not look at me with such contempt," she said darkly. "I know you believe Fanny is better off with you, but you are not a doctor. You have not the medical knowledge necessary to continue to manage her. As she ages, she will only need more assistance."

I scoffed. "That is your justification?"

"I need not justify anything. I am her mother, and I know best."

"Yet you cannot calm her when she is in distress."

"Sometimes you cannot either," she snapped. "Fanny will reach the point where she will best be managed by a medical professional. Given her hysterics in this house just a few days ago, I daresay we are very quickly reaching that point."

She could never find out about Fanny's little outburst in the garden with the neighbors. I closed my eyes and drew in a breath, praying for patience. It would help nothing to villainize Mother and force her into a defensive position. "We will never agree on that score." I leveled her with a look. "What is your plan?"

She watched me for a minute. "Had you secured a husband, I would not need to go to any such extremes. Now I fear we will need to deposit Fanny in a hospital so we may go to London in search of someone to marry you. How else are we to survive?"

Survival. It was the chief motivation for both of us. In that, I found a likeness in my mother. Our choices for handling the poor cards life had dealt us could not be more different, though. To her, once Fanny was out of the way, we would have no trouble moving in polite circles until I could convince someone with enough money to save us from destitution.

She didn't know of Daniel's offer to give us the dower house and an income, but she wouldn't like it anyway. It was not enough for her. The woman had lived in grand houses with a vast fortune at her disposal for the entirety of her life. She couldn't fathom economizing or downsizing our lives if we had any other option.

"Was this your plan all along? To bring us here until you could formulate an agreement with Mr. Waterley to take Fanny?" It made sense now why she had been easy to convince when I wanted my sister to join us. She never wanted Fanny to leave the house, let alone the county. But if I brought Fanny to Northumberland, then she was already near the madhouse originally contracted to care for her. In a foreign house, my sister was easily distressed, the environment bound to incite fits that would only further demonstrate she was in need of a doctor.

"Are you asking if my plan was to find a way for my daughter to be properly cared for?" Mother asked coldly.

Her question rattled me. Was Fanny not receiving proper care? Was I holding my sister back by not allowing her the medical attention she needed? I shook my head. The stories I had heard and the articles I had read proved my convictions were correct. Madhouses were no place for my sister. Mother's feigned tenderness could not cover her selfish heart.

"I will do whatever it takes to keep her with me."

Mother started walking toward the door but stopped and looked over her shoulder. "Then I suggest you find a husband, Verity." She disappeared, leaving the door open and my heart in utter, torturous dismay.

Find a husband? Could it be so simple? Marriage to Daniel would keep us comfortably at Lamouth. Mother could continue her existence as a wealthy matron, and I could be safe with Fanny in our home. Marriage to another man had the potential to save us or condemn my sister. If he took issue with her the way Colin had, she would be no better off than she was now.

I stood in the middle of the room, staring at the doorway my mother had disappeared through for so long that I hardly noticed when it was filled with another shadow.

Daniel's voice broke through my reverie, calling my attention to the way he leaned against the door frame, his arms casually crossed over his chest. His shirtsleeves were rolled up to his elbows and he had yet to don his coat again. His waistcoat defined the width of his chest, and he looked far more roguish than he had any right to. "You are deep in thought," he muttered. "It gives me leave to wonder what you could possibly be ruminating on with such focus."

I looked up and held his brown eyes, shadowed and solemn. He was handsome, his features striking. I knew he had a life before I met him, a history with women and cards and poor choices I knew little about. His reputation had not been false, and marriage to him could mean the potential of suffering with infidelity for the rest of my life if he succumbed to old habits.

But after we had children, it could be a marriage in name only. My body flinched at the very idea, but I shoved aside my sensitivities. Fanny's *life* hung in the balance. I lifted my chin, holding his dark eyes. "I was contemplating how best to convince you to reconsider your stance on marrying me."

CHAPTER TWENTY

DANIEL

If it wasn't for the solemn expression on Verity's face, I would have assumed she was doing her best to make a joke. I decided to turn it into one instead. "I often incite such desire for matrimony when I've shed my coat."

Her line of sight dropped to my arms before rising to my face again. "I hate to disappoint you, but your roguish dress today had nothing to do with my new resolve."

I stepped slowly into the room, rocking on my feet as though I was debating something of great depth and not this woman's blunt declaration. A declaration I did not find as unattractive as I had the first time she made it. It hardly mattered. I was no more eligible now than I was then. "Would you care to enlighten me about what made you reassess your resolve on this matter?"

"I rather wondered if you would care to explain how your nearest neighbor is somehow involved in a local lunatic asylum, and you did not think I would care to know."

My feet stilled, glued to the Aubusson carpet across from her. "I'd like to say it was an attempt to spare you further pain."

"Being ignorant of this would only leave room for potential

problems. In the future, I would appreciate being informed of any dangers to my sister."

"Will you take comfort in the notion that I do not deem Waterley a danger to your sister?"

"He might not be. But my mother very much is, and she has been in communication with one of the Waterley men for some time now." She passed trembling fingers over her brow and rubbed at her temple. "Waterley Hospital is where my late husband arranged for Fanny to be taken."

Hollowness crept into my stomach, opening a chasm and making me sick. It was abundantly clear Verity believed a separation from her sister to be untenable. After watching them together, I could see why Fanny depended on her so greatly, and why Verity would fear not being there to support and advocate for her. I took a step forward. "I did not know."

A tremulous, humorless smile curved her lips. "I imagine not."

"You are shaking."

"I am." She held her hand in front of her, palm facing the floor, and watched her fingers tremble before curling them into a fist. "My mother intends for me to feel powerless so I will dance to her tune. She has thus far accomplished her goal."

"What can I do to support you?"

She lifted her gaze, watching me.

I felt I owed her something of an explanation. I was not a knight in armor, coming to her aid. There was no rescue planned. But I would assist her in any way I could. "You and your sister have come to feel special to me, Verity. You are both friends of mine. I understand I am in a position of power regarding your home, and you will not accept my charity"—I raised my hands before she could argue—"which I wholly understand. If our plan to prepare the dower house for you and supply you with an income is not sufficient, what more can I do?"

"I will not repeat the uncomfortable proposition I gave you on my first night here. But might I ask why an arrangement between us is so repulsive to you?" Her confusion was admittedly adorable.

If I had even an ounce of self-respect, I would have walked from the room immediately. As it stood, I was a glutton for punishment. Marriage to Verity sounded like the best choice I could make—selfishly—but it was impossible. She deserved far better than to be forever connected to me.

"Repulsive is not the right word," I said.

"Oh?" She crossed her arms over her chest. "Then what would you call it?"

"Impossible."

"Will you explain why?"

Could I explain it to her? I didn't often make myself vulnerable to other people and the potential of doing so now made me anxious. I crossed the room toward the fireplace and ran my fingers along the enormous carved mantelpiece. I had a sudden, deep yearning for a glass of rich burgundy, and it occurred to me that, aside from wine with dinner last night, I had not drunk anything for the last two days.

Distraction could be good for some things, I supposed. It was pleasant to have my wits so fully about me.

I heard Verity's footsteps coming toward me and turned away from the fireplace. Her face was determined. It was the same expression I had seen when she was forced to defend her sister. Verity was no stranger to fighting for what she cared about.

"Is it the issue with the heirs?" she asked.

"What heirs?"

"I will accept that answer as a no," she muttered.

I shook my head, pushing aside my confusion. "You are too good for me. You do not realize this now, because you are desperate to protect your sister, but you would later regret a match between us." I was bound to disappoint her the way I'd disappointed my father, my mother, my sister. It was a pattern in my life I'd proven time and again.

Verity's mouth opened, hovered, and she closed it again. A line formed between her eyebrows, and she tilted her head to the side. "I will not accept that answer."

"It is the truth."

"How? We hardly knew one another that first evening."

"Oh, well, that time I rejected you out of hand because I thought you were a fortune hunter. I had no desire to shackle myself to someone who cared so much for money. I quickly learned my initial impressions of you were very wrong."

"That is a relief. A fortune is the last thing on my mind. I won't deny it would greatly ease my burdens, though, if I acquired one."

"Yes, your burdens," I said, leaning my shoulder against the wall beside the mantel. I was much closer to Verity now than a moment ago, and I wondered if it bothered her. She made no sign of it, though, and did not attempt to step back.

"If you truly believe that to be the case, that I am too good for you, then you do not know me at all."

"I think I have a fairly good idea of your character," I said, my voice quiet. "Anyone who would do what you did merely so they could create security for their sister has a good heart."

"Or insufficient morals."

"That is not the case here. I think desperation is more apt."

She wrinkled her nose. "Do I reek of it? Desperation has been my companion these last twelve months."

I reached forward and fingered the edge of her black sleeve. "What color will you wear tomorrow?"

Her breath caught. "What is your favorite color?"

"I do not have one."

"Impossible," she said quietly. "Everyone has a favorite color."

"I am one of a kind."

"You *are*. Do you not know that?"

"Flattery will not win my hand."

Verity shook her head, chuckling. "It is embarrassing to ask you to marry me over and over again and continue to be rejected. Will you not put me from my misery?"

"I thought you promised you would never ask to marry me again."

"And you said 'pity,' if I recall correctly. Now I know you were joking."

My chest squeezed. "You don't. Not really."

"Come now, Daniel. You cannot have it both ways."

"What?" I asked, stepping toward her. "I cannot be drawn to you and simultaneously understand that it is not in your best interest to be connected to me?"

She tucked her chin. "So this is about reputation? You must know I do not care for such things. I do not travel a great deal. I have hardly left Lamouth. My reputation is of no great import."

Her dedication to caring for her sister had ruled so much of her life. "Have you wanted to travel?"

"It is an appealing thought, but I cannot see how it would be possible."

"It could be, if you wanted."

"Perhaps, but I am content in my position. I will not forever pine for a life I do not lead. My home is comfortable, my days full of beauty and joy. What more could I need?"

I stared at her. The simple, easy existence she described was inordinately attractive. "Do you realize how enviable it is to be so content?"

"There is no reason you cannot feel the same."

I gave a quiet scoff. My father's voice ran through my mind. *Why must you be so irresponsible, Daniel? Why can you not be more like your sister? Why do you insist on making careless decisions? You know better.* I ran my hand through my hair. "Some of us do not have the self-possession to be so easily happy."

"Because I—"

Voices filtered through the open doorway and Verity's head flipped toward it. "Drat. Can we not have one full conversation? I hate being forever interrupted."

I wasn't ready to finish our conversation either. I turned toward the mantel and fit my palm to the medallion on the end, pressing hard to release the hook. It gave way and a panel in the wall relaxed, creaking forward. I swung it open like a door.

"What the devil?" Verity said.

I ignored her unladylike speech. The noises in the corridor were growing louder. My mother was on her way toward us, it seemed, my housekeeper in tow.

I lifted an eyebrow and nodded toward the small room. "No one can interrupt us in here."

The woman was desperate enough to take me at my word and stepped into the room. I followed her in and swiftly shut the door, hooking the wooden mechanism back in place. It would appear like a wall to anyone looking from the sitting room.

"What—"

"Shhh," I said quietly. I could hear my mother's voice on the other side of the thin wall. I pressed my ear to the door and heard her speaking to Mrs. Hale, but could not determine what they were saying.

It was dark in the small room, but we had enough space; I wasn't touching Verity.

"What is this place?" she whispered.

"The castle was originally built as a monastery. When it was converted into a house, these small rooms were thought to either be places to hide priests or possibly private prayer rooms. We aren't quite sure."

"What is preventing your mother from looking for us in here now?"

"I'm not sure she was looking for us. She knows of the room, so I suppose she could open the door and discover us." I quieted immediately as I heard her muffled voice come closer. We kept silent until the voices receded.

Light peeked through the cracks lining the doorway, but it wasn't enough to see anything. I faced the direction I thought Verity was standing, grateful for the darkness. This would be easier to admit without being able to read her expression. "I have a long history, and when you ask me to marry you, you do not know what you are offering to tether yourself to."

"I have long since heard of your reputation, Daniel. I am not so innocent as to believe you don't have a past."

"Then you'll understand why you cannot tie yourself to it."

"Why can you not understand that perhaps I am willing to forgive your past?" she said, her voice laced with slight exasperation.

"You do not know what you're saying."

"You do not give me enough credit."

I ran a hand over my face. "Verity, listen. I am not good enough. I make mistakes with startling regularity. I succumb to the temptation of drink and cards." *And women*, though I'd like to have enough faith in myself to believe that was entirely in my past now. "I enjoy *hunting*."

"Then you are wholly unsuitable for Fanny."

I chuckled. "I am too old for Fanny." I had never once considered the girl in a romantic light. "I regard her highly and it pains me to know how appalled she would be if she were to learn of the depth of my appreciation for a good meat pie."

"Your secret is safe with me." I could hear the lovely smile in her voice.

"Can we let the matter rest, then?" I asked. "I do not want to put you in a position where you will later regret making an alliance with me."

"I want nothing more than to secure my life and my sister's. An alliance with you would do that."

I shook my head, though I knew she could not see me. "Perhaps I don't want to be married for my property either," I said quietly.

Verity sucked in a quiet breath as though I had stung her. I could not take back the words, but I didn't want to. I was surprised to realize how much I meant them.

"You are right," she said. "You deserve—what is that sound?"

"What do you mean?" I fell silent, listening. I heard a faint clicking noise and then a small squeak. "Oh blast, I think it might be—"

"A mouse!" Verity screamed.

CHAPTER TWENTY-ONE

VERITY

I f there was one thing I could not abide, it was the feeling of knowing there was a rodent in the room that could very well climb up my leg if it so chose. I jumped toward Daniel, grabbing for him. "Mouse! Open the door!"

"I cannot see," he said, his voice much calmer than the situation warranted.

There was another squeak and the sound of scurrying. I squealed, pulling at Daniel's shirt in my haste to be free of this wretchedly dark room.

"Come here," he said firmly. In a woosh of motion, I was lifted from the floor, one of his arms under my bent knees, the other behind my back.

I hurried to throw my arms around his neck and closed my eyes, my heart hammering.

"I cannot breathe," he said, and I lessened my hold slightly— only enough to give him room to draw in air.

We stood that way in the dark, Daniel holding me up while I clung to him. I could feel the rapid beating of his heart against my side, the warmth of his skin against my palm at his neck, the movement of his muscle with my other on his back. His firm grip revealed how steady a hold he had on me. If I was not set down soon, I might do something foolish. As it stood, it was taking every bit of my self-possession to refrain from leaning in and inhaling his scent.

"Will you not open the door?" I asked.

"I need a free hand to do so."

Drat.

"May I set you down?" he asked.

"No."

Daniel gave a short, surprised laugh. "Then I suppose we must stay here."

"With a mouse?" I whispered.

He was quiet for a moment. "I no longer hear it."

We were both silent. There was no scratching, squeaking, or pattering of tiny footsteps. "That does not mean the mouse is gone. It could merely be lying in wait for my feet to touch the floor again."

"I forgot what devious creatures mice could be."

"Do not say rude things," I whispered. "You do not want to provoke its wrath."

"Oh, of course. How foolish of me. I will take better care of what I say in the future about the dastardly rodents."

My hands slid lower on his back. "Could you perhaps open the door while holding me?"

"No. Are you ready for me to set you down?"

"No."

"As much as I am enjoying this—"

"Are you?" I asked. I was increasingly aware of the feeling of his arms around me, holding me so close to his chest, the smell of his spicy cologne and the cadence of his heart. Mother's earlier decree surfaced in my mind—if I wanted to save Fanny, I needed to find a husband. A wicked idea came to me, and I raised my hands to the back of his neck, resting my fingers around it. My fingertips slid into his silky hair, and I heard his breath hitch.

"Enough of that," he said brusquely.

I spoke with affected innocence. "You do not want me to hold on to you? Are you going to open the door now?"

"You are not that naïve, Verity. You know what you are doing."

He was right. My intention was purely to see if I could persuade him to kiss me. I couldn't help but grin, and I was glad of the darkness to hide it. "I'm only holding on so I do not fall."

"You are doing much more than that," he said quietly, his voice rough.

I brought my other hand to his cheek, grazing my thumb over his forehead and his cheekbone, feeling the contours of his face. My chest settled, my breath slowing. "I would not be a demanding wife, Daniel. I would care for you, but I would not force you to remain at Lamouth either. You could play cards with your friends or whatever it is you wish to do. I would not tie you to my apron strings."

He was quiet for too long, his breathing refusing to slow, and I wondered if I was offending him.

I leaned in a little. It had been over a year since I'd kissed a man—*well* over a year, since I'd refused to speak to Colin after he tried to have Fanny admitted to a madhouse. These things came naturally, though, did they not? There was no sense in worrying I'd forgotten how to kiss.

"You are not playing fairly," he murmured.

His words pricked at my conscience. My face hovered just before his, and I waited. I would not kiss him unless he wanted to be kissed. I might have proved my willingness, but Daniel needed to move the rest of the way and close the distance. I found I hoped, with every tense muscle in my body, that he would kiss me. Not for the purpose of securing his promise to marry me or any such thing, but because I wanted *him*.

The realization struck me. I had feelings for Daniel? He was handsome and ridiculously charming, there was no denying that, but my attraction to him was deeper than appreciating his fine looks. His smile made my heart light, and his caring nature and the attention he paid Fanny were genuine. An image flashed in my mind of Daniel teaching her to fly a kite just hours ago, and I knew with surety that my attempts to persuade him to matrimony were much more selfish than I'd previously admitted to myself.

"You cannot know how deeply I want to kiss you right now, Verity." His voice was raspy and he swallowed hard. "I cannot." He leaned back, turning his head away from me and letting out a full breath. "If I explain how to do it, do you think you could pull the lever to unlatch the door?"

I felt summarily dismissed. Twice now—more than that, really, but it wasn't worth counting—I had all but thrown myself at Daniel and been rejected. Fresh on the heels of suspecting my feelings for him ran deeper than I'd realized, it was a hit to not just my pride, but also my heart.

I cleared my throat. "You may set me down."

His hands tightened subtly. "Do not take offense, Verity. You are beautiful, kind—"

"That is enough of that," I said, wiggling and pushing at his arms. I did not need to be consoled in that manner. "You may set me down now."

"Verity," he pleaded.

I wiggled until he relented. The next thing I knew, Daniel was at the doorway, doing something to the mechanism and pushing it open. We were flooded with light. He let me step out first, squinting against the brightness in the room.

Daniel passed me and crossed to the window, pulling the drapes closed. "Just until our eyes are used to the light again," he explained, before returning to close the door to the secret room. "No mouse that I can see. Little devil must have fled."

Embarrassment burned through me. I moved to leave the room.

"Please wait."

The pleading in his voice made me stop. I turned back to face him.

"You do not know my history." He stepped closer, pain washing across his face. "I could not . . . I will not take advantage of you while you are in a vulnerable state. I did that once, and it has haunted me ever since."

"You need not tell me."

"I want to." He started rolling down his shirtsleeves, focusing on them instead of holding my gaze. "When I was younger, I was quite reckless. My friends and I were forever daring each other to do foolish things. We drank too much, and my father warned me constantly to take care. But why should I? I was invincible." He spoke bitterly.

"That is not uncommon for young men," I said, trying to gentle my tone.

"Perhaps not, but I could see the path my behavior was taking me down and I recognized my father's wisdom. I was not of strong enough character to refuse my friends, however, and regardless of the logic in my parents' wisdom, I did not temper my behaviors."

"Do you temper them now?"

Daniel paused, looking at me with confusion. "That isn't relevant to the point I am trying to make."

"I disagree. You are claiming your unsuitability is because of your past. I am attempting to make the argument that your present behavior is more relevant to the topic at hand."

His lips parted in preparation to argue, his brown eyes watching me.

Fanny swept quietly into the room, and I spun to face her. "All finished with the chickens?"

She sent me a fleeting look of mild confusion. I supposed I

didn't sound as natural as I'd hoped. "It is time to draw," she said.

Drawing. The schedule. It took a moment for my mind to float back down to me, for apparently it had been lost in the clouds. I *never* forgot Fanny's schedule, but the mouse and the dark room and possibly the handsome gentleman had all contributed to putting it momentarily from the front of my mind. I needed to focus better. "Of course. That is why I have been waiting for you here."

Daniel looked from me to the fireplace. "We should've stayed in the room," he muttered.

I ignored the comment and moved to sit with Fanny at the small table. Daniel's fingers reached out as I passed and brushed the back of my knuckles lightly. Fire swept over my skin in the form of a shiver, and my breath hitched. I cast a glance at him over my shoulder, but he was not looking at me. He was looking at the floor, his brow bent in concentration.

Focus, Verity. I turned my attention to Fanny. She pulled paper and her graphite pencils from the pile on the table where we had previously left them. She started to sketch with her right hand, her left spinning the paper in different angles as she worked. It was truly marvelous watching her images come slowly to life in this manner.

Daniel cleared his throat softly. "We will continue our conversation at a later time?"

I nodded.

His face bent into a grim smile. I had the impression he didn't want to leave by the way he hovered, unmoving. His eyes dropped to Fanny's paper, and he stepped closer. "Is that . . ."

"It is your kite," Fanny said. "I have no talent with people, so I will leave it."

"Have the chickens fly it?" I suggested.

Fanny laughed. She tilted her head and looked at the

drawing already in progress. "Yes, they shall. Can you imagine chickens flying a kite?"

"It is absurd," Daniel said, humor in his tone as well. "You're very talented, Fanny."

"Thank you." She paused and reached for her stack of papers, then combed through them to pull out a handful of pictures she had drawn while at the castle. "May I show you more?"

"I'd love to see them." Daniel pulled a chair close to Fanny's other side and took a seat.

Fanny showed him each of the animals she had been working on, then spread them on the table. "Which is your favorite?"

"Must you always ask that?"

She looked at me. "I like to know."

I chuckled.

"It is impossible to answer," Daniel said, looking at all of them. He dropped his finger on the one directly in front of her. "I think I will like the kite best."

Fanny nodded. "That is likely because you have a greater connection to it."

"I think you're right." He looked at it for a while longer, and I imagined his concentration was elsewhere. He seemed to shake himself and stood. "I have matters of business to attend to, so I shall see you both later. Good day, ladies." He dipped in a bow and left.

Fanny resumed work on her kite, giving me silence to ruminate on the events of the last few hours.

Daniel was unwilling to marry me. Mother had made a valid point—the only thing that would give us stability and security now was marriage. But I couldn't risk marrying anyone else. Colin had seemed perfectly kind and even lovely toward Fanny. His small comments and side glances should have given me a hint of his true feelings toward her, but I did not discern them until it was too late.

I would not repeat that mistake again. Yet if Mother was determined to install Fanny in a madhouse, there was nothing I could do about that either. Only Mother had legal control over her daughter, and Fanny was years from reaching her majority.

Drat. I needed to find another solution. I looked at Fanny's innocent face, no crease of concentration marring her eyebrows. Drawing came as naturally to her as breathing, and it was clear it took no significant effort. Her relaxed manner in Daniel's company and the way she had found a rhythm at Arden Castle proved the harmonious nature of the place. "You've enjoyed your time here, have you not?" I asked.

Fanny did not look up from her drawing. "It has been amiable."

We had needed to adjust our schedule and expectations upon first arriving, but once those were accomplished, I had been impressed with Fanny's malleability. It gave me hope. It allowed me to believe she could find similar contentment in another house. Maybe a very small cottage with our own hens. We could locate birds and lure them to our house much like Mr. Ramsey had done at his gardener cottage. Perhaps Mary would even come with us.

My mind worked around the new problem. Such a cottage presented a perfectly lovely image, but I did not know how we could afford it.

I would devise a plan, though, because one thing had become perfectly clear to me. If Mother did not value Fanny's safety, I no longer needed to concern myself with making sure we had a place to go that Mother would approve of. She need not come with us, but could remain at Lamouth. If not in the big house, then in the dower house once it was repaired.

My new goal was finding a suitable situation for my sister and me.

CHAPTER TWENTY-TWO

DANIEL

The first thought I had upon waking up was wondering what color Verity would wear now she was out of mourning. I sat at the desk in the study mulling over what my favorite color was. I had not been lying to her. I did not know if I possessed one. The door was propped open so I could see the foot of the stairs from this angle, and I watched it, hoping she would come down soon.

I had never before put such effort into catching a glimpse of a woman. If anyone were to accuse me of sitting here merely so I could see Verity, I would resolutely deny it. Honestly, had I lost my wits? It had taken every ounce of control I possessed to quiet my mind long enough to fall asleep last night. I couldn't stop imagining the feel of Verity in my arms, her hands on my neck, or remove the desire to have her there again.

One would almost imagine I was developing feelings for her, which was ridiculous.

Footsteps sounded on the stairs, and I came to attention immediately, craning my neck slightly to better see.

Dean appeared, looking toward the study. He startled to find me staring at him. I straightened at once, chagrined. It wasn't his typical practice to use the main stairs, and if I hadn't known better, I would believe he'd done it merely to give me a start.

He came into the study, Oscar trailing behind him.

"Yes?" I said impatiently, rubbing the hound's head when he trotted up to me.

"Will you be wanting the bronze waistcoat for dinner this evening, sir?"

"I have no care for what I wear, Dean. You know this."

"Generally speaking, that is the case," he said, nodding slowly. "I did not know if your dinner plans tonight were cause for more attention."

"What dinner plans?" I asked skeptically. Oscar leaned into my hand, forcing me to rub his ears again.

"The guests, my lord. The Misses Kelby and Miss Martin."

"Oh yes, of course. *Those* guests." I clenched my teeth, and it took great restraint not to break a tooth. Meddling Mother, again.

Dean blinked at me. "Were you perhaps unaware, my lord?"

"It is very likely that was intentionally the case."

His face crumpled in feigned apology. "Did not mean to overstep my bounds, sir. Only wanted to prepare the proper clothes."

I opened the top drawer with exaggerated flourish and pulled out my father's old pocket watch, flipping it open to check the time. I looked back at him. "Twelve hours before dinner?"

Dean grinned with unabashed humor. "Never could read time very well."

"Thank you for the warning."

He bent in a bow and turned to leave, but stopped at the door and looked back.

"Yes?" Oscar slumped down over my feet. He was much heavier than he realized.

"You were talking in your sleep last night, sir."

"Oh?" I asked wryly. "What was it I said?"

"That was the strange thing, sir. You only repeated the word 'fairy.'"

"Odd, that." I looked at the pocket watch in my hand and waited for Dean to leave. Did he suspect I'd been saying Verity's name? Clever man. I clicked the watch open and closed a few times, then realized how ridiculous I was being. Sitting around, waiting for a woman merely so I could catch a glimpse of her?

I opened the drawer and tossed my father's pocket watch into it before slamming it shut. "Dean!" I yelled. Oscar gave a short, surprised bark before laying his head back down.

My valet stepped back into the room so quickly he must've been hovering outside the door. "Yes, my lord?"

"Change of plans. I will go riding now."

"Yes, sir." He left to prepare my riding clothes. I dropped my head into my hands and rubbed my temples. Everything was mashed together. What I suspected to be feelings for Verity warred with my desire to remain alone, incapable of bothering anyone. I had proven through my callous treatment of Miss Waterley that I did not deserve a lady in my life of such esteem, and Verity was quality personified. But her plight was not lost on me either. She wanted security and believed I could provide it.

Her promise not to bother me was nearly laughable. How could I be married to one such as her and not desire to spend all my time with her? I knew exactly how we would spend it, too, with a walk in the morning, the hens afterward, followed by a stint of drawing.

I shook away the thought and pushed back my chair, slipping my feet out from under my now slumbering dog. The bureau against the wall contained a deep amber bottle, tucked into the corner, and it did not take long to retrieve the brandy, open it, and raise it to my nose for a whiff. I wanted a taste, but not just a little. I wanted glass after glass until the uncomfortable feelings were muted. The smell triggered a physical longing in my stomach. It was my habit to dull my frustrations with alcohol so I would not vent my anger on my mother. She had long been a matchmaker, attempting to find me a suitable wife, and I did not want to lash out at her, so I had turned to drink instead.

The covert way she had invited the Kelbys and their goddaughter to dinner drove me to this cabinet. Avoiding my feelings for Verity drove me here. Wanting an escape drove me to this bottle of brandy. It was a habit so ingrained in me, I didn't consider what I was doing until I held the bottle in my hands.

But if I drank enough to be foxed, how would I face anyone tonight? How could I speak to Verity? How would I face Fanny? Verity's question from yesterday pecked at me like an obnoxious little bird.

I did not temper my behaviors.

Do you temper them now?

It was such a harmless question, but within it lay the power of choice. I had allowed my past to define me and my character. When faced with discomfort, regardless of the knowledge that it would disappoint my mother, I fell into the habit of being the disreputable lout she expected. Why? For fear that my attempts at reformation would fail and I would disappoint myself as well as her?

I looked wryly down at the bottle and brought it back up to my nose for another delicious whiff. Yes, if I tried to be a better man, I was most assuredly going to fail. I shoved the cork into the bottle and put it into the cabinet.

Brandy no longer sounded appealing at present. I left the room and raced up the stairs toward my chamber. A long bruising ride was in order.

When I rounded the corner, I pulled up quickly to avoid running into a woman.

No, not just *a* woman. Verity.

And she was wearing blue. A rich, deep shade that complemented her sparkling green eyes. She laughed, her hand fluttering to her heart. "You gave me a fright."

"Forgive my haste."

"It is no matter." She smiled and moved to step around me.

I turned as she walked and watched her. "Where is Fanny?"

"She's gone down already to search for that starling. I think she'll have me climbing trees before long."

"I happen to be an excellent climber." I gave a flourish as if I was reporting a particular skill. "If you need help in that regard, send for me."

Verity laughed, the sound driving a pleasant wisp of warmth through me.

"Perhaps I will come by once my ride is through to see if you are in need of assistance."

"That would be most kind of you, Daniel." She curtsied in farewell and continued down the stairs. I watched her walk away, wishing I was holding her hand and guiding her. I shook my head, hoping to dislodge the pleasant fantasy.

A long, *long* bruising ride was in order.

Despite helping the women search a great deal after my ride, and again the next day, and then the next, Fanny could not find her starling.

"Are you certain your friends have not used the bird for target practice?" Fanny asked with slight condemnation while we walked back to the house on the third morning.

In all honesty, I could not promise such a thing. It would surprise me greatly if they had. I cleared my throat. "It is highly unlikely."

Fanny frowned. "But not impossible."

"If birds migrate," Verity said, "then perhaps the starling only wanted a new home."

"But to leave the nest?" Fanny stopped, looking back over her shoulder. "Do you think she laid any eggs before she disappeared?"

Oh, bloody h— I swallowed my curse before I could speak it aloud and leaned closer to Verity, catching a whiff of her faint floral scent. I knew it came from Pears soap, and somehow that made it even lovelier. As a man who used cologne, I understood the desire for assistance in smelling nice. Verity had no such dependencies. She was merely clean.

It was symbolism at its best. She had a clean soul, and I used artifice to appear as a decent person.

"Did you want something?" she whispered.

I'd been distracted and stood there, smelling her, for far too long. "Fanny will want us to look at the nest now."

Fanny turned toward us as if she'd heard us, but she was too far away. "We really ought to check."

"We should have wagered something," I said. "I would have won."

Verity shot me an amused smile but ignored my comment.

Fanny made a humming sound, looking toward the animal enclosures, then back toward the copse. Her schedule pulled her one way and her desires another. I waited for Verity to soothe Fanny into changing her schedule, but she merely waited, her lips pressed softly together, watching her sister.

Fanny's hands started shaking in front of her stomach, her gaze shifting between the trees and the direction of the animal pens. Would Verity step in now? Should I?

Verity spoke gently. "You are the mistress of your time."

"The mistress of my time," Fanny repeated.

"Shall we look quickly for the nest?" I softened my voice much as they both had done.

Fanny gave a distinct nod and started walking toward the

trees. "It will not take long." She was probably telling herself that, not either of us.

I offered Verity my arm, and we followed Fanny until we reached the tree where they had first seen the nest. I scanned the fields surrounding us, glad not to see any friends or neighbors in the area. Fanny went to the base of the tree and rested her hand on the lowest branch, looking up as though determining how best to check the nest.

I might be considered unprincipled by some, but I was in no way going to allow a seventeen-year-old young lady to climb the tree when I was present. I shrugged from my coat for better shoulder mobility and handed it to Verity. "Do try not to proposition me this time," I said.

She folded my coat over her arms, her mouth fighting a smile. Color filled her cheeks, lending her beautiful countenance a sweetness.

I winked, and she looked away. But I was glad to see her smile remain.

It took a moment to roll up my sleeves before I approached the tree and began to climb.

"Be careful," Verity said. "We do not want to carry you home with a broken ankle."

"Have some faith in me," I joked, climbing higher.

I wasn't entirely sure, but I thought I heard her say, *I do.*

It did not take long to reach the branch where the starling had built her nest. I looked down and stilled, counting four smooth, oval, blue eggs. When I lowered my gaze and caught Verity's, she seemed to sense what I had found.

"What is it?" Fanny asked, anxious.

"Eggs."

CHAPTER TWENTY-THREE

VERITY

It came as no surprise that Fanny felt the best thing would be to leave the nest where it was for one full day before saving the eggs—with avid observation, of course. I hoped the mother would arrive soon and relieve us of any duty.

Daniel had returned to the house for a blanket, and we set up our watch party in the shade of the trees, away from the nest but close enough to see it. Fanny watched it resolutely, her attention unwavering.

"What shall we do if the mother does not return today?" I asked.

"She must," Fanny said.

I shared a look with Daniel over my sister's head.

"We shall see," he said. "It is not time to worry yet."

Daniel's tree climbing was impressive, so naturally we passed the next hour sharing stories of our silly childhood exploits. I learned of the time Daniel convinced his sister to play hide-and-seek in the attic and left her there for nearly an entire day. He learned of the time I built a tent in my bedroom for Fanny and me to sleep in, then refused to sleep anywhere but the tent for almost a week, despite the fact that Fanny did not like the confining walls and wouldn't join me.

"Your nanny allowed you to sleep in it for so many nights?" he asked.

"My father was indulgent. I wanted to sleep in the tent, so he allowed it." My heart panged sharply, missing him. We'd both lost our fathers, I realized, my sorrow extending to Daniel. "What was your father like?"

Daniel gave a light scoff and looked away. His eyes were heavy. "My father was an intelligent man, and he found reason to teach a lesson in every circumstance."

"He must have cared for you deeply in order to put such effort into guiding you."

Daniel looked at me wryly. "That is the debate, is it not? Was he critical because it was his aim to improve my character or because he could not abide having a soulless son?"

"Could it not have been both?"

"Perhaps, though one is more forgivable than the other."

"In what way?"

Daniel was quiet for a moment. He looked from me to Fanny, watching her sit quietly and hum to herself, her attention rapt on the nest. "In one instance, his aim was improving me for the sake of *me*, the other was far more selfish. He wanted me to improve for *his* sake."

I hadn't thought of it in that way, but I understood. "The latter perfectly describes my mother," I said quietly, so as not to be overheard by my sister. It was impossible to know when Fanny was lost in her own thoughts and when she only appeared that way. Her observations often surprised me, proving that she paid attention far more than I ever expected.

Daniel looked from me to Fanny, lifting his eyebrows and nodding slightly toward her.

"Yes. Our mother is more concerned with the way others view our family than with our personal feelings. It has caused much heartache for my sister and me, but sometimes I feel I cannot fault her for only doing what she knows. She has never lived in a home that did not contain more pride than love. How can she know better?"

"You claim her ignorant? That is charitable of you."

"It is much easier to live with," I argued.

"I understand that." Daniel reached over to the grass and pulled a weed, peeling the stem into bits. "For all my anger, I recognize I deserve a large share of the blame. Once, when I was a lad, I'd been very naughty—I cannot recall why, now, only that I'd done something to greatly anger my father. He revoked my riding privileges, which was a great offense at that stage in my life." He smiled, but it held more sorrow than humor. "He promised I could ride again after I had written a letter to my mother apologizing for my behavior, and another to him, listing the ways I had erred and how I could right my wrongs."

"Were your riding privileges returned to you immediately, then?"

"No. That would've meant admitting my wrongs, and I was far too stubborn. I did not ride for a month."

"A month?" I laughed. "I am not sure stubborn best describes you, Daniel. Is there a stronger word than that?"

Daniel tossed the obliterated weed and leaned back against his palms. "Obstinate?"

"I hope you have improved since that episode."

"Hardly." He laughed. "I nearly ran from Arden the other night when I was warned by my valet the Kelbys and their goddaughter were to dine."

"But you didn't," I said. "You remained, which shows growth of character. The dinner was not so terrible, was it?"

"My dinner partner made it bearable."

I blushed, looking down at the grass near my feet.

Daniel cleared his throat. "The Kelby sisters are kind, if a little overbearing."

"One must commend their singular focus."

"In finding a match for me? Yes, that is focus, indeed."

The older women were eccentric, which could very well be part of the reason no one seemed to mind when they pushed their goddaughter mercilessly at Daniel. "Miss Martin seems guileless. Your mother must approve of the match if she invited them."

"I am certain she does. Miss Martin is all things amiable. Biddable. Accomplished. Pretty." He spoke the words like small darts thrown at a target board.

Good heavens. I did not realize jealousy could rage so hot within me. I hoped I looked calm on the surface, dropping my attention to the faint amber pattern on my gown.

"And above all, a veritable child," Daniel said.

I looked at him, something lightening in my chest. "She is out in Society. Evidently she attended the Season this year."

"She is still young." He looked at me. "My tastes run older than her."

His gaze lingered on me, and I averted my eyes. It wasn't fair of him to say such things when he continued to refuse my proposals.

Oh, heavens. *Proposals*? Plural? I was utterly ridiculous.

Fanny looked toward the stone wall, her brow wrinkling. "Someone is coming."

Horses neighed, clomping across the field on the other side of the wall. Four men were passing through Mr. Waterley's land, and they hadn't seemed to notice us.

"They might not see us," Daniel said softly. "The wall could be hiding us."

Was that hope in his voice? It mirrored my emotions perfectly. I wanted them to pass unhindered, and I imagined Daniel and Fanny felt the same, for we were all quiet.

Mr. Waterley looked directly toward us, as if he could sense our thoughts bending toward him. Daniel was quick, lifting his arm in a wave and rising to greet the men. He hadn't at all made it seem like he didn't wish to speak to them now.

Mr. Waterley, Lord Belford, Mr. Egerton, and a man I assumed to be his twin brother all rode up near the wall.

"Join us, Palmer," Mr. Egerton called, lifting a gun a little to show they were about to leave on a hunting expedition.

Daniel shook his head. "I will not leave my guests, gentlemen."

Mr. Waterley's gaze slid to Fanny and remained there. I wanted to move in front of her, to shield her. How much did he know about my sister? Had Mother contacted his uncle prior to us coming here? It was clear he knew who she was. Unless his tastes ran toward girls who paid him no mind—for his attention was intentionally settled on Fanny.

"Are you having a picnic?" Lord Belford asked, his jolly expression evidence of his general kindness.

Daniel hesitated. "Yes."

Mr. Waterley looked from Fanny to me. "Where is the food?"

"It will be here shortly."

"Odd place for a picnic," Lord Belford said, then seemed to shake the thought. "But I never was one for eating outside. Insects and whatnot—you know."

There was a beat of uncomfortable silence before Daniel spoke again. "I would wish you luck today, but you will not need it."

Mr. Egerton grinned. "Waterley might. The man's been dashed distracted lately."

Mr. Waterely made a loud scoff. "For that, I shall put you to the blush." He dipped his head in a nod to Daniel, then to Fanny, then to me. "Good day."

The hunting party left shortly, and Daniel returned to our blanket, standing above us. He looked distracted, uncomfortable, his hands clasped behind his back but his shoulders tense.

I stood, brushing my hands down my gown to smooth the rumples. "You appear uneasy."

He tried to smile. "It is very likely nothing worth fretting over."

"But you *are* fretting. What is it?"

"Waterley." He ran a hand over his face as he watched them disappear from view. "He mentioned recently his need to marry a fortune. I did not think much on it then, but his behavior has been strange of late, and I wonder if he is in more of a bind than he let on."

"Because of what Mr. Egerton said about his being distracted?"

"Partially, though I've noticed it as well. It gives me leave to wonder if his fortune hunting is born of greed or necessity."

"Does he not own the neighboring estate?"

"He does."

I swallowed, avoiding looking at Fanny. "And the . . . asylum. Does he not have any stake in that?"

Daniel looked down at me, his eyes holding compassion. He did not speak for a moment, instead seeming to decide what to say.

"You need not censor yourself on my behalf," I said.

"That was not my intent," he said quietly. He looked at Fanny. "Waterley owns the asylum, but he plays no material part in the running of the place. His uncle is the overseeing doctor."

That should have brought me comfort, but it only made my muscles tighten. "If he is in need of money, what is he capable of doing? Filling his hospital with more patients? Raising the prices of their care?"

"Taking a bride with a sufficient dowry," Daniel supplied.

"Yet he has come to Northumberland with a hunting party."

"Do not forget Miss Malton. I haven't any idea of the state of her finances, but she could be his intent."

Silence whispered between us on the faint breeze, the

sounds of nature rustling around us as Fanny fidgeted quietly on the blanket.

"If you believed that, Daniel, you would not sound so uncertain."

He lowered his wry smile to me, settling it over my countenance. His fingers traced up my forearm, coming to rest just above my elbow. He gave me a gentle squeeze. "Fanny is safe while she is in my home. I will not allow anything to happen to her."

The words were a balm to my worried heart. I could not reduce the adoration and gratitude swirling warmly through my body—not even to save my own pride. I cared not that this man had resolutely decided against any liaison with me; my feelings for him were amplified by his compassion. Father had always loved Fanny, and when he was alive, I hadn't any reason to worry for her safety, not until my husband had taken things into his own hands and Mother had done nothing to stop him. With Father gone, Colin gone, and only Mother remaining, Fanny's safety was constantly on my mind.

It was something of a respite to stand beside Daniel and feel the truth in his words. His confidence and understanding lightened my heart in a way I had never before felt.

"I believe you."

Daniel laughed. "Well, you should. I mean it." His smile gentled into contentment, his eyes dropping to my lips. Was he thinking about the moment when the mouse had driven me into his arms? I certainly was.

"The mother is not returning. We could be making too much noise," Fanny said, though clearly she meant that only Daniel and I were making too much noise. She turned her head toward us, but kept her gaze from our faces. "I am hungry."

I waited for Daniel's contentment to slip, for a thread of frustration or irritation to break through his countenance, but his grin only widened, amusement lighting his brown eyes.

"Shall I fetch some food for us? I would not wish to be called dishonest, and I did tell my friends we were out here for the purpose of a picnic."

"Yes," Fanny said, returning her attention to the tree. "Picnic."

"That would be kind," I said. "Perhaps it is better if I go. Fanny does not tolerate most foods. Her diet is particular."

"What will she eat?"

"Biscuits," Fanny said, interrupting.

Daniel laughed. "Understood. Anything else, my lady?"

Fanny did not reply. She likely believed he was addressing me, though she would be mistaken. His attention was still on her. "She does not answer to that," I said. "She never has. Mother did not enforce its use with Fanny."

"Why?" Daniel asked.

"It had been her way of differentiating between us, I believe. She did not elevate my sister to the status she deserved, so others do not look at her as though she is a lady."

"Except when she was introduced to me."

"Yes, but that was different. My mother wanted you to perceive our family in a positive way. It served her purposes."

His mouth bent in a frown, a disturbed wrinkle lining his nose. "That is . . ."

"Yes," I agreed, unwilling to say more or disparage my parent further. "Regarding our picnic, bread, cheese, or apples will suffice. Nothing with meat, and no pies or anything that might have ingredients Fanny cannot identify."

He seemed mildly surprised. "What does she typically eat for her dinner, then?"

"Gruel."

"And breakfast?"

"Gruel. I try to supplement it where she will let me, but she has difficulty with most food. It has been easier to keep to a diet we can rely on."

His lips quirked into a gentle smile. His gaze lingered on Fanny for a moment before returning to me. "Do not forget the biscuits."

"Of course not," I said, the lightening in my chest making me oddly emotional. There was no accounting for why I felt like crying out my gratitude to him. All Daniel had done was accept our oddities without question. No suggestions, no believing he knew better. Simple, gentle acceptance.

"I'll return soon." Daniel bowed farewell to both of us and walked away. I watched him until he disappeared, then sat on the blanket beside my sister.

"I like Daniel, but he needs to speak quietly if he does not want to keep the mother starling from the nest."

A smile came unbidden to my lips. "I like Daniel, too."

There was a breath of silence. "I know."

CHAPTER TWENTY-FOUR

VERITY

We were able to convince Fanny to admit the eggs were abandoned just before the sun began its final descent for the evening. Daniel fetched a small crate and filled it with straw from the stables, then climbed the tree again to retrieve the eggs. The nest was impossible to maneuver through the hole in the tree, but he did his best to pull out fragments.

I shook out the blanket we'd been sitting on and began to fold it while Daniel climbed slowly down the tree with one hand, the other holding the eggs, padded by bits of nest, against his chest.

"Be careful," Fanny admonished, taking me by surprise. She stood at the base of the trunk, gathering her skirt to collect the starling eggs.

I pressed the blanket into her hands. "Here, this will be better." She took the blanket, dropping her skirt to cover her legs.

Daniel's feet hit the ground. He tucked the eggs in the center of the blanket, and Fanny knelt before the crate with them. She created a cocoon of straw and carefully placed the eggs inside, their shiny blue surface standing out against the golden straw.

"What do you know of hatching starlings?" I asked. I wished we had Lamouth's gardener here to instruct us. I depended on Fanny's knowledge entirely in this arena.

"They must be warm." Fanny kept her gaze on the eggs. "I will sleep beside them."

"You cannot do that. They're animals, Fanny. They must stay outside."

Her arms went protectively around the box.

"They'll be warm in the stables," I assured her.

Daniel took a step toward me, lowering his voice. "It does not offend me if she brings them into the house. It is a castle, after all. I'm certain they wouldn't be the first farm animals to grace its halls."

"Perhaps in the past, but now it is not the thing to bring wild starling eggs inside."

He tilted his head a little to the side. "Not usually, no. But if she needs to watch over them closely so she can be aware when they hatch—"

"It is not a good idea." I'd spoken too crisply, cutting Daniel's words off at the hilt. Fanny's attention to the birds spoke of a single-mindedness that made me nervous. My mother would not be pleased about this turn of events. The more I could do to keep the peace, the better. "Animals stay outside."

"Oscar does not," Fanny argued. She straightened her shoulders, her brow pulling together. "Which means Oscar could be a danger to these little ones."

"So you agree? They'll stay in the stables?"

"We can find them a safe place," Daniel said.

"A safe place," Fanny repeated, picking up the box. She started toward the stables.

I bent to retrieve the discarded blanket while Daniel shrugged his coat back on.

Daniel fastened his coat buttons as we walked. "You are forever devising reasons for me to need mobility in my arms."

It had not been my idea for him to shed his coat or climb the tree—he'd done both of those of his own volition. I would never argue with his choice to remove his coat so his arms could move easily, though. My lips formed a soft smile. "Impressed by my superior cunning?"

"Deviousness is a more appropriate descriptor, my lady. One would question whether you disposed of the starling yourself merely to force me to climb the tree multiple times."

I laughed at the absurdity of his joke. "Watch your volume or my sister might believe you. I cannot risk making an enemy of her until we are safely home again."

He chuckled. "Do you often make an enemy out of Fanny?"

"I often tell her things she does not like to hear, which causes her to mutiny."

"That surprises me." He peered at me. "I have seen nothing but your attempts to placate her."

"More often than not, mollifying Fanny is my only option." I watched her walk ahead of us for a moment, the crate of eggs held against her chest. "That is how it feels, at least. When we are in a safe, familiar environment, though, I try to help her push the boundaries of what she typically finds comfortable."

"'You are the mistress of your time,'" he quoted.

"Yes." My stomach gave a little flip. He listened closely. It was evident that while Daniel often tried to play the devil-may-care lout, he paid attention to Fanny and me. He was not as careless or reckless as he wanted others to believe.

"It is a good, guiding phrase to teach her."

"I can do better than that, but sometimes those things which we find to be obvious are more difficult for Fanny to under-stand. Her mind works logically and so much on a schedule that I have tried to find ways to help her practice flexibility while also making plausible sense to her."

We turned the corner out of the trees to find the sun setting behind Arden Castle. I admired the oranges and yellows splashed across the sky as if with watercolors, the clouds shadowed and wispy, adding dimension to the sunset. I inhaled the fresh air and exhaled my earlier frustrations. When I looked at Daniel again, he was watching me. "What is it?" I asked.

"You are an admirable woman, Verity."

Heat rushed to my cheeks. "I was not speaking with the intent of making you admire me. Indeed, I believe my dedication to Fanny might be considered excessive to most."

"Trust me. I suffer no illusions where your intent is concerned."

I eyed him warily. "Is that enigmatic statement meant to provide me with some relief? I fear it only does the opposite."

"I meant it precisely how you think I meant it," he said quietly, looking at me.

I couldn't hold his gaze anymore, so I watched Fanny's sure steps ahead of me on the garden path toward the house. "You are a flirt, Daniel Palmer."

"Indeed."

His lack of argument disappointed me. Had I wanted him to admit he meant the words in all sincerity? That he was developing feelings the way I was developing them? It was absurd. Ridiculous. My current situation provided no room for such delicate feelings, anyway. It would do nothing but distract me from my main objective—to protect my sister.

It took the better part of a half hour to find a situation for the eggs that pleased Fanny: an empty stall in the stables with extra straw to keep them warm.

Once they were situated, I pressed my hands together. "Shall we go change for dinner now?"

Fanny watched the eggs, crouched low to see them. "I would like to eat here."

Daniel stepped away, and I was grateful he seemed to sense my desire for space.

"We can return first thing in the morning to check on them, but we need to go to the house for dinner."

"I would prefer to remain out here."

"I understand that. However, you are not an animal, and this building is for animals. I promise we will return first thing in the morning."

"If they hatch—"

"If they hatch in the night, you will be able to feed them immediately in the morning. The extra time will not harm them."

She bent to check the eggs once more before rising. "Very well."

It was with relief that I walked back to the house with her, Daniel just behind us. He paused in the entryway, forcing me to stop and look at him.

"I will see you both at dinner tonight?" he asked.

"Fanny eats in our room," I said, though he knew that. She walked ahead of me, mounting the stairs.

"She is welcome at the table. I understand she is not out yet, but—"

"Thank you, but it is not allowed." I tried to smile.

"Allowed? It is my table."

"Yes, but she has far too many food aversions to make dining in company a pleasant experience for her. My mother made the rule a few years ago, and it has been for the best."

Daniel looked to where she was disappearing at the top of the stairs and lowered his voice. "I am happy to provide a different meal for her than the rest of the table receives. If she would like to spend time with us, she is more than welcome."

I hesitated, unsure of how much to share. "Her diet is only part of the problem. We had a situation once when Fanny ate with us and the duck was brought out. It distressed her terribly in front of my mother's guests."

"I see."

215

"It had been our local vicar and his wife, and neither of them were as mortified by Fanny's outburst as my mother or my late husband had been. But we decided then it was best for Fanny to eat in the kitchen. For Fanny's sake, I never argued the point."

"I can see why she might dislike being in the dining room. Her love of birds is . . . strong."

"That is putting it mildly," I said, softening my words with a smile.

"I will not press you further on this. Please tell me if there's anything more I can do."

"You have done enough, Daniel."

He bowed softly, and we parted ways.

When I reached the top of the stairs, my mother's voice whispered sharply, snagging my attention. "Verity, come." She turned back into her room, and I followed her.

When I closed her door, I startled to find fire in her snapping eyes. "How much did you tell the earl of Fanny's past?"

"What do you mean?"

"What have you told him?" she repeated.

"I've told him nothing, Mother." I was tempted to explain to her how we had spent our day, but anything so eccentric as watching a nest for such a long period of time would only deepen her unpleasant mood.

"If you allow him to learn we have madness in our blood, do you think he will take you for a wife?"

I stepped back and bumped into the door, reeling as though I'd been slapped. "It hardly matters. My sister is not mad."

Mother shook her head sadly. "I wish she were not, but you know as well as I do that she is. You truly believe the earl will remember Fanny's sweet-tempered heart and forgive her madness when it sets off? That he will not believe her more suited to medical care after he sees her upset and unreachable? You cannot claim such ignorance after watching how others have reacted to her fits."

By others, she meant Colin. Her words were a harsh reminder of the possibilities of trusting others. Colin had been kind and generous with his time toward Fanny until she had become inconsolable, humming and quaking. I owned that she had appeared utterly disturbed, but I had not expected Colin to be so repulsed by her.

Fear crept into my chest. I couldn't disagree with my mother. It was impossible to know how anyone would react until they were in that very situation. Even when Fanny had become upset here in the kitchen, Daniel had not been present to witness it.

Then again, he had seen bits of her discomfort in snippets, and not once had he seemed repulsed.

Daniel was a good and kind man. He deserved for me to think the best of his character. But my mother was correct, and I could not discount the possibility that his opinions would change.

"What would you have me do, Mother? I am trying my best to balance Fanny and the earl. But she is unchanging and he is uninterested in marriage."

"Then *make* him interested," she said quietly. "You are running out of time." She walked over to her door and opened it, waiting for me to leave.

I stepped like a ghost across the corridor to my own chamber, my mind in a whirl. I allowed Mary to help me dress for dinner while Fanny sat at the table, sketching eggs in a crate full of straw. It was not until I sat at the dressing table, watching Mary style my hair for dinner, that Mother's words settled in my hollow chest, driving cold ice through my veins. *You are running out of time.*

What clock had she begun, and what would happen when the time was up?

My attention wavered at dinner, my mind snagging on Mother's threat and unwilling to move past it. Lady Moorington seemed to keep the conversation moving nicely, but I had a hard time following it while I analyzed those words: *you are running out of time.* She meant to scare me into action, I knew that much. Daniel had already proven he wouldn't marry me, which meant I needed to contrive another plan to care for Fanny, and it was very clear that returning to Lamouth permanently would not be an option—not while Mother was there.

But where would we go? Could I contrive employment elsewhere? Daniel had been willing to hire me and allow us to remain at the dower house at Lamouth, but would that be too close to Mother? What would she be driven to do in order to drag me to London in search of a husband and a fortune?

By the time we removed to the drawing room following dinner, I was devising a plan to excuse myself early. My worrying had given me a headache, and I was in no fit state to be in company. I adjusted my shawl around my shoulders, ready to crawl into bed and succumb to sleep.

"Shall we play whist tonight?" Lady Moorington asked when we settled in the chairs.

The door cracked open before anyone could give her a response. The butler stepped inside and looked at me. "A message for you, my lady." He wasn't holding any paper or salver, so I stood and crossed the room toward him.

I noticed Mary standing in the doorway and slipped into the corridor beside her, nodding my head to Worthlin. "Thank you."

Mary chewed on her lip, worrying me.

I waited for the butler to walk away. "What is it, Mary?"

"It's Fanny, my lady. She's missing."

CHAPTER TWENTY-FIVE

VERITY

Search first, panic later. I repeated the words to myself while I regained my equilibrium. I would gather information and form a plan before succumbing to a fit of hysterics. Resolutely, I focused on breathing steadily. "Please explain."

Mary nodded. "Nothing seemed out of the ordinary when she ate her dinner. Then she remained at the table in your room to draw. I took the dinner tray downstairs to the kitchen as I always do, and when I returned, she was gone. I looked everywhere. The sitting room, the kitchen, your mother's bedroom—anywhere I could think she'd gone. Fanny isn't anywhere to be found."

My mind conjured an image of Mr. Waterley binding her wrists and tossing her into the back of his wagon, carting her away. I shook it, banishing it at once. *Search first, panic later.* I looked over my shoulder at Mother, who was watching me through the open doorway with a grim expression.

Could she possibly know already? Was this what she meant by the downturned lips and slightly hooded eyes? Or perhaps it was the root of the ominous warning: time was running out because she had already sent for men to take Fanny away. My

219

hands shook, my feet glued in place. I didn't know whether to run and look for Fanny or turn and beg my mother to explain.

Search first had been my advice to myself. I would heed it.

"Mary, you look again inside: upstairs, in the kitchen, the sitting room—every place you've already looked in case you crossed paths with her and she has since returned. I will look in the stables."

She started to move but looked back, surprised. "Why the stables?"

"The starling's eggs. She could—" I swallowed. "I sincerely hope she is looking after them now." It was a possibility, at least.

She nodded, agreeing with me.

"Now, Mary," I said with quiet urgency.

My maid turned down the corridor and disappeared through a dark paneled doorway, which I assumed was the entrance to the servants' staircase.

I spun toward the front door of the house, but had not taken one step before I heard my name behind me.

"Verity?" Daniel asked.

I squeezed my eyes closed. Mother's warnings from earlier about how people could change, how it was impossible to predict how they would react to any given situation, were fresh in my mind when I turned to face him.

His concern was evident. I looked beyond him to the drawing room, but could not see either of our mothers from this angle.

"Is something wrong?" he asked.

"It is likely nothing."

He hesitated, seeming to sense my tension, or perhaps just the eagerness I felt to be on my way. I hadn't turned back to fully face him. "May I help?"

"I do not—" My hands curled into fists, my nails biting into my palms. This could be the moment where he found us wild, where his opinion of Fanny could alter. It was a risk I had to take. "My sister is missing. It is likely nothing. I am going to look at the stables."

"I will accompany you."

"You need not—"

"I am not letting you walk so far in the dark alone, Verity." He spoke calmly, his dark eyes roaming my face. "May I please accompany you?"

"Yes." I turned and walked swiftly towards the door, not bothering to wait for him. He did not need me to. He caught up quickly, reaching the door before me and opening it so I could continue through. We went down the stone steps and crossed the gravel drive. My shawl fluttered off my shoulders and flew behind me, but I didn't turn back for it. I would find it later. First I had to find Fanny.

"Worthlin told you she was missing?" he asked.

"No, my maid did. She has checked all the rooms in the castle Fanny would be familiar with and grew concerned." My breath came in shallow spurts. My lungs struggled, unused to being called upon so heavily.

"Fanny is likely with the eggs," he said. "She had difficulty leaving them behind."

"I had the same thought." My voice rose higher each time I spoke. "It could be nothing. She is probably safe."

"I understand you are telling yourself these things more than you are telling me," he said kindly, "but be comforted to know they are all true."

They *were* true. I hoped that would bring me some comfort, but I would not be able to untense my entire body until I saw my sister again.

I could not inhale deeply enough nor walk fast enough. My lungs were not expanding to capacity. The stables were in sight, and I rushed toward them, uncaring if I looked ungraceful or gangly. I'd never been good at running—I hadn't occasion for it. I tore through the stable doors, my lungs on fire, my gaze searching wildly over the empty room for my sister.

"She isn't here," Daniel said, checking the stall where we'd tucked the crate with the nest of eggs.

I turned, stepping outside, scanning the dark horizon. Helplessness welled up around me like a dense bank of smoke. Fanny's absence was thick, pressing against my chest. I banished the flashes of men taking her away, doing my best to shove the unwelcome fears from my mind.

"Perhaps the tree?" Daniel suggested.

My mind spun. Tree? Or a wagon driven by one of Mr. Waterley's lackeys? My stomach was sick, and I struggled to move.

Daniel moved to stand directly in front of me, pulling my focus from darting around the dark grounds. "We will keep looking, Verity. She cannot have gone far."

"You do not know that."

"It does no good to give up now."

I closed my eyes, drawing in a breath. He was correct. We had not exhausted the property yet. Every moment we wasted was a moment she could be alone and upset. "My maid is searching the house. I will check the tree." I started toward it.

Daniel jogged to catch up to me. "Has this happened before?"

"A handful of times, but never like this."

"What is different now?"

"We are at a strange place," I said between heaving breaths. "There is a—a threat to her safety."

"What threat?"

Could he truly not know? After I was so angry with him the other day and the conversation we had during our picnic, I expected him to have some understanding of the situation. "Your neighbor."

"Waterley?" He scoffed. "The man might be greedy, but he would never take your sister—"

"Unless my mother asked him to," I said, running ahead. My stomach grew sicker, recalling the last time Fanny had gone missing and I'd run after her, pulling her from the wagon before the men could take her away, my father berating Colin for stepping out of bounds. My heart clenched, remembering the confusion she'd had then and the anger I'd felt toward my mother and husband.

"Your mother?" he asked, shocked.

I swallowed thickly. "She has done this before."

Daniel's head whipped toward me.

It was not the time for explanations, which he seemed to sense, for he did not press me for further information. I needed to see the tree, to find Fanny. I prayed with every step, lifting the hem of my gown and pounding my feet into the ground. I could hear Daniel running beside me, but I paid him no mind.

When I reached the trees, I realized my idiocy. I hadn't brought a lantern, and it was too dark to see.

Daniel took my hand, and I almost jerked away on impulse. "I know the way," he said.

I let him lead me through the trees, searching as we moved for any motion or sound from my sister. We made it to the stone wall, and Daniel held fast to my hand. I let him lead me along until we came to the place where we had seen the starling's nest.

"Fanny!" I called. I didn't see her anywhere.

Daniel released my hand, walking a little away to search. My heart beat out of my chest, a combination of nerves and exercise my body wasn't accustomed to.

"Fanny!" I called again.

"Verity?"

I froze. The voice was quiet above the blood pumping in my ears. I looked up and spotted my sister's lavender gown swinging high in the tree. "I cannot move," she said, her voice shaky.

"Are you stuck?"

There were too many beats of silence. "Yes," she finally called back timidly.

I turned to Daniel, but he'd already shrugged off his coat and tossed it over the wall. He strode to the tree and pulled himself up swiftly, climbing with the surety of a man who had been called to action. "I am coming, Fanny. Stay where you are." For such a tense moment, his voice was surprisingly even.

I wrapped my arms around my waist, squeezing my sides and stepping back to watch them. Daniel made it to Fanny's feet and seemed to hesitate, tugging on a branch that looked too thin before trying a new one. He put his foot on a smaller branch, butting it right next to the trunk. "Be careful," I called.

"All will be well." His confidence was inspiring. He spoke to Fanny softly, though I couldn't hear what he said. My blood still pulsed loudly in my ears, washing like waves crashing against a rocky beach.

It probably only took a few minutes, but it felt like ages while Daniel guided Fanny down the tree one branch at a time. My entire body was shaking by the time her feet touched the ground. I crossed the distance in two large steps and pulled her toward me, crushing her into a hug despite knowing she did not appreciate them.

"You frightened me."

"Sorry," she muttered.

"I thought . . ." The words shriveled on my tongue. I could not share my fears with her. I shook the awful image from my head of Waterley taking her away, of my mother's grim expression that must've been due to her general discontent with me, and enjoyed the relief of holding my sister in my arms.

I tightened my hold around her. "I am so grateful you are safe." Hot tears threatened to roll down my cheeks, but I did not allow them freedom. I drew in a shaky breath and leaned back. "What were you doing?"

"The eggs need more of their nest if they are to be warm."

"It was too hard for Daniel to remove the nest from that small hole, remember?"

"I learned that," she said, looking up at the tree. "I worry for—"

"You can give them my shawl. If we wrap it around the eggs, it will act as a nest and keep them warm." I believed the straw to be sufficient, but Fanny clearly didn't.

"Truly? Thank you."

"Yes. Let us go retrieve it. It fell from my shoulders some-where near the front steps of the house. I am certain it is there still. But we must hurry. We need to inform Mary you are safe, or she could still be looking."

Fanny lowered her head, looking at the dark ground.

"You must tell us when you do things like this," I admon-ished. "You cannot leave without informing someone, or you worry us."

"I will in the future."

"You *must*. Do you understand that? It was so frightening to not know where you are."

She would not look at me. "I understand."

Daniel stepped behind me to pick up his coat and put it back on. He buttoned the front and joined us, the moonlight washing over his face. "This removal of my coat is becoming quite a habit."

I appreciated his lightness. He hadn't thus far been repulsed by Fanny, and all I could sense in his countenance now was relief. It gave me leave to appreciate him fully. But I could not give ventilation to my deepest gratitudes presently, not when my body was coming down from the highest sense of anxiety. Instead, I settled on continuing his joke, though I could sense how tired my voice sounded. "One might wonder why you ever put it on in the first place?"

He gave a soft chuckle. "I often ask myself the same thing."

CHAPTER TWENTY-SIX

DANIEL

Verity located the shawl quickly and gave it to Fanny. While they went to the stables to tend to the nest, I went inside the house and asked Worthlin to locate Mary and inform her Fanny was safe.

My feet crunched on the gravel drive as I made my way back to where the sisters were. Verity's fear had been complete, its depth taking me by surprise. When she mentioned Waterley, I'd thought she could not have been in earnest. That she believed her mother would contract with him to take Fanny away? That didn't sit well in my stomach.

I would like to think Waterley would have some compunction about following through on a directive like that, even if it meant adding to his coffers. I had known the man my entire life, and while he had made some questionable choices, he was not evil.

But according to Verity, this was not the first time Lady Huxley had done something like this. Would Waterley even know to question the orders if they came from his uncle? I shook my head. It would not be Waterley anyway, would it?

Rather a hired man. Though his uncle had fetched people occasionally himself, so it was not outside the realm of possibility.

Lanterns hung in the stables, sending a warm wash of light over the stalls, and the horses arched their heads into the walkway in their curiosity. I walked down the straw-strewn path until I reached the empty stall at the end and leaned against the door, observing the women. Fanny crouched at the crate, arranging the emerald shawl to her satisfaction. Verity stood behind her, her arms crossed over her chest and a tired expression on her face.

"Is everything in order?" I asked.

Verity looked at me, but Fanny didn't. "The shawl should help." Verity shot me a tremulous smile. "I admit it looks much warmer now."

"Shall we return inside?"

"You've told Mr. Worthlin to pass on my message?"

"Yes, he is locating Mary straightaway."

She gave a faint nod, but her mouth was again turned down at the ends. An overwhelming urge to pull her into my arms and lend her comfort came over me, bringing a rush of surprise with it. The way she held herself, her arms around her waist, struck me. Who was there to comfort Verity? Fanny loved her sister, of that I had no doubt, but she was not a physically affectionate person. If anything, she was the opposite, purposefully avoiding it.

Verity deserved to be embraced as well. I knew I was drawn to her. I could not seem to look at anything else when she was in the room, and I had a hard time thinking of other things when she was out of it. The desire to hold her was overwhelming in its magnitude, taking me by surprise.

"Are you ready, Fanny?" she asked. "We will check on them first thing tomorrow after breakfast."

Fanny hesitated, arranging the shawl in silence. After a few more minutes, she stood, turning to leave. She didn't say anything, passing her sister and me and walking toward the exit.

Verity gave a little sigh and followed. We walked silently back toward the house, Fanny ahead of us.

"When I am not here, do you walk by her side?"

Verity looked at me sharply, confusion on her brow. "No. Not usually, at least. She does not enjoy conversation unless it is necessary, and she usually goes at her own pace." She gave a faint smile. "Is that not obvious?"

"Yes. It was just a curiosity."

When we reached the base of the stone steps, Verity turned and pinched my sleeve to halt me. "Daniel?"

"What is it? You look so worried you're starting to worry me."

"I only wanted to thank you. I do not know what I would have done had you not been there." She shook her head and wrapped her arms around herself again. "No, that is false. I would have had to climb a tree."

"I am glad you weren't forced to resort to that. Some of those branches were not strong enough to hold my weight." I gave her a humorless laugh. "It is a miracle one of us did not crash to the ground this evening."

She closed her eyes and drew in a shaky breath. "I was so scared," she whispered.

Hang convention. I reached forward and pulled her into my arms, sliding my hands across her back and pressing her into an embrace. She collapsed into me, and I held her up while her shuddering breath vented fear and exhaustion and anxiety onto my shoulder.

"She is safe now," I murmured into her hair. She smelled of a blossoming garden and reminded me of a sunny summer day behind Arden. "You are safe."

"For how long?" She shook her head and leaned back, but didn't step out of my arms.

I looked down at her. The overwhelming temptation to kiss her overcame me, and it took every ounce of strength to resist.

"As long as you are in my home, you are safe," I promised.

She looked sadly away, and I hated the impression I received that she didn't agree. Not that she didn't trust *me*, perhaps—rather that she felt it was out of my control. I searched for the words to argue against what I imagined she might be thinking when she pressed gently against my chest and stepped out of my arms.

"Forgive me, Verity. That was inappropriate."

"It was exactly what I needed. Thank you." She turned and walked up the steps.

I swallowed a joke about how this private moment between us was only lacking a marriage proposal. It wouldn't be humorous now, not when I almost wished it wasn't a joke.

Verity was mounting the stairs toward the bedrooms when I made it inside and shut the door behind me. I couldn't follow her up, and I assumed she wanted to be alone with Fanny, but I wanted to go with her. That was unusual for me. I was unused to desiring any sort of emotional connection with a woman.

Instead, I stood near the bottom of the stairs and waited until she disappeared before I sought refuge in the study. The bottle of brandy beckoned me from the bureau. I pulled it from the cupboard, uncorked it, and splashed a finger full into a glass. Picking up the cork, I rolled it through my fingers, glancing between the half-full bottle and the glass. I never stopped at one. It was far more comfortable to lose myself than to sit in my discomfort.

But running from my feelings and my problems had never actually helped, anyway, had it? All the brandy did was postpone whatever disappointment, disgust, or irritation I felt towards myself.

Maybe if I sat in the discomfort tonight, I could move on from my disappointment more quickly. If Verity had given me an opening, I would have kissed her. I wanted to kiss her, and I never trifled with ladies. It was clear my control was growing weaker.

I shoved the cork into the bottle and put it back in the cabinet, then carried the glass to my chair and slouched against the smooth leather cushion. I closed my eyes and took a sip. It settled on my tongue, and I swirled the brandy in the glass before resting my forearm against the chair and letting it hang over the side. Drinking for the enjoyment of the beverage instead of with the intent of succumbing to oblivion was an entirely different experience.

The drink provided no comfort. It didn't bring me any sense of satisfaction. What I wanted was to be upstairs with Verity and Fanny, an odd notion for me.

A light scratch at the door stole my attention, and I turned my head in time to see my mother open it softly. She seemed hesitant, stepping quietly in and closing the door behind her, watching me with slightly widened eyes as if attempting to gauge what sort of mood she would find me in. She had been here playing hostess for weeks. Had I just now noticed the eggshells she walked on around me?

"I just received a concerning bit of news from Worthlin," she said, regally stepping forward.

I gestured to the chair opposite me. She seemed surprised but covered it quickly. "Lady Frances was lost outside near the wall dividing our land from Waterley's. Her maid couldn't find her and was worried, so I helped Lady Verity search."

"That was kind of you."

I ignored the comment. It was what any gentleman would do. "She's been found and returned to her room."

Mother seemed to weigh her words. "Lady Verity takes a great deal upon herself."

I gave a gentle scoff. "That might be putting it mildly." I looked at the brandy in my glass. "Has Lady Huxley said anything of note about her?"

"Nothing directly. I believe her questioning about your responsibilities and attachment to this estate revealed some of her intentions."

"What would those be?"

"To contrive a match between you and one of her daughters. I'm not sure she has a preference on which, though it seems she believes Lady Verity might have more of a chance of winning your favor."

I tipped my glass back and swallowed the rest of it before setting it on the table with a light thunk. I wasn't particularly inclined to give that woman anything she desired, but this was one thing we did agree on. Of the two, Verity was the one who had any chance at all of receiving an offer of marriage. I could not look at Fanny in any way except as an older brother might.

"Does the lady hold your esteem?" Mother asked, watching me closely.

"You must know she does, Mother." I spoke softly, but it was a truth that settled in the room, bringing silence with it for a spell.

"I was beginning to wonder. I hadn't expected you to remain at Arden as long as you have, especially after I invited Lady Huxley and her daughters to visit. When you stayed, involving yourself with your guests so fully, it took me by great surprise. Especially in light of the hunting party so close at hand."

"I do not have a taste for hunting at present."

"Which is odd, you must admit. What *do* you have a taste for?"

A quieter life, I almost said. It was part of the reason I had returned to Arden—so I could relax, slow down, and no longer need to be the center of every social event my friends hosted. I'd been running so hard for so long I had forgotten how good it felt to slow down until I came here. I mulled over this until my mother spoke again.

"Your father would be angry if he knew I was about to confide in you." Her voice was gentle, the words measured as if she still didn't know whether she wanted to speak them as they left her mouth.

I sat up.

"He was not always perfect," she said, giving me a look. "When we were first married, he spent quite a lot of time with his friends in much the same manner you seem to do. We were often separated, and your father never gained a reputation for being a cad, but he certainly had his share of larks. He drank to excess with his friends and made some foolish decisions in those years."

"You cannot be describing my father."

She wore a sad smile. "I am. It was a rather short career in recklessness, and he ceased altogether when you were born."

My stomach clenched. I said nothing, allowing her to talk. My mother did not typically confide in me in this manner. She would not be doing so now unless she had something important to share.

"Your father met you as a precious little babe, and he made the choice at once to cease his reckless behaviors. He focused on learning the intricacies of running Arden and how to profit from the land. He was not always the humble man you knew."

"You say that as if you believe it is a choice and not inherent behavior."

"It *is* a choice, Daniel. You choose how you want to act, whom you want to be, the type of man you want to present to the world."

"Perhaps I need to have a son, then."

She looked at me long enough that I began to squirm. "That

is not at all what I meant. You have the choice, Daniel. You can choose to spend more time in worthy pursuits as you seemed to have done this week. You can choose to have one glass of port after dinner without finishing the bottle. You can *choose* to forgive yourself for your past mistakes and be a better man."

Her words slapped me. "How do you know I haven't forgiven myself?" I asked hoarsely. She was correct, but I thought I'd hidden my regrets deeply, burying them in a devil-may-care attitude. I thought I'd been successful.

My mother's knowing eyes proved differently. "I love you, Daniel. It does not matter what ill choices you make or the amount of times you run away, your actions will never lessen my love for you. Your worth is not defined by your mistakes. *That* is what is inherent. Everything else, you choose. I am challenging you to make the difficult choice and be a better man." She stood, her shoulders bent with exhaustion. "When Lady Huxley and her daughters leave, I intend to do the same. I will visit Jane and Ewan before returning home. You are welcome to join me."

I gave a soft nod, still running over the words she said.

She crossed the small space and bent down to kiss the top of my head, an action she had not taken in many years. "I love you, Daniel."

"Thank you, Mother," I said, struggling against the emotion building in my chest. "I love you, too."

She gave me a sad smile and left the room. Aside from a few moments, I had been making the choice all week to stay home, to spend time with my mother and guests, and to avoid drinking to excess. How did I feel? Was it a sustainable change in behavior? My gaze flicked to the bureau against the far wall, the one holding the bottle of brandy. I'd only taken one glass, and it had been enough.

Oscar trotted into the room through the narrowly open door and slumped on the carpet at my feet. I bent down and scratched him behind the ears. "What do you think, boy? Can a man change?"

He bent his neck, turning to look up at me, before slumping back down on the floor. I sighed. I didn't know whether to trust it either.

CHAPTER TWENTY-SEVEN

VERITY

Since discovering Fanny in the tree last night, I had spent every spare moment devising and dismissing ideas for how I could provide for our future. Mother was not to be trusted any longer, and the sooner I devised a way to claim independence, the better. Selling the sapphire pendant and diamond earbobs Colin had gifted me was the only viable option I had come up with—they could keep us comfortable for a few years, I imagined. I hadn't the slightest idea how much they would fetch. It would be enough to start us in a cottage somewhere, but it was in no way a permanent solution.

After my mother's ominous warning that I was running out of time—or Fanny was running out of time—I thought a temporary solution was enough for now.

Fanny walked beside me as we made our way toward the house after visiting the chickens. The starlings had yet to hatch, and Fanny desired to continue her schedule as usual, altering it only to check on the eggs hourly.

It would certainly provide us with a good deal more exercise, but aside from that, I was unable to find the benefits of arranging our day in such a way.

Lady Moorington was in the entryway when we returned to the house. Fanny passed by her and moved to the stairs without comment. The countess smiled at me, so I halted, dipping in a small curtsy. "Good day, my lady."

"The sun is so warm and lovely today, it gives me hope the rain is behind us for good. I thought it might be nice to take a drive." Her eyes flicked to where Fanny was mounting the stairs before returning to me. "Would that be agreeable? I thought to have Cook pack us a bit of a picnic."

"Has my mother been invited?"

"Yes, and she believes her ankle injury is acting up."

This ankle injury was news to me. In all likelihood, it was feigned with the design of remaining indoors. I wanted to ask if Daniel would join us.

It seemed Lady Moorington read my mind. "My son has agreed to accompany us."

A drive sounded lovely in this weather. I welcomed the chance to see more of the local countryside, but convincing Fanny to leave her eggs was another issue. "I am not certain my sister would be agreeable to the scheme, but I can ask her."

Lady Moorington smiled warmly at me. She was regality personified, with such elegant bearing and kind eyes. "Shall we agree to meet outside in a half hour if your sister approves of the outing?"

"That would be sufficient." If I could not convince Fanny to leave by then, I likely would not be convincing her to leave at all.

I found her in the sitting room, sketching the mother starling standing on the end of a branch. Pulling out the chair, I sat beside her. "Lady Moorington invited us on a picnic. I know it would change our schedule for the day, but it would be nice to leave the estate for a bit. Perhaps we would see other local birds."

She paused, but her attention stayed on the paper, the pencil hovering above the beak she was shading.

"When we first decided to come here, we talked about making a study of Northumberland birds. It is difficult to make a study when all we have seen are starlings and chickens."

"And swallows," she added.

"Yes, and the swallows near the garden. Perhaps we will see what else there is nearby."

"We draw now."

"Usually, that is the case. I thought we could draw when we return."

She pulled out her watch and consulted the time.

I held my breath, hoping I had convinced her. "We need to change now if we want to have enough time to check on your eggs before we leave."

"I would prefer to draw," Fanny said.

My stomach clenched. "You could bring paper and a pencil to sketch in the carriage if we see birds. It would be easier to add them to your report if you draw them immediately."

The idea seemed to bring her some excitement, her eyes widening and glancing quickly at me before settling on the watch again. She was likely debating the merits between doing what most appealed to her versus what she felt she had to do.

I reached across the table but didn't take her hand. "Fanny, our schedule changes quite often while we're here. Have you noticed that?"

"Yes," she whispered, "and it causes me great distress."

My heart pulled toward her. "Sometimes those changes have led to more special experiences, though, have they not?"

She thought about it more. "Special experiences?"

"Finding the starling. Flying the kite. Saving the eggs. Those were all the result of a change in schedule, of you becoming the mistress of your time. Perhaps we ought to try to change your schedule every so often to see if it is something that pleases us."

"Us? Would a carriage ride with Lady Moorington please you?"

Her thoughtfulness warmed my chest. "On a lovely day like this? It would. I think it would please our hostess very much, which is important to consider."

She looked up at me. "Will Daniel be there?"

"I believe so."

She sighed. "Then we may go." She stood, gathering paper and pencils. "I would like to visit the eggs before we leave."

"Of course," I said, fighting a grin. My heart swelled with appreciation and achievement and victory. "I think we are going to have a lovely day."

Daniel

I wasn't fond of Mother's idea to take an open carriage ride through the country lanes until I discovered her intent to include our guests in the invitation. I sat across from Verity now, the sun beating down on us, my attention roaming the straight planes of her nose and jaw, her pink lips. She was far more beautiful than the scenery around us.

"I was told your castle began as a monastery," Verity said, directing the question to my mother.

"It did. When it became a private home, there were many improvements made, and it was greatly fortified to withstand attacks. I believe it has retained its general appearance as a fortress quite well, though the monastery is harder to sort out until you are inside."

"It is such a grand building. I imagine its history is just as rich."

A carriage came our direction from the opposite way, and I

recognized the yellow lacquered side instantly. The top was removed, leaving its occupants open to the elements, much as ours was. Two of its women were elaborately, vibrantly dressed. "Blast."

"Language," Mother whispered.

"My apologies." I watched the carriage to see if it intended to slow at all.

To my dismay, it did. Miss Edith waved a handkerchief in the air, and her coachman stopped their carriage on the side of the road, ours slowing to match.

"Lovely day for a drive," Miss Kelby said. "We were just on our way to call on you."

Mother smiled graciously. "What a treat that would have been."

"We wanted to invite you to dine with us before the assemblies."

"A splendid idea." Mother looked at me, raising her eyebrows. Had she not been so refined, I thought she would have resorted to nudging.

I cleared my throat. "I am not certain if our entire party is attending the assembly."

Verity smiled apologetically. "No, I am afraid my sister and my mother do not plan to attend."

"We are glad to welcome anyone in your house who chooses to go," Miss Kelby said. "My goddaughter, Miss Martin, would very much enjoy having another young lady at the table. Would you not?"

All eyes turned on Miss Martin. "Oh yes, I would." Her eyes were wide in genuine interest. I imagined after her godmothers' company all day, she would not mind another young lady at all.

Verity's mouth tightened. "I must ensure I can leave my mother."

"Of course, of course, dear."

That was an excuse. Was I the only one who could see it? She likely meant whether she could leave her *sister*.

The Kelby women spoke to my mother for a moment longer, but I watched Verity's troubled gaze flit between Miss Martin and Fanny. When she raised her eyes and met mine, I lifted an eyebrow slightly. She shook her head softly, as if to say it was not the time to discuss what was on her mind. I liked to think she would be willing to discuss it later, though.

The Kelby sisters bid us farewell, and their carriage went on its way.

"If they intended to visit us, does this mean they will turn around and follow our carriage?" Fanny asked, taking me by surprise. I hadn't realized she'd been paying attention.

Mother laughed, and the sound eased through my chest and made me smile. "I suppose that means they might," she said.

"Shall we ask Tom to lead us down to the ruins for our picnic?"

"Oh Daniel, what a fantastic idea." Mother pressed her hands together. "It would be such a treat to show Lady Verity and Lady Frances the old ruins. They are a romantic sight."

"Are there birds there?" Fanny asked.

"I suppose there might be," I said. "We can look. Would you like that?"

Fanny looked at her lap. "Yes."

"Then it is decided." I waved to get my coachman's attention and directed him to take us to the ruins. A gentle breeze rolled over us as the sun beat down overhead. Green hills rose around us in every direction, yellow grass combing the sides of the road, making the landscape wilder than it was near Arden. The ruins came into view, crumbled rock bleeding down into overgrown grass.

Verity drew in a slight intake of breath. I had to admit that the scene would border on romantic, had I not been sitting beside my mother. "Shall we walk around before pulling out the baskets of food?"

The women agreed, and I helped each of them out. Fanny went off immediately toward the rocky outlines of old buildings.

"She was hoping to see more local birds," Verity explained.

"I shall keep my eye out for them."

Verity walked away with my mother to see the stones closer, and I followed them at a sedate pace. Regret pulled at me as I watched them chatting comfortably. I had spent so much of my time avoiding my mother's matchmaking attempts or comparing myself to what I thought she wanted me to be that I was never able to enjoy the time I spent in her company. It was not until our conversation, when she had told me how much she loved me, that I realized how deeply I had needed to hear those words—how long I had been running from them.

If I could turn back to the day she'd arrived at Arden weeks ago and enjoy her company better, I would. Since her marriage to my stepfather, I had allowed distance to grow between us. In my anger toward him, I was still allowing it to fester.

I had not liked the man or my mother's ability to marry him so soon after my father died, but I did love my mother, and she deserved my respect and attention. She would soon be leaving, and her time in my home felt wasted now—an opportunity squandered.

The rest of the hour passed in pleasant conversation as we walked around the ruins. We pulled out baskets of small hand pies, slices of bread, ham, cheese, plums, and bottles of wine. Our party enjoyed pointing out a handful of birds for Fanny to sketch, but the trouble in Verity's eyes and the discontent in my mother's led me to believe no one was quite as happy as they seemed.

I spent the return drive deciding not to waste another moment in the short time I had to spend in my mother's company. I owed her an apology for my behavior. Her revelations about my father had been harder to swallow than I thought, and they pricked at me like a woodpecker. Father had been such an upstanding man of superb character in all the years I had known him. If he could choose to be so, could I not do the same? Was it even possible for me?

When the carriage pulled up to Arden Castle, the front door of the house opened and a large man stepped onto the front portico. My stomach clenched involuntarily and Mother's slight gasp only heightened my irritation. Her husband darkened my doorway with his unreasonable height and too-wide grin.

"I came immediately to share the good news," my stepfather, Lord Moorington, bellowed. His deep voice carried easily, and his joy was unmistakable.

I hopped down from the carriage and helped my mother out. She crossed the gravel and held both of her hands out toward her husband in a motion that churned my stomach. "Has the babe arrived?"

"Just a few days ago," Lord Moorington said, his eyes twinkling. "And it was not just *one* babe."

Mother gasped. "Oh, blessed heavens! Come inside, dear. I want to hear everything." She stopped just before the door but did not release his hand. "Where are my manners? Allow me to introduce Lady Verity and Lady Frances, daughters of the late Lord Huxley."

Moorington looked at me quickly, putting all the pieces together before bowing to the ladies and saying everything which was proper in greeting. He was the perfect gentleman in every way except for one. He was not my father.

"Ladies, a pleasure."

"Do not concern yourself with us," Verity said. "Go and share your good news."

Mother gave her a grateful smile and went with Moorington into the house. I watched them leave, my gaze hovering on the door they had disappeared through. My house was tainted now, ruined by the presence of a man I loathed. A true usurper.

Verity spoke again, pulling me from my trance. "We are going to the stables to check on the eggs if you'd like to come, Daniel."

I faced her. "I would like that above all things."

CHAPTER TWENTY-EIGHT

DANIEL

Horses neighed, begging for attention all along the stalls. Men moved about, working while Fanny sat on a saddle blanket nestled beside her crate, watching the eggs. Periodically she would adjust the shawl Verity had donated or move the straw, anything to ensure the eggs were warm enough.

I sat beside Verity against the opposite wall on a crude bench of crates I had tossed a saddle blanket over. It was far from comfortable, but I would remain here all day if it meant enjoying her company.

Verity smoothed a lock of auburn hair away from her face. "Your stepfather seems a very jolly sort."

My mood darkened immediately. "I think becoming a grandfather would do that to most men. Ensuring the line undoubtedly brought him even more joy."

"It is not insignificant to receive security, Daniel. Or perhaps the relief of knowing his children are secure is what brought him such happiness."

I couldn't argue that. As much as I wanted to make Moorington out to be the villain, none of her reasons were absurd.

"His estates were in peril when he courted my mother, and

he would not marry her unless I provided a healthy sum," I said. "It never felt right to me."

"Is he a wastrel? Did he lose his fortune in cards?"

"No. Just ill luck, I believe."

Verity was silent for a moment. "I do not know the circumstances entirely, but as an earl with property and tenants depending upon him, the need for security does not seem an awful trait. Money is a large part of most marriage agreements."

Must she be so level-headed? I considered the point, trying to determine if I was being unreasonable. "Logically, I understand my dislike of him is largely because of my loyalty to my father, but my emotions do not always react to logic, and it is hard to see him as anything but a usurper in my family."

"I can understand," she said, watching her sister through the open stable door.

My mouth turned up at the edges slightly. "Because I usurped your family's title?"

She looked at me sharply. "Not at all. It is not your fault you were the next male descendent in the Palmer line." She narrowed her eyes. "Is that why you refused the earldom? You thought we didn't want you to have it?"

"No. In all honesty, the thought had crossed my mind. But it is more than that. I am not noble enough for such a calling, Verity. I am not made for it." Mother's claim about the power of choice rang through my mind. I shook it away. "One cannot choose to be noble. Nobility is decided upon birth."

Verity's expression shifted. "Is that another logical thought of yours?"

"No." I shook my head. "It is the truth, and I did not say it merely so you would disagree with me. Enough about my situation. If it is not my place in your family line that you related to, then what was it?"

"Illogical thoughts. Feelings that fail to make sense." Sorrow bent her mouth. "Today, for example, we stopped to speak with the Kelbys and Miss Martin gave such a pretty answer when she was called upon to speak, it made me dislike her so completely for no fair reason at all."

"Despite her attempts at securing me for her husband, I am not intending to marry the girl," I said, giving the words an air of flirtation.

Verity laughed, the sound echoing through the stables. "That sort of jealousy was not what plagued me."

"Pity." I had meant it as a joke but felt disappointment all the same.

She lowered her voice to a whisper, her mirth seeping away, replaced by a serious tone. "It is unfair and illogical of me, and I recognize that, but I cannot watch Miss Martin function so smoothly and capably, with such pretty manners, and not be jealous." Verity paused, watching her sister through the open stall door. "I cannot help but wish Fanny could be more like her." Her whisper grew so quiet I could hardly hear her. "I hate myself for it, but I feel those things all the same."

I took her hand in mine, curling my fingers around hers.

"The moment the thought enters my head, I banish it immediately." Verity gestured lightly toward Fanny with her other hand. "I would not want her to be anything other than the beautiful soul she is. She is so perfect, and she brings such joy to my life. But that doesn't stop me from wishing life was easier for her, from seeing Miss Martin and wishing Fanny had as simple an existence."

I waited to be certain she was finished before speaking. "You are envious of the wrong young woman, Verity."

She tipped her head to look at me, her eyes shining with emotion. "What do you mean?"

"I struggle to believe Miss Martin has anyone in her life who loves her as fiercely as Fanny is loved by you."

Tears rolled over Verity's cheek, and she slipped her hand free of mine to wipe them away with the back of her wrist.

My mother's face flashed in my head. *I love you, Daniel*. Was that not enough?

Verity gave her head a small shake. "The godmothers might give me a little competition."

"In their attempts to secure me, perhaps."

Verity's laugh was sudden and loud, and I couldn't help the grin spreading over my lips at retrieving a genuine laugh, soothing the soreness in my chest. I hadn't any idea why the Kelby sisters wanted me for Miss Martin's husband, anyway. They had been our neighbors for as long as I'd been alive and knew all of my past—including what I had done to Miss Waterley.

"Will you consider accepting the earldom?" Verity asked, taking me by surprise.

My teeth clenched in immediate reply. "I would not be good at it."

"I heartily disagree."

"You do not know my entire past, Verity."

"You already know my feelings on that." She reached for my hand this time, and I welcomed it, her fingers fitting so perfectly around mine. "There is nothing you could have done that would preclude you from deserving this role, Daniel. Who decides what we deserve, anyway? You have been given this opportunity to do good, to serve. What do you choose to do with that power?"

Choose. There it was again, someone telling me it was within my power to decide. Was it so easy? Could it be as simple as deciding I would take on the mantle, attend the Lords, pass laws that meant something, take care of my tenants . . . all the responsibilities I knew were waiting for me, that I was ignoring?

Verity knew of my reputation, had spent time with me, and still found me worthy? Was all that remained finding myself worthy?

I looked down into her eyes and realized with a startling surety that my feelings for her were growing stronger. Was this love? It was different from what I felt for my mother and my sister and my nephew. It was the warm and solid knowledge that Verity meant something to me. "You will come to the assemblies?"

She looked startled by my change in conversation. I could not very well say I was falling in love with her. Instead, I would ask her to dance.

"I am afraid to leave Fanny. My mother has deemed it inappropriate for her to go while in mourning, and I fear leaving Fanny at her mercy."

"Did you never leave Fanny home to attend the assemblies at Lamouth?"

"Occasionally. Mary would stay with her."

"Can Mary not do the same here?"

She chewed her lip. "I suppose, but my mother mentioned . . ." She looked away, clearing her throat. "I am making something out of nothing, perhaps. Suffice it to say I am worried for Fanny's safety. If I was to leave and something happened to her, I would never forgive myself."

"But if Mary was with her, she would be safe."

"If Mary promises not to leave her side."

"Then we will extract such a promise from Mary. I can ask Worthlin—"

"No," she said quickly. "I do not wish to embarrass my family. If Mary vows to remain with her the entire time we are gone, then I see no reason why I cannot come."

"Splendid. I hope you'll dance with me."

Fanny's voice stole our attention. "Are the eggs warm enough?"

"I am not sure," Verity said, rising and brushing her hands down her skirt. "How can we determine whether or not they are?"

Fanny pressed her fingers to the eggs, her brow troubled. "Mr. Ramsey would know."

"Yes, he likely would." Verity looked back at me and added in an undertone, "Our gardener."

"We can question Ludell," I offered.

"The man who oversees the animals? That is a good idea."

Fanny stood and followed us from the stables.

"Anything to postpone facing my stepfather," I said with a too-wide smile.

Verity didn't return it. "You might feel differently if you shared your feelings with him."

I laughed. "In theory, perhaps."

She gave me a look of long suffering before quickening her step to walk beside her sister. I trailed behind them, wondering if she was correct, but unwilling to test the theory presently. *One thing at a time, Verity. You can help me improve one small bit at a time.*

Ludell was not as much help as I'd hoped he would be. His experience was that eggs needed a mother to keep them warm constantly. He had little faith in Fanny being able to replace the mother the eggs had lost. When the women began walking back to the house, Ludell pulled me aside to tell me they had likely been a lost cause when we retrieved the eggs if the mother had been gone for multiple days.

"You might hope for a miracle," he said when I bade him a good day.

"I am."

Oscar greeted me when I entered the house. I watched Fanny and Verity disappear upstairs before I went to hide in the study, my dog at my heels. I opened the door and froze, surprised to find Lord Moorington sitting in one of the leather chairs in front of the empty hearth.

First he infiltrated my family, and now my father's space? Unbelievable.

I started to back out of the room when he shifted his gaze to me and lifted his hand in a halting gesture. "Do not leave on my account, son."

Son. He had no right to call me that. "Is there something I can do for you?"

"A spot of whisky wouldn't be amiss."

I crossed to the bureau, grateful I had a task to occupy me so I would not snap at him. "No whisky, but I have brandy here."

"That'll do."

I pulled two glasses and the brandy from the cupboard and set them all on the shelf. I uncorked the bottle, pouring the first glass. My hand paused above the second glass, and I looked down at the round, empty space waiting for liquid. Generally speaking, sharing a glass of brandy with a gentleman was completely above reproach. Something within me wanted to know if I could do what Mother and Verity seemed to think I was capable of—make the choice for myself.

If I tested this on something so small and inconsequential as sharing a glass of brandy with the earl, I was less likely to berate myself for failure.

I put the bottle and the empty glass away and carried the brandy to Moorington before sitting in the chair opposite him. Perhaps my next test would be to see how long I could sit in this man's company and pretend to enjoy myself. "Congratulations on the new heir," I said.

He took a sip. "Twins."

"I heard. An heir and a spare. How fortunate."

His eyebrows pulled together before his forehead cleared. "Twin *girls.*"

I wished for that glass of brandy now, if for no other reason than to give my hands something to occupy them instead of staring blankly at Moorington while I realized what he'd said. The man had twin granddaughters and he was still so over-joyed? It did not make sense. It implied he was happy for the sake of grandchildren, not for securing the line of his earldom. He was not as shallow as I'd believed.

"I trust you have been taking care of your mother? She seems tired."

"She has spent the last week entertaining Lady Huxley," I muttered. "I haven't been in their company for the entirety of that time, but I imagine it is a taxing undertaking."

He nodded, a smile pulling at his mouth. "I know the lady. I can see how that would be the case. Her daughters are much the same?"

"Not to my knowledge. I have enjoyed their company. They seem very different from their mother."

He nodded. "Perhaps they take after their father, then."

"I wouldn't know." Was our interview nearing an end? Had I passed? I searched for a reason to slip away, but my mind was blank. I could not even discern why he'd wanted to speak to me in the first place.

Perhaps a new topic of conversation was in order.

Lord Moorington's son had once been betrothed to my sister, before Jane married her Scotsman. I knew his son had married someone else, and it was on the tip of my tongue to ask if Moorington approved of the bride, but given his joy in the twins' birth, I thought that answer might be obvious.

"We intend to visit Jane before returning to Surrey," he said. "Your mother mentioned she invited you."

"I do not plan to join you at present."

"That's what I feared."

"*Feared?*" I gave a little laugh. "I thought you would be grateful."

Moorington swirled the brandy in his glass before tipping it back and drinking the remaining contents. He set the cup on his knee, holding the glass and watching me. "I do not dislike you, Daniel."

"Which is in no way indicative that you enjoy my company either, my lord."

He was quiet, watching me with unflinching focus. He allowed us to sit in the silence until my insides squirmed. I did my best to appear calm on the surface, but discomfort was steadily rising within me.

At length, he stood, crossing to the bureau to set his glass down. When he walked to the door, he paused and turned back to face me. "I will make two things perfectly clear, then I will never speak on this again." His voice was sturdy, solid.

I wanted to say something flippant, but I refrained, biting my tongue. It did not feel like the time for jokes.

"I never have, and never do, intend to replace your father. I loved my first wife, and I count myself fortunate and blessed to have found love again after her death. It is different with your mother than it was with my first wife, but my love for her is no less. Every choice I make is with her happiness in mind." He stood in the doorway, watching me as if to seal his words with a resolute stare.

After another minute, he gave one little dip of his head and left. His words had hit their mark. I was glad someone loved my mother so deeply, and was not at all surprised the man was capable of doing so. My grudge over his required settlement seemed petty now. Did it matter if the man needed money at the start of his marriage? He wasn't the fortune hunter I'd thought him to be—not when his love was so pure. As much as I didn't want to admit it, I believed I'd wronged him.

Resentment sat on me, but it did not fit as well as it had before. It was time to let it go.

CHAPTER TWENTY-NINE

VERITY

"Promise me, Mary," I said, holding my maid's gaze with unblinking ferocity. "Promise me you will not allow Fanny from your sight until I have returned from the assemblies."

Eyes wide, head shaking slowly, Mary vowed. "I won't. I swear it."

It was more than just the fear that Fanny would slip outside to check the eggs and end up stuck in a tree that forced me into such a wild retrieval of promises from my maid. My stomach was utterly sick with apprehension.

Mother had been taken ill with a headache this morning after breakfast and stayed in her room for the duration of the day. I had gone to check on her just before readying for the ball and found her sleeping. One would think finding her in such a state would lend me some comfort, but I was uneasy all the same.

I closed my eyes and waited for Mary to finish putting my hair up.

"All will be well," Fanny said, sitting at the table and sketching.

"Then why am I full of fear?"

"Because you think I will climb a tree again and need Daniel's help to climb back down."

I let out an involuntary chuckle. "Do you promise you will not partake in any such foolishness?"

She looked at the darkened window, her brow furrowed. "It is an impossible thing to promise. If there is a fire that forces us outside and one of the barn cats climbs a tree and finds itself stuck, I will attempt a rescue. But I own the scenario is highly unlikely."

"Yes, Fanny. That *is* highly unlikely." I shared a look with Mary and couldn't help smiling. I inhaled slowly, hoping to release my anxiety with my exhale.

I walked over to Fanny and drew her into a quick hug before kissing the top of her head. "Do not give Mary too much trouble."

She looked at me with offense. "I never would."

"I know." I smiled.

Mary walked me to the door. "Enjoy yourself, my lady."

"I will try." The diamond earbobs I would soon be attempting to sell dangled from my ears. My burgundy gown shone in the candlelight when I moved, and my hair was styled with extra care. I felt ridiculous, putting such effort into my appearance for a country assembly. But I hadn't done it for the assembly—not really. I'd done it for Daniel.

He would not marry me, but we could enjoy this evening. Then, when it was all over, I hoped he would be able to direct me in the sale of my jewelry. There must be some sort of man of business I could hire to arrange the sale for me. I hadn't the least idea what the earrings or necklace were worth, nor how to obtain the money. But I had a feeling Daniel would know.

Lord and Lady Moorington were waiting in the drawing room when I joined them, and Daniel stood at the hearth, his coat crisp and black against a clean white cravat and an emerald waistcoat. His hair looked darker in the evening light, his eyes a deeper brown. His brow was furrowed in concentration as he stared at the mantel he leaned against, his attention so rapt he had not noticed me walk in. My breath caught at how inordinately handsome he looked, and I forced myself to look away before I could reveal my emotions to his mother.

"You look beautiful," Lady Moorington said, crossing the room to take my hand. "I am glad you opted to join us."

"Forgive me. I did not mean to keep you waiting."

"Not at all," Lord Moorington said. "We are right on time. Shall we?" He offered his arm to his wife.

Daniel approached, circumventing his stepfather to offer his arm to me. His gaze was direct, meaningful. "You look beautiful, Verity."

"Thank you. I find I must retract my earlier statement. It appears I *am* fond of coats on occasion."

A grin broke through his grim countenance. "I hadn't realized you weren't fond of them."

"Truly? And here I thought we'd established my feelings on a man in his shirtsleeves, Daniel."

"You are talking nonsense."

"I am trying to tell you that you look handsome, but evidently I'm failing at it."

He nodded, passing a hand over his clean-shaven jaw. "No, I received the message. Thank you."

He helped me into the carriage opposite Lord and Lady Moorington, and we were off.

Dinner at the Kelby house was every bit as entertaining as I'd anticipated it being. Miss Martin was quiet, polite, and everything an earl should want in a wife. Her godmothers were complimentary and sweet and did not allow anyone else to get a word in.

When we reached the assembly hall, I realized the benefit of attending a ball in which I did not know the local Society—I did not have to dance often, and my feet were saved from overtiring. I danced the first set with Daniel, sat out the second with Lady Moorington, then danced the third with her husband, who was surprisingly light on his feet for such a large man. I could not help but like Lord Moorington. I sensed an uneasiness between him and Daniel, but he was cordial and kind, in my opinion. The way he cared for his wife was sweet.

"What are you ruminating on so deeply?" Daniel asked, coming to stand beside me. We were tucked against the back wall near Lord and Lady Moorington while they chatted with some neighbors, just far enough to be out of earshot, though in perfect view.

"Your stepfather, actually."

Daniel's countenance shifted, shuttering as if he had just closed the windows over the conversation.

"I sense it is not a topic you take to."

He tried to seem nonchalant. "I have no opinion on the matter."

I laughed lightly. "That is clearly false."

Daniel watched his mother and her husband for a minute before his shoulders relaxed, lowering away from his ears. "In truth, I am making a great effort to let go of my negative opinions of the man. He loves my mother. I cannot hold anything against him for that."

"It would be challenging to watch my mother marry again. I do not judge you for your feelings."

"I used to care much more than I do now. I mistook the type of man Lord Moorington was initially, and I have since seen how wrong I was." Daniel watched Lord Moorington as he spoke. "I want my mother to be happy, and he gives her joy."

"What about you, Daniel? What would make you happy?"

He looked down at me, his clear brown eyes roaming over my face. He seemed to be struggling with the question. Or perhaps he was struggling with how to answer it.

I lowered my gaze. "Forgive me. That was impertinent."

"No." His fingers brushed over my arm as though he meant to hold my hand, but then decided against it—no doubt because of our public setting. "You are one of the only people who could ask me that and receive an honest answer."

"Which is?"

"You. You already have brought happiness into my life. You and Fanny together have given me something to think about other than myself. Had I known the type of person you were when you first *approached* me"—he said the word with meaning, and I knew he was referring to the night I went to his room—"I may have given a different answer."

My breath caught, lodging in my throat. My lips parted. "Do you mean it? Am I understanding you correctly?"

"Verity, I think I am falling—"

"Lord Huxley," a deep voice boomed, startling both of us. Mr. Waterley came toward us, his sister on his arm. Daniel flinched. There was some sort of history there, something he had yet to tell me.

Miss Waterley untangled herself from her brother's arm and bobbed in a curtsy. "Lord Huxley, a pleasure." She dipped a curtsy to me, and I returned it.

"I hope you've enjoyed your time in the country," Daniel said.

"Immensely." She looked from Daniel to her brother. "We've discussed making our home here more permanent. I've grown bored of London."

Daniel smiled, but it seemed forced. "You will no doubt feel the same of Northumberland before too long."

She twinkled up at him. "I shan't. I will admit, I expected to see more of you, my lord."

Confusion bent his eyebrows. Daniel opened his mouth, then promptly closed it again. He turned toward me. "Shall we dance, my lady?"

Again? I was about to argue about the propriety of dancing a second set when the pleading look in his eyes touched me, and I put my hand on his arm, letting him lead me toward the center of the floor.

I leaned in and lowered my voice. "People might talk."

"Let them. It is far better to give them a thread of truth about us than to reignite old rumors."

"Concerning Miss Waterley?" I asked.

"Yes, and my ill treatment of her. I deserve how deeply she has hated me for the past ten years, but giving me attention now? I can only wonder what she wants from me."

"I highly doubt you deserve her hatred. In any case, she doesn't seem to dislike you at all."

"Believe it, Verity." He swallowed, looking at me closely. "I ruined the girl. We were found together during a dinner party at my house. I would have married her then, but we were both far too young and my father did his best to hush it up, despite how much she begged for a union." His mouth bent in disgust. "The decade that passed since then has dulled the rumors, but the truth still remains."

Shock rippled through me. He'd ruined her? But she was a lady of quality. He did not trifle with ladies . . .

Daniel caught my eyes and flinched. "You were right. We should not have started the second set. You do not deserve to have your reputation linked to mine. I am not worthy of you."

I took his hands to keep him from walking away. "Do not leave me here. Do not walk away."

He lowered his voice, whispering. "You might not see this now, but doing so would be a kindness to you."

"To me? To abandon me in the middle of the dance floor surrounded by strangers would be a kindness?"

He looked grim. "It is far better than linking your name to a rake."

"You are no longer a rake, Daniel, and you have not been for some time, I wager. Besides, I care not for your past." I squeezed his hand until he met my eyes. "Daniel, believe me. I care not for anything but for the man you are today."

"But if you knew what I did—"

"Did you hurt her?"

"No." He swallowed. "It was entirely a product of young infatuation . . . on both sides. Which I heartily regret."

"Then I do not need to know more details than what you've already shared." I swallowed, hoping he read the sincerity in my eyes. For all that Miss Waterley must have suffered at the time, she seemed perfectly happy now, surrounded by gentlemen who would gladly take her arm. Mr. Egerton had been most attentive to her when we'd seen them together. She was no longer suffering.

If anything, the woman had reappeared in Daniel's life because marriage to him now would make her a countess. The timing was too suspicious to be anything else.

"Has she been a social pariah her entire life?" I asked.

"No," he said, his brow bent. "Her brother has provided her with multiple Seasons, and she has not lacked for beaus."

"Then you must admit you have not ruined her life." By the sound of it, Daniel was only a boy himself when the events occurred. I tightened my hold on his hands, willing him to meet my gaze. "It sounds as though you need to forgive yourself."

The music started, and the dance began, moving us together and apart enough to make conversation more difficult. Daniel's expression was solemn, his eyes unwavering in their devotion to watch me. I found I didn't care what anyone else thought or what assumptions they made when we began our second set. I cared for this man, and I believed he was coming to care for me too.

It had grown abundantly clear to me that the only thing standing in Daniel's way was himself.

"Do you respect my opinions?" I asked.

"Yes," he said, confusion lacing his tone.

"Then you will agree I know my own mind."

His smile was soft, curving his lips slightly. "That is abundantly clear."

"Then do not question what I feel for you."

Daniel grew quiet. He watched me while we moved through the motions, heedless of those around us. His hand gently guided me, softly pressing into my arm, my waist, my back.

I felt his breath on my neck when he turned me around, and my eyes settled in the far doorway snagging on a familiar looking man. "Was that—"

We moved away, and I craned my neck to see the doorway.

"What is it?" Daniel asked.

I reached for his hand and pulled him out of the line to the sound of a few audible complaints nearby. "Your valet is here, I think." I gestured to where I'd seen him.

"Yes," he said with some surprise. "It's Dean."

Daniel pulled me through the room. His fingers curled around mine, holding firm until we reached his servant. "What is it? Is anyone hurt?"

Dean looked at me, and my body flushed with ice.

He swallowed. "Your sister has been taken."

CHAPTER THIRTY

DANIEL

My arm went around Verity in case she swooned, but I should have known better. Despite her sudden rigid posture, she did not falter at all. Instead, she lifted her chin. "Who took Fanny?"

Dean's expression was grim. "Two men. I didn't recognize them." He paused. "They had permission from your mother."

Verity's jaw went hard, like she was clenching her teeth together. She stepped past Dean toward the front door and the street.

I looked at my servant. "Find my mother and inform her we are leaving, then meet me outside. I want to hear every detail of the events that transpired while we travel."

"Yes, sir." He slipped away immediately, weaving through the crowd to locate my mother.

I followed Verity and found her climbing into our carriage. The coachman stood near the front, preparing to mount his seat.

I stood at the open door to the carriage. "What do you intend to do?"

"Find her." She was resolute, calm by all appearances. I could well believe she was an utter mess of nerves, though. "Medical help. That will be my mother's claim." She spoke calmly, but I could hear the fire bubbling under her words.

"Do you know where they've taken her? Who would've taken her?"

"She had an arrangement with Mr. Waterley's uncle last time." Verity shook her head slightly. "Rather, my husband made the arrangements. I imagine my mother approached them about that same agreement. She warned me time was running out. She must have had this planned."

"Then I know where we need to go." I leaned back out of the carriage as Dean came toward me, my mother and stepfather just behind him. *Blast.* I did not need them interfering now.

"Would you like me to send a carriage for you, Mother?" I asked.

"We are coming with you."

Just as I feared. "We are not going home."

"Oh?" Her sleek dark eyebrows lifted. "Are you intending to fetch Lady Frances yourself?"

I sent a glare to Dean.

"Never mind your anger. I forced him to tell me." She waved away the words. "Where would she have been taken?"

"Waterley's asylum, most likely."

My mother drew in a quick, surprised breath.

Moorington shifted on his feet. "She is not mad, I take it?"

"Far from it." I was glad to see our coachman settling himself in the driving seat, nearly ready to leave. "It is my belief her mother wishes to have her restrained for selfish purposes."

Moorington gave a resolute nod. "Then we need to save her from such a fate."

My begrudging respect for him grew. "You would take my word for it?"

Moorington inclined his head, looking me squarely in the face. "I've never doubted you, son. Just some of your choices."

I had to respect that. I understood it, at least. "Mother, I am not sure this is the place for a woman—"

"If Lady Verity is going, so will I." She stepped past me and helped herself into the carriage.

Dean returned, and I waited for him to approach me. "We haven't the room anymore."

"I rode here, sir. I'll follow you."

"No, go home and wait for more instruction. But tell me everything you know first."

"I already have. Two men came. Mary couldn't stop them. Lady Huxley gave her permission for them to take Lady Frances. Indeed, sir, I think she sent for them."

I nodded to Dean, who turned away to fetch his horse. "With haste," I called to the coachman before sliding into the carriage and shutting the door behind me. I sat beside Verity, across from my mother and her husband, our shoulders jostling as the conveyance rolled forward.

I reached for Verity's hand and pulled it onto my lap, covering it in both of my own. "We will retrieve her."

"We must," she said quietly, looking out the window.

"Indeed," I agreed. "We must."

It took the better part of an hour to reach the Waterley Hospital Lunatic Asylum. The building was a perfect square, three floors of six evenly spaced dark windows, except for a handful that glowed orange with candlelight.

It was a grim-looking house, and I feared for what state we would find Fanny in. "Will you wait in the carriage, Verity? I am afraid it will be difficult for you inside."

"I've heard stories," she said quietly. "I know how terrible these places are."

"Then you'll understand why I think you should remain here with my mother."

She shook her head stubbornly. "I will retrieve my sister. Her needs are more important than my sensibilities."

I expected that answer, but I'd wanted to try all the same. "I cannot argue with that."

We filed from the carriage, followed by Moorington and my mother. I shot her a look, and she lifted her eyebrows again. "If Lady Verity comes, I come."

We went to the door, and I banged against it with the knocker until it opened to a man with long gray hair tied back in a queue. "I need to speak to Dr. Waterley."

His wrinkled face scrunched. "It is late—"

"You can retrieve a patient for me, or you can retrieve the doctor."

The man seemed unsure. He glanced at Moorington behind me, and I was grateful for the earl's immense size. He was physically intimidating.

"Wait here," the servant said. He returned shortly with Dr. Waterley behind him.

The man was tall and slender, a frown constantly marring his brow. "Palmer?" He pulled up quickly upon seeing my mother. "Mrs. Palmer. Excuse me, it is Lady . . ."

"Lady Moorington," she supplied. "And my husband, the Earl of Moorington."

Dr. Waterley bent at the waist. "To what do I owe the honor?"

Mother did not allow her confidence to waver. "We have come to retrieve a patient. Lady Frances Palmer."

The doctor's eyes flicked to me, then back to my mother. "I am afraid that is out of the question."

Verity straightened. "You confirm she is here, then?"

"Yes, but we do not allow visitors in the evening. You'll have to return tomorrow."

"We're not here for a visit," Verity said. "We are here to retrieve her and take her home."

"Again, that is out of the question. She has been placed under our care by her mother, and no one else has the authority to remove her from it."

Verity took a step forward, and I grabbed her hand to hold her back. I lowered my voice. "You have no legal rights here."

"Allow me to see her."

"I am afraid I cannot," the doctor said.

"You can," Verity snapped. "You choose not to. I will not leave your property until I have assured myself of her safety."

He wavered, his gaze slipping from Verity to Moorington, then my mother.

Moorington stepped forward, waiting on Verity's other side, his hands resting behind his back. We stood sentinel, supporting her. Against Dr. Waterley and his aging servant, we were a force to consider seriously. "It should not take long to reassure the young lady of her sister's safety," Moorington said, a threat in his tone I admired.

Dr. Waterley hesitated further. "Very well," he said at last. "Follow me." He turned down a corridor before moving up a set of stairs, and our entire party followed him. Distant sounds in the house set an eerie feeling in my bones. Floorboards creaking, muffled moaning. The sound of metal scraped behind a door we passed and a door slammed somewhere down the corridor, causing me to flinch.

Dr. Waterley pulled a set of keys from his pocket and stopped midway down the corridor. A light sputtered in the sconce on the wall, highlighting his movements as he located the correct key and slid it into the lock, unbolting the door.

Verity brushed past him before he had the door open all the way. "Fanny?"

The room was dark. I pulled the candle from a wall sconce and stepped past the doctor into the room.

Fanny sat on the edge of the bed, hugging her knees to her chest and whimpering. A thick chain ran from her foot to the bedpost, shackled around her ankle. Verity's arms immediately went around her sister.

Dr. Waterley cleared his throat. "You've seen she is safe. Now the patient needs her rest."

Verity's attention snapped to him. "Unlock her at once."

"It is for the safety—"

"Unlock her *now.*"

He waited a moment, clearly unused to being spoken to in such a manner. "Only the patient's mother can remove her from the premises."

"You will be receiving a letter from her mother tomorrow."

"Then she will be released tomorrow," he said, though it was clear he did not expect this to be the case.

I would have picked up Fanny and bolted out of there, except for the chain around her ankle. "Is that necessary?" I asked. "The woman is hardly a threat."

"It is customary."

Fire flowed through my veins, and it took great restraint not to throttle the man. "I asked if it was *necessary.*"

Dr. Waterley stepped back out of the room, refusing to answer me. If this was standard practice, then his asylum would need to be analyzed regarding their upkeep of regulations. "I am locking the door, whether or not you are in here."

Verity's eyes flashed, but she did not move away from her sister's side.

I was tempted to remain with them, but I could not help her from within this room. I handed Verity the candle and stepped from the room. "Verity—"

The doctor swung the door closed and locked the bolt in place before putting the keys in his pocket.

"You will be hearing from the magistrate," Moorington promised in a startlingly low tone.

Dr. Waterley's hesitation gave me one moment of hope before he started walking down the corridor toward the door again. "I have done nothing illegal, sir. Return with the girl's mother or a formal release letter, and we may have a different conversation."

"You intend to keep her locked up all night?" Moorington asked.

"It is standard practice—"

"And Lady Verity?" I questioned. "You intend to keep *her* as well?"

He looked at me. "She chose to remain."

We'd reached the front of the house again, and Dr. Waterley gestured to the door, which his servant opened. Mother walked out, followed by Moorington.

I glared at the doctor. He'd lived in the house beside ours for most of my life, raising my friend and attending dinners and card parties in our drawing room until he came to manage this asylum. He had been something of a friend to my father. But now? Now he repulsed me. I hadn't realized that Verity had just cause for fear at my house, that this monster was willing to take her sister away and chain her up like a wild dog. I wanted to spit at his feet, but refrained. If only just.

I walked out and followed my mother and Moorington to the carriage. When we reached it, I turned back to look at the house, my body shaking in anger.

"Should we have offered him money?" my mother asked.

Her husband slid an arm around her back. "I do not think any sum would compare to the income the girl will bring him over time."

"Weasel," she said.

I climbed into the carriage, and they followed me before we took off. "What do you intend to do?" Mother asked.

"Have a conversation with Lady Huxley. She will be persuaded to sign for Fanny's release."

"You are confident." Mother certainly sounded worried. "That woman is unfeeling."

"She'll agree," I said, looking out the window as the carriage started moving. "I have something she wants."

CHAPTER THIRTY-ONE

VERITY

One small flame flickered on the nub of a candlestick resting on the floor beside us. I sat beside Fanny on the wooden floorboards near the foot of the bed. I was grateful Daniel had given me the light before the doctor shut the door, if only so I could see Fanny's face long enough to ascertain that she was well. Or as well as could be expected.

"I did not climb any trees," Fanny said.

A watery chuckle slipped through my chest. "Thank you for keeping to your word. If it would have meant evading this situation, I would have welcomed finding you in a tree."

She did not respond to this. "You did not need to stay."

"I could not leave you alone."

"The doctor means to help me. Mother told me so. He helps others with poor understanding as well. But he took my watch." Her hands started shaking. "And I am very uncomfortable with this lock around my ankle."

Fire tore through my chest. "It will not be much longer, Fanny. Daniel left to retrieve the necessary paperwork so we can take you home."

"Daniel," Fanny repeated softly. "Home."

It would not be too long. I had faith in his ability to remove us from this place. I could not discern where it stemmed from, only that I did not doubt him. I imagined we had a long night of waiting ahead of us, though.

Mother would not be easily convinced.

I closed my eyes, feeling warm tears trail over my cheeks. If I had not gone to the assemblies, this would not have happened. I could have kept her safe. "Can you forgive me?"

Fanny tilted her head to the side. "You didn't do anything wrong."

"I left you."

"To dance with Daniel," she said simply. "I am happy you went to dance with Daniel."

I gave a chuckle. "I did not go merely to dance with Daniel, Fanny. I went to the assemblies in town."

"Did you not dance with Daniel?"

"I did, but . . . I only meant that dancing with him was not my primary objective . . . Oh, very well. It was. How long have my feelings been so obvious?"

"I do not know about your feelings," Fanny said. "I like Daniel. He is kind."

"He is very kind, and he will find a way to secure our release."

"And then you will marry him?"

"I would like to. He seems to have a different idea, though." I sighed, leaning back against the footboard. "We might have to find our own little cottage, Fanny, for just the two of us."

I was glad to already be wearing my earrings. I would not need to return to Arden Castle, but we could leave at once for Lamouth after we were let out of this horrid place. We could retrieve the sapphire necklace and, together with the diamond earrings, they would provide for us until I could contrive an income.

"A cottage?" Fanny asked, yawning. "I would rather live with Daniel."

As would I. "Shall we try to get some rest?"

"Verity?" Her voice wobbled, aching my heart. "I am afraid for my eggs."

I stifled a laugh. It was not in any way a humorous situation, but that had not been what I'd expected to hear. Of course she would be in such danger and think of the little starlings.

"Fanny, they might not survive," I said gently. "They could have been too long without a mother already when you saved them."

"I thought of that, but I can hope."

"Yes, my dear. You can hope."

Light snuck through the narrow window and illuminated the small room with hazy morning sun. Fanny had curled up on the bed and fell asleep a few hours ago. I sat against the wall on the floor, listening to the sounds of the other patients in the nearby rooms and on the floor above us. Someone had cried for well over an hour, yet no one came to their aid. With every hour, my concern grew and expanded. Daniel could have returned home and traveled back at least twice already in the amount of time that passed.

What kept him away?

This room resembled a jail more than a home. It in no way seemed like a hospital. I didn't know if I could ever forgive my mother for forcing Fanny into this. I understood her ignorance, her insistence that doctors could help Fanny more than we could—she would be unable to consider anything else, since she could never calm Fanny. I wanted to extend grace for that, but she had been selfishly motivated, forfeiting any patience I had for her.

Instead, shielding Fanny from pain was my priority. I did not want her to understand what her mother had done to her, but she seemed to know. At this point, all I could do was shield her from our mother herself.

A key rattled in the lock, and I stood, shaking Fanny on the shoulder. "Wake. Someone is here."

Fanny groaned, turning over on the bed and blinking sleepy eyes up at me.

The door opened, and Daniel stood there, his stepfather right behind him in much the same stance they had last night. Relief swept through me in a cascading wave, but I kept it at bay. I would not allow myself to feel it until Fanny and I were outside.

"Unlock her," Daniel said, his voice steel.

Dr. Waterley's servant stepped forward with a set of keys and bent to unlock the shackle at Fanny's ankle, his gray, stringy hair falling in his face. When he had it unfastened, she scooted away from him and bent to rub the tender skin.

"That is all," Daniel said, waiting for the man to leave. He looked at me, his dark brown eyes pools of warmth. "She is free to go."

I crossed the room and threw my arms around his waist. "Thank you." My words were muffled, my face buried in his chest. His arms came around me, pressing into my back briefly before I stepped out of his hold.

"Can we leave now?" Fanny asked, her voice subdued.

"Yes," I said, sharing a smile with Daniel and Lord Moorington. "Let us go."

We followed Daniel and Lord Moorington down the corridor before I remembered the watch. "Wait. They've taken her pocket watch."

Daniel reached into his pocket and pulled it out, the long chain swinging as he handed it to Fanny. "Dr. Waterley returned it."

"Without provocation?" I hadn't expected that.

Daniel looked at Lord Moorington. "No, he was certainly provoked."

Lord Moorington wore a self-satisfied smile. "The magistrate will be performing an inspection on this location later this morning. It is better for us if Dr. Waterley doesn't catch word of it before he arrives."

The fresh air outside was soothing after spending such a length of time in the unclean, moldy house. I had only been locked in that room for a matter of hours, but bringing my sister out of it provided me a great deal of relief. My heart hurt for the people who still remained.

When we reached the carriage, Fanny climbed inside and Lord Moorington followed her, seeming to sense that Daniel wanted to speak to me.

He took my hand and pulled me further away from the carriage. We could still see it, but they would not be able to hear us. "Your mother will not be at Arden when we return."

I felt an inordinate sense of relief, knowing I was not going to be forced to leave the estate immediately. I wasn't ready to give up Daniel's company quite yet if I could help it. "What do you mean?"

"It was part of our agreement."

My hands curled into fists at my sides in anticipation. He had taken away my opportunity to vent my anger and frustration at my mother, but perhaps that was a good thing. "How did you convince her to agree to it?"

"I told her that you and I were to be married, and I would assume responsibility for Fanny. I paid her a good sum for the honor."

My breath caught. *Married.*

He watched me warily. "It was a risk, but I hoped the idea has not grown repugnant to you."

"You know it did not," I said breathlessly.

He chuckled and rubbed a hand over his chin. "I did not know it, but I hoped. After admitting my stupidity where Miss Waterley was concerned, I hoped I had not changed your opinion of me beyond repair."

"If you think I would be so easily altered, you cannot know me that well."

"I didn't think so. Which is what led me to believe I could trust in myself and my ability to care for you. My mother has kindly reminded me I have to make the choice to be the type of man I want to be. Beside you, I feel capable of making those choices for the better."

"You are not just committing to a life with me, Daniel."

He looked at the carriage across the drive where Fanny was waiting. "I know," he whispered. "I care for you both."

My heart swelled, hearing the words I knew in my heart already. "You will stop refusing to be the earl now?"

His mouth curved into a smile. "Yes, my lady."

"Thank heavens."

He laughed, sliding his hands around my waist and pulling me toward him. "Will you become my wife, Verity?"

"It would be my honor."

His gaze locked on mine, all humor draining immediately from his expression, replaced with gravity. His brown eyes darkened, becoming pools of warm drinking chocolate, and his lips hovered over mine. I swallowed hard, feeling the emotion buzz between us like a swarm of honeybees, setting my hair on end in anticipation.

Before I realized what was happening, my lips were met by his smiling ones. He poured warmth into me, like a hot drink slowly filling my veins. I responded in kind. His hands slid down my back, and his kiss slowed, adopting a reverence that proved how deeply his feelings ran. I had never been kissed like this before, but I had a feeling I would be kissed like this for the rest of my life.

"Does this mean you are going to marry Daniel?" Fanny called, her voice filtering out of the carriage.

I felt his lips smile against mine. He gave me one last lingering kiss before leaning back. "Yes, Fanny," he called, not removing his eyes from me. "Would that be all right with you?"

"It would." Her distinct matter-of-fact tone was comforting.

"Then it is settled," Daniel whispered, holding me close. "We shall have the banns read immediately."

I reached up on tiptoe to press another kiss to his lips. When I leaned back, he sighed.

Daniel moved toward the carriage, but I pulled his arm to halt him. "My mother?"

"She has agreed that a house in London was much more to her taste, and now she can afford it. I thought you would not want her near Fanny for a while."

"I would be happy if she never saw Fanny again."

"But that is not your choice to make," Daniel said gently, "is it?"

I huffed. "No."

"We will worry about the future at a later date. Her money will run out, so I thought we could devise a situation where your mother could become a companion eventually. But we would need to find the lady."

"My mother, a companion?" I laughed.

"She might have forced me to pay her for the honor of becoming Fanny's guardian, but I refuse to provide for a woman who would treat Fanny in such a way. She will not receive another ha'penny from me."

I leaned up and pressed a kiss to his mouth. "I think we will get on very well."

"We already do, love."

"Shall we?" Moorington asked. "Your mother will be worried."

"I need to see my eggs," Fanny said.

"Of course," Daniel replied, helping me into the carriage and allowing me to settle beside my sister. "Visiting your eggs will be the very first thing we do when we return home."

Home. It sounded very nice to me.

CHAPTER THIRTY-TWO

VERITY

My nails were slowly becoming chewed little stubs while I vented my anxiety on them instead of the people around me. The smell of pigs drifted on the slight breeze, but I didn't pay it any mind. My attention was on the hen house.

"It will work," Fanny said with certainty.

I looked at Daniel, who merely returned a shrug. Wonderful. Very confidence-inspiring of him.

Mr. Ludell leaned against the far fence, watching just as we did. He'd advised us against this course of action. Mother hens sometimes pecked at foreign eggs. Other times, they adopted them. We were sincerely hoping for the latter. If it was the former, I did not know what that would do to Fanny.

"Perhaps she will not notice the new eggs," Daniel said quietly, watching the hen.

"The bright blue, small, shiny eggs we hid beneath her?"

He gave a slight chuckle. "Very well. She will notice them."

"She will know," Fanny said. "Mr. Ramsey told me chickens are one of the smartest birds."

I watched a hen peck at the ground incessantly on the far

side of the yard and questioned Mr. Ramsey's wisdom for the first time. I wished he were here to aid us in this dilemma, but Mr. Ludell had been knowledgeable enough, if a little negative-minded.

Daniel slid a little closer to me, reaching down to brush his fingers softly against mine. I looked up at him, but his attention was still on the hen we'd selected as the starlings' new mother—the compassionate one, according to Mr. Ludell.

"We've an hour," Mr. Ludell said. "She'll either accept them or not within the next hour."

"Shall we occupy our minds elsewhere, then?" I asked. "There is nothing more we can do now."

Fanny continued to watch the hen sitting on her brood of eggs in the henhouse. "I would prefer to remain here."

It was nearly time to leave for drawing, but it seemed she did not mind the alteration in schedule. "Because you are the mistress of your own time," I said.

"Mistress of my own time," she repeated quietly, her fingers finding the pocket watch. She checked the time and slid it back into her dress. Her shoulders tensed, the discomfort evident in the way she held herself. This flexibility of mind was likely not going to last for much longer—not after the importance of the starlings wore off, at least. Any improvement of flexibility was an improvement, though.

Feet crunched on the gravel drive just opposite the animal pens, and Daniel turned to look over his shoulder. "Blast. It's Belford."

I squeezed his fingers before pulling my hand free. "You may go. I will apprise you of the eggs' situation when we have further information."

He smiled, gave me a gentle bow, and turned away. I listened to their footsteps recede together and stepped closer to Fanny—as close as she would allow.

"How are you feeling today?" I asked. Only one day had

passed since we'd brought her home from the asylum. Her ankle was still red and tender, but it was her mind and the state of her emotions regarding our mother I was most worried about.

"Good."

"Have you given any further thought on where you would like to live after Daniel and I are married?"

Fanny stared straight ahead. I would have wondered if she'd heard me, but I was used to waiting. "I miss Lamouth. I miss Mother. I like it here."

Well, lovely. "Then you will be happy wherever we are?"

"I should be," she said. "But I cannot predict the future."

I bit back a smile. "Very valid point." I cleared my throat. "And Mother? You . . . you *want* to see her again?"

Fanny's forehead furrowed. "Someday."

Relief flowed through me. It was not something I would have to address today. Fanny was certainly more loving and far more forgiving than I was. If it were in my power, I would keep them separated for the rest of our lives. But Daniel was correct, and I needed to accept that Fanny had the ability to make decisions for herself. I slid my arm over her back, feeling her stiffen, and gave her a gentle hug. "I love you, Fanny."

"I love you, too, Veri—look!" She pointed to the hen, who was now bending her neck to look at the eggs.

I tensed, crossing my arms and squeezing my sides. A breeze picked up a loose lock of hair and drew it over my forehead, and I tucked it back away.

"She left them unharmed," Fanny whispered. "She has adopted them as her own." The hen looked down at the eggs, arranging them with her beak, then sat again, and my entire body relaxed.

"You've done it," I said. "Now we need to hope it is not too late for the eggs."

"Hope," Fanny repeated. "I can hope."

Emotion bubbled up to my throat, and I cleared it away,

wiping at the moisture in my eyes. Hope had been instilled in my heart again, our future and happiness secured. I could not be happier.

Daniel

I showed Belford into the study and poured him a glass of brandy. "The hunting party didn't attend the assemblies in its entirety. We missed you there."

"Stuffy things, those assemblies," he said, wrinkling his nose. He accepted the glass and took a sip. "Waterley took his sister, though."

"Miss Malton as well?"

"Yes. She went with them."

I hadn't seen her, but my attention had been stolen rather completely by Verity. Oscar trotted into the room and came to rest near my feet. He lifted his enormous head and laid it on my lap as I absently scratched his ears. My hand felt empty without the glass, but I'd made the choice not to drink unless I was eating a meal, and I thought it would serve me well.

"Listen," Belford said, rearranging himself on his seat and clearing his throat, "I came to warn you. I am not one for inserting myself where I do not belong, but I could not allow this to lie."

My head swarmed with possibilities, but I removed them all. If an old rumor was surfacing, I had confidence Verity would not throw me away over it. She had proven her steadiness of character, and I had faith in her. "What is it?"

"Miss Waterley. She has it in her head you'll make good on your past . . . indiscretions . . . and offer for her. They need money, you know, and she would like a title. Waterley's wasted his inheritance at the races, and now they are in a scramble."

"I hadn't known that." Though in all honesty, I was not very surprised. He hadn't ever had a great deal of self-possession. "They're bound to be disappointed."

Belford shook his head, his golden locks shifting. "I would not put it past the chit to do whatever she could to entrap you, Palmer."

I cleared my throat. "It's Huxley, now."

Belford's pale eyebrows rose. "About time. What made you accept the change?"

I shot him a grin. "Lady Verity."

A slow smile spread over my friend's face, and he hit his knee. "You've fallen for her?"

"I have. We're to be married as soon as the banns can be read."

"Then you will not worry yourself over any of Miss Waterley's plans."

"She can attempt whatever she'd like. Perhaps you can save her the trouble and announce my engagement when you return to their house."

Belford nodded, then emptied his glass. "Egerton will be thrilled. The chap has proposed to her twice since she arrived last week."

"Perhaps next time she will accept him, then."

"Perhaps." Belford shook his head, watching me. "Never thought I'd see you married, Huxley."

I sat in the feeling of being called by my title, glad not to feel any revulsion. It fit well. The degree to which I looked forward to enacting change and participating in Parliament surprised me, but I imagined it was the hope Verity and Fanny had given me for a brighter future. My first order of business would be to strengthen the regulation process for asylums. I knew there was one in place, but after what I had witnessed at Waterley Hospital, it was clearly not being enforced as well as it needed to be.

Belford stood. "That is a weight off my shoulders."

I thanked him for coming by and saw him out before returning to the study and sitting behind the desk. The furniture had not shrunk at all, and I had in no way grown, but it felt as though it fit now. I no longer felt dwarfed by the enormity of the man who'd last resided here, no longer felt as though I was lacking in comparison. He'd had his share of mistakes, and he'd chosen to grow and change. I only wished he had confided in me instead of berated me while he'd been alive. I would have been far more interested in listening.

I opened the top drawer of the desk and pulled out his pocket watch, turning it over and running my finger along the engraved casing. It was high time I stopped running from his memory and embraced it instead. I slid the watch into my waistcoat pocket and attached the chain, enjoying the heaviness of my father's watch against my stomach.

The door swung open and Verity stood there.

"Did it work?" I asked, immediately rising from my chair.

She smiled, and the room suddenly seemed brighter. "Thus far it has. The hen did not reject the eggs or peck them open, so Mr. Ludell believes we can count it as a success."

I stepped around the desk and crossed to meet her halfway. "What an utter relief."

"I won't be able to relax until the eggs have hatched and Fanny has moved on to her next obsession." She stepped into my arms, sliding her hands around my waist. "Any word from the magistrate?"

"Not yet. Moorington believes it will take more time to complete the investigation and submit their findings. We must be patient."

"I cannot think of those people chained and crying without wishing the process could be sped in some way."

"We have done everything we can," I reminded her, resting my chin on the top of her head.

"Not *everything*. We could bring them all here to the safety and security of Arden Castle."

"Well, not really. That wouldn't be legal."

Verity stilled, pulling back slightly to look up at me. "What if we *did* do something of that nature?"

"What do you mean?"

Her eyes were round and bright. "We could begin an asylum of our own. Hire a good doctor. Create a safe space for the people who truly need it. No chains, no locking of doors unless it is necessary for their safety. Nothing barbaric at all."

"No putting people on display like animals," I muttered.

"Precisely."

I ran a hand over my jaw, considering the idea. "We do not need two houses. Though it wouldn't be possible at Lamouth. I'm certain the entailment would become problematic."

"No. And this is your home, so I would never presume—"

"You are not presuming anything, love. I think it is a wonderful idea. We must speak to my mother."

"To gather her permission?"

"No." I smiled. "It is our home, and she will not oppose what we want to do with it. I think she has wisdom to share. She could help us solidify our plan before she leaves to see Jane." I swallowed. "Both she and Moorington would likely have a good deal of advice to give us."

Verity grinned. "I am glad to hear you say that. But we are in no great hurry. Did you not hear? Your mother intends to remain until after the wedding. She has written to Jane to invite her to come here as well."

"Of course she has," I said dryly.

"Are you upset?"

"No. It brings me inordinate joy. But I cannot say so aloud, can I? What would that do to my reputation?"

"You can say anything you'd like to me. I won't reveal your beautiful, golden heart to anyone. I promise."

I leaned down and kissed her, wrapping my arms around her back to bring her as close as possible. "I love you, Verity."

"Good. I love you as well."

EPILOGUE

VERITY

One Year Later

I walked through the kitchen slowly, my hands linked and resting on top of my softly rounded stomach while I perused the excess of food Cook had made for the party today. Cakes, jellies, pies, tarts, and biscuits filled every bit of space on the long worktable, plated beautifully and ready to be carried to the tables outside. The savory portion of the meal was already being conveyed upstairs, along with orgeat and lemonade.

"You've outdone yourself," I said, sidling up to the older woman, her frizzy red hair tied back and mostly hidden beneath a white cap. It was impossible to hide all of it away, and vibrant coils broke free in random intervals around her head.

Cook swiped her wrist across her forehead and sent me a cheeky smile. "Only the best for my little Fanny."

"You realize Fanny will not be a patient in the hospital, do you not?"

Cook's eyes narrowed. "Is this party not for her?"

"She has helped plan and execute it, but it is for the opening

289

of the hospital. It is for all the patients we've brought here this week." I swept my gaze along the overladen table once more. "You made all this for Fanny?"

"To *celebrate* Fanny," she corrected, an indulgent smile brightening her florid face. It had not taken too long at Arden Castle for the servants to care for Fanny the way the servants had at Lamouth Park. Once they understood her, they opened their hearts to her easily.

"But she would not even eat most of these things."

Cook's lips pressed together and she pointed her wooden spoon my direction. "She tasted a tart yesterday. Swear on my best pot, she did."

I could not control my own surprise. "Did she spit it out?"

Cook's eyes slid to the side.

Ah, ha. She *did*. I suppressed my amusement.

"It is still a success, my lady," Cook pressed.

"Of course it is. Any improvement is a success."

She looked satisfied by my agreement.

"Lady Huxley?"

I turned to find Mary waiting in the entrance to the stairway. "Yes?"

"Lord Huxley has asked after you, my lady."

"I'm on my way. Where might I find him?" I followed her up the stairs, my lungs not quite up to snuff now that a baby felt the need to press against them.

"Just outside, my lady."

"Thank you, Mary." I huffed, reaching the top of the stairs, and found Daniel coming toward me, his steps quick.

"You ought to be sitting down somewhere," he said, anxiety creasing his eyes.

"I am no invalid," I muttered, but I allowed him to take my arm. "Cook has overdone it, I think."

His dark eyebrows rose slightly. "You might change your opinion when you come outside."

I stopped, tugging on Daniel's sleeve so he would stop beside me. The corridor was quiet, most everyone outside where the party had already begun. "What do you mean by that?"

"You recall how we sent all those invitations to our friends and family to invite them to celebrate with us?"

"Yes." I had penned each of them, and it had taken ages.

He lifted one shoulder. "Well, they have come."

"What, all of them?"

Daniel slid his hand around my neck, brushing his thumb softly against my cheekbone. "Most of them, yes."

"And Fanny?" Anxiety crept through my stomach. That many people gathered on our lawn meant quite a crowd—a potentially overwhelming crowd.

"She is with Mother, eating a plate full of berries," Daniel said.

"And her art?"

"I am certain we won't have any remaining at the end of the day."

I closed my eyes, leaning forward to rest my forehead against Daniel's shoulder. It had been his idea to sell Fanny's artwork to fund a scholarship for those who might not be able to afford care but were in need of it. Once the hospital was full and running smoothly, Fanny meant to teach art classes to the interested patients, who could choose if they wanted to submit their work for sale as well. If today was a success, I planned to host various garden parties or autumn fêtes where the artwork could be displayed and sold.

It was a dream, a loose plan, but if Daniel was to be believed, it just might work. My chest filled with warmth when his arms came around me.

"Your dream is becoming a reality," he whispered into my hair.

"Because of you," I countered. I leaned back to better see his chocolate brown eyes. "It is all thanks to your kindness and generosity."

"I would do anything for you and for Fanny, love. You know that."

"I do." I reached up on tiptoe to kiss him, my body filling with love, warming me from my toes to my heart. When I leaned back, I smiled at Daniel's lazy grin.

He took my hand and started pulling me toward the door. "Dr. McEwan is speaking with Jane about Scotland. I think we ought to guide him to a different conversation before he is reminded of how much he loves his homeland and leaves us."

"Gracious, we cannot give him that option," I said with mock outrage. "We would be nothing without Dr. McEwan."

Daniel guided me down the steps and around the house toward the garden where the party was set up. People milled around, eating from small plates, sitting beneath awnings or walking about the flowered paths. A good number of people perused Fanny's animal paintings, and I spotted her sitting with my mother-in-law, as Daniel had mentioned. My heart buoyed to see so many people here, celebrating and supporting our endeavor.

When Daniel and I had sat down with Lord and Lady Moorington to initially present our idea to them, they had been entirely supportive, but their advice was not without warnings. Neighbors could be upset about the concept, Mr. Waterley could fight it, obtaining the proper approval could be difficult— but while we had faced some of those difficulties over the previous year, it had not been the trial we expected.

Mr. Waterley no longer was on speaking terms with Daniel after his own hospital was put under review and closed down, but we had absorbed most of his patients and they were now being properly cared for, so it was not entirely a loss. We recently heard that he had married not too long ago and headed for the colonies. I was not sorry to lose him as a neighbor.

We approached Jane, who sat in the shade of a tent beside Dr. McEwan. "The heather is lovely," she said, nodding. "When the fields are entirely purple, it is my favorite time of year."

He smiled fondly.

"Do not put any ideas in our dear doctor's head, Jane," I scolded, moving to sit beside her on a vacant chair.

She shot me an apologetic smile. Her raven-colored hair was swept up in an elegant style, and she glanced back at the doctor. "You would never leave your patients for your homeland, would you?"

"Of course not." He wore a kind smile that matched the twinkle in his eyes. It was those very features that made me believe he was a good man when I first met him, and I had not been proven wrong. The strides he had already made with Fanny's comfort made his addition to our life worth the cost. She was even eating at the dinner table with us now. In my efforts to protect her, I'd found I held her back in some ways, but Dr. McEwan was helping me to let go and Fanny to find her independence.

Daniel stood beside me, resting his hand on my shoulder. "Would you like me to fetch you a plate?"

"That would be lovely."

"Oh, be a dear and fetch me something as well," Jane said. "I'm famished."

"I'd be honored. Where is your derelict husband, anyway?"

"Keeping Lachlan out of your rose bushes. He believes he is a cat now, and evidently they enjoy crawling through bushes."

"Lachlan loves Fanny. We could ask her to entertain him for a while," Daniel suggested.

Jane smiled. "Perhaps later. I do not wish to pull Fanny away from Mother just yet."

Daniel leaned down and pressed a kiss to my temple before leaving to fill a plate. I watched him go while Jane and Dr. McEwan resumed their conversation. My gaze slipped among the groups of friends new and old, neighbors, parishioners, some family members of our patients, and a few patients themselves. The love and support we had received was enough to fill my cup and my heart for months.

The party lasted most of the day. When the afternoon aged into evening and most of the guests had left, I found Fanny walking toward the house. I said goodnight to my mother-in-law and father-in-law and caught up to my sister. "Where are you off to?"

"I want to draw."

Of course she did. It seemed to be her favorite activity for calming her mind. "Did you notice that all of your paintings were bought?"

"No." She continued to walk, and I followed her up the steps into the house.

"You've done a lot of good for the people who cannot afford to pay their own way."

She smiled, looking down at her feet. "I am glad people like my paintings. Shall I do more of them?"

"If you'd like to, that would be lovely."

She yawned, and I followed her up to her bedroom, ringing for Mary and waiting until she was situated with her drawing supplies before bidding her goodnight and leaving the room.

Daniel was waiting in the corridor for me, and I nearly screamed when I closed the door and found him standing there. "You gave me a fright. Be careful, darling. We do not wish for anyone to hear screams coming from our house. It might scare the patients."

He grimaced. "I did not consider that. Where is our little starling?"

"In her room. Mary is in with her." He'd taken to calling Fanny that after her project with the starlings, which had led to two surviving birds. The other two eggs never hatched. I let out an exhausted sigh.

"Tired?"

"Yes," I said, not bothering to hide my yawn.

"Then allow me." Daniel slid his arm under my knees and lifted me in his arms.

I threw my hands around his neck and stifled a squeal. "I am perfectly capable of walking to the next room over."

"I know, but then I wouldn't be able to do this." He stopped at our doorway and leaned forward until his lips met mine. He kissed me, pulling me closer to his chest. When he leaned back, he looked at me, unmoving. "It is going to be difficult to leave Arden now."

"I was thinking about that," I said quietly, resting my hands on his back. "What if we do not make Lamouth our permanent residence? We can move about at will. Here, there, London. Whichever strikes our fancy."

"You propose keeping three homes, Lady Huxley?"

"I do." I grinned. "Only because I do not wish to leave the hospital forever."

"Fanny would certainly appreciate that."

"We might be able to convince her to come to Lamouth with us, too, if we promise to return shortly."

"Yes, but remember what we talked about. Giving her independence is good, too."

"I know." I pouted. "I will just miss her."

"And she will miss you, which is why I never expected us to be away for long, anyway."

I drew in a quick breath. "You mean it?"

"Of course I mean it. I love Fanny too, you know."

"I know."

He reached for the handle and opened our door, then carried me inside and set me on the edge of the bed before returning to close it.

"It is too early to go to sleep," I said.

"Not for a woman growing a baby," he argued, crouching down to untie my shoes.

I must have looked as tired as I felt. I glanced down, watching Daniel slip my shoes off before he pulled my feet onto the bed and began to rub the tension away. "I love you, Daniel."

He looked up, his dark hair falling over one eyebrow, his dark brown eyes caught on me. "I love you too."

AUTHOR'S NOTE

She would not have been diagnosed in this way in 1819, but Fanny would be considered high-functioning autistic today. As a mother of a beautiful girl with autism who also loves animals with everything in her heart and has incredible drawing talent, I knew that creating Fanny's character would be both difficult and bring me immense joy. My own sweet daughter helped me develop Fanny, choosing which traits the character should have and the difficulties she should face. Fanny is a product of my experience with many children and teens on the spectrum, a culmination of the challenged and triumphs I've witnessed them facing. Fanny is not a direct reflection of my own child, but a combination of many people I know and love.

While she is meant to represent a large group of people, it is called a spectrum for a reason, and Fanny in no way embodies everyone's experience with autism. I hope her representation has at least given you a glimpse into the trials and joys faced by some special needs people and their families, especially if it differs from your own experiences. We all need to have compassion and patience for those we may not understand.

On the other hand, I hope Fanny's character has also allowed those of you with similar experiences to rejoice and laugh at the familiar grievances she endured. There is beauty in shared trials and experiences, and I hope you found beauty in Fanny.

During the Regency era, asylums had already begun to be reformed. There were yearly inspections done by a group in London or magistrates out in the country in an attempt to regulate the severe conditions patients were previously found in. But even with those regulations, people and doctors took advantage of the patients—or greedy men would accept any woman, so long as her husband could pay the fees, whether or not she was mentally stable.

An alternative for someone in Fanny's situation would have been to place her in the custody of a family who lived in the country and was willing to accept money in exchange for taking care of the family member. Jane Austen's brother and uncle were in such circumstances and cared for by a family in the country until they died.

In this story, I wanted to highlight the asylums and the lack of options someone like Fanny faced, especially when her mother cared more for her reputation than her child. (Yes, she was awful. As a mother of an autistic child, I can safely promise most of us are not that way.) I've heard autism referred to as invisible, because in some cases unless you are aware of the diagnosis, it is not obvious. Fanny is a representation of that, depicted in her appearances of rudeness or rigidity with her schedule. Had I given her a more severe diagnosis, she would have been forced to an asylum or the care of a poor family in exchange for money. I wanted Fanny to remain with her sister, which is why I chose to make her high-functioning. And once Daniel and the servants of Arden understood her, they were able to have flexibility and compassion for her.

I hope we can show that flexibility and compassion for

others, whether or not they hold any diagnosis. We never know what other people are struggling with, and it is a good reminder to love everyone. Thank you for reading my story, and I hope you were able to identify with or better understand what some families with special needs might face.

ACKNOWLEDGMENTS

First thanks goes to the Castles & Courtship authors. You are all a joy to work with and I love each and every one of you! I'm so glad to have found this group of ladies who have fostered such a healthy and positive working relationship. Y'all are the best!

Thank you to all of my beta readers for your feedback and willingness to read my terrible beginning draft! Nancy Madsen, Heidi Stott, Emily Flynn, Alison Moulton, Brooke Losee, Melanie Atkinson, and Kerry Perry. Thank you Susan Frederickson for rushing through a last-second read when I was feeling stressed.

Thank you to my critique group for helping me get the beginning off to a solid start: Martha Keyes, Deborah Hathaway, Jess Heileman, I value your feedback so much!

Thank you Karie Crawford and Theresa Schultz for your polish and Ashtyn Newbold for the gorgeous cover!

Biggest thanks goes to Jon for helping me feel confident enough to write this story. To Audrey for being my plot chat buddy and giving me permission to tap into your beautiful brain. To my kids for going to the park so I have a quiet house to work (we all win in that situation). To Lucy for all your head tilts, they are my favorite.

To my Heavenly Father, for endless grace and the gift of hope.

To ARC readers, bookstagrammers, and readers, thank you for taking a chance on my story. You are my people!

CASTLES & COURTSHIP SERIES

An Amiable Foe by Jennie Goutet

To Know Miss May by Deborah M Hathaway

A Heart to Keep by Ashtyn Newbold

A Noble Inheritance by Kasey Stockton

The Rules of Matchmaking by Rebecca Connolly

A Suitable Arrangement by Martha Keyes

An Engagement with the Enemy by Sally Britton

Charming the Recluse by Mindy Burbidge Strunk

Each book is a stand-alone romance and they can be read in any order

ABOUT THE AUTHOR

Kasey Stockton is a staunch lover of all things romantic. She doesn't discriminate between genres and enjoys a wide variety of happily ever afters. Drawn to the Regency period at a young age when gifted a copy of *Sense and Sensibility* by her grand-mother, Kasey initially began writing Regency romances. She has since written in a variety of genres, but all of her titles fall under clean romance. A native of northern California, she now resides in Texas with her own prince charming and their three children. When not reading, writing, or binge-watching chick flicks, she enjoys running, cutting hair, and anything chocolate.

Printed in Great Britain
by Amazon